GRANDVIEW DRIVE

GRANDVIEW DRIVE

~~SHORT STORIES~~

~~A NOVEL~~

FICTION

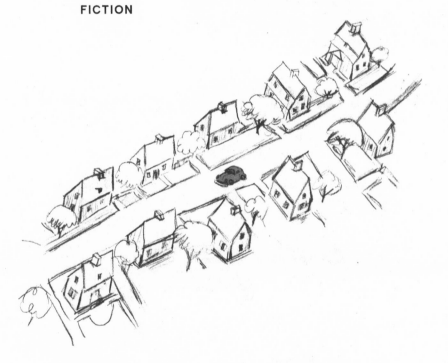

TIM BLACKETT

NIGHTWOOD EDITIONS

2023

1 2 3 4 5 — 27 26 25 24 23

Nightwood Editions
P.O. Box 1779
Gibsons, BC VON 1V0
Canada
www.nightwoodeditions.com

COVER DESIGN: Angela Yen
TYPOGRAPHY: Carleton Wilson

Nightwood Editions acknowledges the support of the Canada Council for the Arts,
the Government of Canada, and the Province of British Columbia through the BC
Arts Council.

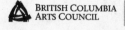

Canada Council   Conseil des Arts
for the Arts   du Canada

This book has been printed on 100% post-consumer recycled paper.

Printed and bound in Canada.

LIBRARY AND ARCHIVES CANADA CATALOGUING IN PUBLICATION

Title: Grandview Drive / Tim Blackett.
Names: Blackett, Tim, author.
Identifiers: Canadiana (print) 20230444164 | Canadiana (ebook) 20230444180 |
    ISBN 9780889714649 (softcover) | ISBN 9780889714656 (EPUB)
Subjects: LCGFT: Short stories.
Classification: LCC PS8603.L268 B73 2023 | DDC C813/.6—dc23

For anyone who has ever felt alone.

CONTENTS

CONTENTS

GRANDVIEW DRIVE

Standing there in the window, throwing her head back in laughter, sending bits of spittle and food shooting out of her mouth before placing a hot dinner in front of her thin husband and her bookish kids, the woman looked happy. Earl had driven past the corner of Grandview and Lone an unmemorable number of times. He'd put in his time at work, stop for an extra-hot latte at Starbucks on Main before turning left onto Lone and driving past 2600 Grandview to merge onto Broadview and drive on home. But tonight, with the autumn sun falling hard, this moving portrait in a picture window seemed to project itself into his car as he passed. He could see her apron trying to cover her stomach, her jelly arms jiggling as she set the pork chops on the table, her neck and cheeks shaking as she laughed, her chubby little hands wiping the hair from her face, her pug nose. Not fat, exactly. Rotund. He might not have noticed if she were only fat.

He left work early the next day. He rolled his eyes at the lady in Starbucks rubbing her chin as she asked about the ingredients of pastries. He found himself speeding down Lone. He parked kitty-corner from 2600. He watched her kids set the table then sit with their father to wait for their mother to finish in the kitchen. He watched them eat.

Watching from the street, he wished he had ordered whole milk instead of soy in the latte. He decided he would cancel his membership at Karl's Workout and Fitness on Second. He would eat all day every day until he was ready. Then he'd knock on their door and tell them he was their uncle.

He watched from the road almost every weeknight as the family ate, laughed, sat watching TV or playing cards. He imagined himself sitting with them, inside, sinking his sour-cream-and-onion chip deep into the jalapeno dip and crunching into it for all to hear. He looked them each in the eye, said, I'm so glad I could be here. He brought his girlfriend to their door and said, This is Tina. Tina smiled and kissed his cheek. They all hugged, smiled, ate cake, cookies, drank whole milk.

The woman in the window started closing her blinds. Earl sat for a few nights watching the shadows behind the blinds, waiting for a blind to open again. But they didn't, and he couldn't handle watching shadows anymore. He drove home, unsatisfied, unsettled. He called his mother—no answer, there never was. He watched TV—fake people, far away, with fake smiles. He brushed his teeth. He masturbated. He dreamed dreams he would never remember.

He stopped going to work early. He pressed snooze again and again. He stopped setting his alarm early.

He started turning left onto Grandview after work, driving its three blocks until the houses disappeared and it opened into Grandview Park. The park followed the bend in the road until it found one last long block of houses—what seemed like mansions to Earl—coming to a dead end at the ninth fairway of the Grandview Golf and Country Club.

It took him a few weeks, but he found an arsenal of houses he could imagine himself inside of, being a part of. He drove past 2600 with the same slap of regret he felt driving past his mother's, or even Tina's. He drove past 2604–2624, who almost always had their blinds drawn. He drove through the intersection of Grandview and Lee and parked in front of 2708 where he looked behind and across to 2705.

An old man sat in a rocker reading a book while an old woman sat on the sofa beside him knitting. Earl sat cross-legged on the floor. What book are you reading Grandpa? he asked the old man. The old man looked up. He slipped his bookmark between the pages, holding the book up so Earl could see the cover.

It's *Anna Karenina*, the old man said. The greatest novel ever written. When you're older, you can have this copy. I'm sure you'll agree.

It's his favourite, the old lady said. He's read it a dozen times. I'm surprised he even offered it to you. She smiled. The old man smiled. Earl smiled and played with the fuzz on the carpet.

Once, before he realized parking behind the huge poplar tree on 2704's lawn would block the view from 2700's window, he was watching the old man read, the old lady knit. He heard the clickety-clack of the knitting needles as they built their Christmas scarves. They clicked louder and louder until Earl began to wonder where the noise was coming from. He looked around to find it, and saw a scrawny man with a scraggly comb-over standing in 2700 tapping a yellow coffee mug against the window, glaring a hole through Earl's Buick. Earl spun a U-turn and sped off, screaming left onto Lone without even looking to see if anyone was coming.

He started being careful. He started wearing dark clothes and sunglasses and putting his hood up to hide his face. It made him feel creepy. It made him look creepy. He found places—behind trees or mailboxes, in front of houses that seemed empty all the time—where he could watch in safety. He believed he was invisible, unnoticeable even if they looked right at him.

He parked in front of 2712. The occupants were always home, but every blind was drawn save for the living-room window which had the back of a large flat-screen TV blocking most of the view inside, shading the back walls with a faint, blue glow. From there, he could just see into 2721 where a grand piano sat silhouetted in the picture window. He could also see, in the yard of 2713, two little girls playing: poking caterpillars, rolling in the grass in their little dresses, slipping down a plastic slide set up under a sprinkler, dancing.

Once, he stopped right in front of 2713 to get a better look at them. He got out to buy a cup of *Freshly Squeezed Lemonade* for twenty-five cents. He tipped them five dollars. He imagined how they would giggle and run to hug him if he were their real uncle. He thought he could spend all day watching them frolic.

If he pulled forward just a bit, he could see the man behind the piano in 2721 pacing, waving sheaves of loose paper, looking down at them, then holding them to his side and waving his free hand in the air as he recited what was sure to be the lines of an award-winning play. Earl sat in his car and stared at the man and ran up the walk, pushed through the door.

Where were you? the man said. I've been waiting all evening. He gave the script to Earl. Earl sat on the piano bench and read lines with him. They probably went for drinks after, might have shot some pool.

He most often sat in front of 2712. He could watch the light from the action movie or the news, cartoons, a porno, whatever was on TV, for hours. He knew it was boring. He didn't know why he enjoyed it. Then he saw a man stand up—a jack-in-the-box popping its head from behind the TV—and leave the room, returning seconds later sipping a beer. He saw himself—alone—sipping a beer. So this became his own house on Grandview Drive. This was where the old lady brought her hand-knit scarf on Christmas morning. This was where he brought his girlfriends, made love to them. This was where the scrawny man said, Should be a record-breaker this one, sitting on the sofa sipping from the yellow mug Earl had picked just for him. Where his nieces knocked on the door hollering for him to come watch their latest dance routine on the sidewalk. This was where he lived. Not the place where he ate and spent the nights falling asleep.

He started daydreaming about Grandview Drive at work. He had to rescue one of the little girls from a tree. He read *Anna Karenina*. He bought a yellow mug. He went to pick up his fat girlfriend. They drove to watch an award-winning play.

"Are you okay?" his boss asked him.

"I'm fine," he said.

"You seem… distracted."

"I feel fine—good."

"Well, don't get too stressed. Use some of that vacation time if you need it."

He requested two weeks off and wasted his remaining work hours looking at images of cities that Google told him were the farthest from Macleod. Pictures of skyscrapers in Perth, of houses and buildings packed tightly on a hill in Antananarivo, beaches in Durban.

Sometimes 2721 would put down his script and sit at the grand piano. He stretched out his arms and cracked all his knuckles before placing his fingers on the keys. He shut his eyes and started swaying to and fro like a love song in the spring. Earl turned on the radio, tuned it past all of Today's Best Music, past forty minutes of commercial-free rock, past Rip-Roarin' Rick Morin's Country Roundup, to 99.7 FM, Classical Music, Classical Life. Beethoven's Piano Sonata No. 14 was playing. He closed his own eyes and laid his head back on the rest. For a long time, he watched as the residents of Grandview Drive sat in a dark semi-circle around an open oak casket, weeping. 2721 stood to present the eulogy. I'm sure you would agree, he began his speech, red-faced and somber, we've suffered a great loss today.

He turned the radio to Gold 101.9, All Oldies, All the Time. "One" was playing. He shut the radio off. He sat up and drove away. He drove past the 2800's altogether, past the giant fish tank bubbling in 2812, past the solar panels on the roof of 2815, past the weeds in 2824's flower beds, past Grandview Park even, where the last evening soccer match was ending with a handshake.

He loved driving along the bend, watching the kids bounce around on the jungle gym. He loved how the houses ended with 2832, but started up again at 3000. As if there was a glitch in time that skipped him forward each time he floated through the park. A whole block, an entire world, was lost in the glitch. He saw them mowing their lawns, licking their popsicles, painting their fences, laughing at their children as they pedalled their tricycles, unaware of the man in the Buick skipping through their lives every evening.

The grand finale of Grandview, the 3000s, was Earl's favourite block. Of the ten mansions, five on each side, only 3017 ever had her blinds open. She sat on her couch so Earl could study her profile, her slender neck stretching down, hiding behind the couch with the rest of her, her fire-red hair forever pulled back in a pretty little flame licking down the back of her neck, the light of the lamp sifting through her long lashes, her red, red lips reading along to her textbooks or sipping green tea softly from a mug, her tongue reaching out to grab ravioli from a fork, her pinky finger—every so often—wriggling into her nostril to scratch.

Slumped in his car, he straightened his tie with one hand as he walked up the drive, hiding white daffodils behind his back with the other. Her sunny blue eyes caught him walking. She ran to the front door to swing it open before he could knock. He pulled the daffodils from behind him. She grabbed them, pressed them to her nose, inhaled, then threw her arms around his neck. She kissed him, lifting one of her legs the way girls do when they kiss in doorways, standing on tiptoes with the other.

She looked out the window, caught him staring. He looked down at the steering wheel and fumbled through his pockets trying to find his phone. He found it in his butt pocket, pulled it out, opened it, stared right through it. Eventually, he felt the burning of embarrassment melt away. He looked back at 3017. She was back to her book. She said, Come in. I'll make you some supper.

I was hoping we'd go out for supper.

Oh? Where to?

I've got reservations at Rufus.

Oh my gosh, Earl. You're kidding.

He smiled. He straightened his tie.

Just let me go change! Put these in water for me?

Across the street, 3020, a second floor bedroom light turned on; filtering through the blinds, it was an overexposed photograph shining in the night. He knew this would happen. If he waited until his radio said 10:16 that light would turn on nearly every night. The first time, he was excited. He thought he had found another life to watch. He did watch. She stepped onto a treadmill in front of the window and started jogging. He watched her bounce, her breasts bounce. He sped home to masturbate. He got mad at himself right after, and the next time he parked at the end of Grandview Drive, he could hardly look at 3017. He didn't deserve her. He had let her down. He tried not to watch 3020 bounce. But he couldn't help it. He sat, staring.

He hated himself for staring. He wanted to jump out of his car, run up to 3017, push through the door without knocking. He wanted to tell her she was beautiful, tell her he knows it's a little strange but he feels like he knows her already, he loves her hair, her name, he wants to go out with her, take her bowling, buy her desert, make her grilled cheese for lunch every day. He knows he could love her, she could love him, they could be happy, together.

3017 knocked on his car door. It scared him so much, he hit his head on the glass. He stared at her. She yelled through the window, "Can I help you with something?"

He rolled down the window. "I'm sorry?" he stuttered.

"Well, I noticed you sitting here. Are you lost?"

"Uh… I am. I'm lost." He clicked his phone open. It was still on his email app, no new messages.

"Well, I think you should go." She pointed down Grandview. "Turn right on Lone. It'll take you to Main."

"I'm just… I… Checking out the golf course."

"Oh," she said, and she looked out into the trees.

He backed the car up a little, then turned around and sped off, leaving 3017 with her hands on her hips, the wind tossing her red hair all over. He couldn't believe she had caught him staring at 3020. He would have to forget about Grandview. He would never creep down it again. He'd find a different route home. He would leave town. He wouldn't tell anyone. He'd start life over. He'd park kitty-corner on Lone and be satisfied with watching the family of shadows. He'd go to work early, stay late. He'd focus. He'd call his mother. He'd go back to Karl's. He'd live alone on Broadview Avenue. He'd spend his nights falling asleep to the TV.

He accelerated around the bend through Grandview Park. The light of the moon shone its ghost rays on the empty playground. The weeds waved. The bubbling fish puckered their lips and kissed him goodbye. The solar panels whispered good night and shut off for sleep. The piano man closed his eyes, missed Earl zooming past in the Buick. The old man put down his book, said, Well, it gets better every time I read it. The old lady stood and wrapped a white scarf around her wrinkled neck. Do you think this is long enough? she said. It's his going-away present. The two little girls rolled over in their beds to look out their window; they wished for an extra blessing on their uncle as a star shot overhead. The man behind the flat screen fiddled with his satellite radio as he backed his half-ton into the middle of Grandview, on his way to pick up his pizza.

The car slammed into the truck bed and Earl shot through the windshield. He felt the prick of glass as it shattered and watched the moonlight splinter, refracting off the pieces. He felt the cool autumn breeze wrap around him. He let it carry him over the truck bed. He held his breath. Saw each of Grandview's faces, grave and unsmiling, whispering, We'll miss you, Earl.

I wonder, he thought before he tore his face along the asphalt. Before he crushed his nose, his cheekbones, broke his jaw, sent his teeth fluttering in all directions. Before he snapped his neck and crumpled yard upon yard down the road until he lay wide-eyed and bloody in the middle of Grandview Drive, I wonder if the woman in the window will come out to see.

ALWAYS IN THE ECHO

I have a friend who's survived two separate lightning strikes. I know they say that doesn't happen, but they also say there's a one-in-nine-million chance of it happening. So it's gotta happen if they've got the statistics for it, right? Plus, I know it's true. I went to the goddamn hospital to see him, both times. I've seen the burns and scars, both of his charred watches. I told him once that I figured he was the luckiest man alive, having survived twice.

"Lucky?" he said, and he laughed a weird little hysterical laugh. "I've been hit by lightning two fucking times," he said. "I walk around in a dream. A dream that shifts in and out of nightmare whenever it wants. I shake. I hide in the bathtub the minute I hear thunder. Fuck luck," he said. "Luck is *knowing* the guy who survived two lightning smites. How many people do you know who know a guy who has survived even one smite?" he said.

And so I've always considered myself a little bit lucky. I take risks. I play the lottery. I jaywalk downtown at rush hour. I pet stray dogs, pick up hitchhikers, that sort of thing. I don't go chasing after women. I believe if you're lucky, the right woman will fall into your arms and you'll look her in the eye and say, There you are.

I was watching the news, sipping a beer, when I heard this smash and crash out on the street. At first I thought it was the TV, which was showing a local girl in New York pounding the keys of a fancy old piano, then kicking some guy in a suit in the nose when he tried to pull her away from it. The man reading the news was saying it's all very horrifying, and I had just started to question whether that was the best word to describe this kid when I heard the crash, all faded and dull and miles away... but getting closer, definitely getting closer, sounding nothing at all like a kid kicking a man in the face. So I ran to the window to see what it was.

It was some poor jackass who'd spilt his bike, a Ducati Monster or some nonsense. What he was doing screaming down Grandview, I haven't the slightest. But he must've been going fast 'cause his bike landed in front of my house in a squashed-up bunch of mess, and he shot a full block down, leaving blood and skin and tiny bits of helmet on the street in his wake.

When I got to him, there was nothing anyone could've done. He must've broke nearly everything in him. He was on his back, but his legs were stretched up on either side of his head, back broken to bits like a tortured old ragdoll, bottoms of his feet pointing to the clouds, face all road-rashed up and missing half its skin, eyes just looking past his crotch into the blue, blue sky.

His near-toothless grin sent a tingle up and down my spine as I stood over him, staring, unable to move. It didn't seem real in any way. It felt like I was looking at some kinda prehistoric cave painting—*Bruised and Bloody Carcass*, they might've called it. I don't know what I was thinking, standing there, when this girl, this woman, came running up. You'd think the whole street would've heard and come running, but it's just me and this crumpled jumble of body and guts, and this girl, in the middle of the road. She doesn't say anything, just stands there looking at him, then at me, and I just stare back at her. It's almost like she has a smile on her face. And she says to me, she says, "Lucky he was wearing his helmet."

And I look at her and she's smiling so wide like she just can't hold it in anymore. And I start laughing, just hackling away like a goddamned hyena. And I look at the guy and at her and all around the neighbourhood and I feel my eyes going all wild-like and I start to wonder if a person could actually, like literally, laugh his own head off.

I mean it's not like anything was funny. I just didn't have the first clue what the hell I was supposed to be doing.

Eventually I sat down and she sat beside me, and I was like, "What the hell are we supposed to do?"

"We gotta get outta here," she said, nonchalant as hell.

"We can't just leave him here."

"Someone else will find it," she said. "We shouldn't have to deal with this. It's not fair for us to have to deal with it."

All I think now is we were both terrified. Who would expect to see death all dressed up and grinning on the bloody asphalt? But all I thought at the time was, Who is this fuckin' woman? Who could possibly be so unaffected by this? And I just stared into her beady brown eyes, past her little nose, her plump lips—into her eyes, down into her. She just let me stare, let me dig inside her, just opened herself up to me and let me search through her.

"Come on," she said finally. "We need to get drunk is what we need." She stood and pulled me up and we walked all the way to Bubba's. She wrapped her arm through mine and held my hand with both of hers. It was as if nothing had happened, as if we had met in another lifetime, another world, and we were just fitting ourselves back together—as if she had fallen into my arms and I looked at her and said, There you are. I've missed you.

She told me stories, elaborate, detailed stories as if she were making them up as we walked along. Stories of people I'd never heard of, places I'd never been. Friends from college who moved to Florida. Summer road trips so drunken she couldn't remember them. A night lost in the woods. Skinny dipping with strangers in a lake so thick with weeds it felt like trudging through butter. Her mother's mysterious disappearance. Her father getting lost in himself and taking on the personalities of characters he'd read about, he'd dreamt of, characters he'd write in his journals. I couldn't help thinking I could never keep up. I could never tell stories like this. I lived in my house, sipped Bud Light and watched TV, went to work, came home, waited for a girl to fall into my arms.

I know a guy who has survived two separate lightning strikes, I was about to say, but we had arrived at Bubba's and she was holding the door open for me. "Lucky we came when we did," she said. "My old friend is working." And she pulled me to a round booth in the corner where we hid away from the restaurant. "You haven't said a thing about yourself," she said.

"Oh, I'm boring," I said. "I can't even think of a single interesting thing about myself."

"How'd you get that scar?" she asked, and she touched me just below my left eye. I had never noticed a scar there, didn't even remember getting cut there, but when she touched it, I could feel it, like it was bubbling up under my eye and if I didn't explain it, it would swell up so much so that it would seal my eyes shut and I would never see her again.

"I can hardly remember," I said. "I think I fell out of a tree once." The scar cooled, submerged, fell into the background of things.

"Lucky you didn't stab your eye out."

"I guess, yeah. Actually I've always considered myself a little bit lucky. My friend has survived two separate lightning strikes."

"Whoa. That is lucky. My father says he was hit by lightning. On a night it wasn't even raining."

"Hey, haven't seen you for a while," the waitress said, placing some cutlery on the table.

"Haven't been looking hard enough."

"Ha! *Touché*... Whatcha been doin'?"

"Watched a guy wreck his bike tonight."

"Oh yeah? I bet you did! Was he all right?"

"Hard to say. You got a drink for watching a bike wreck?"

"Oh, I'm sure we got something. Two of 'em?"

"Two of 'em."

"All righty."

"That's your friend?" I said.

"We go way back."

"Ah."

"Wanna dance?"

There was music playing in the background, barely audible above the murmur of the people, but she pulled me out of the booth and started dancing. She closed her eyes and danced a slow dance with her arms in the air, her hips swaying, as if she were alone in a basement dancing to her favourite song on repeat. I had never met anyone so unencumbered by her surroundings, so willing to do what she pleased. She moved around the bar as if it were her childhood home, as if she had it memorized, as if she had spent her life dancing around its tables and chairs, memorizing. If other people were bothered, she didn't notice.

And neither did I. I stood there watching her. I sat back down and watched her. I was utterly enthralled by her freedom, her confidence. Her. Just her. I could have sat there watching all night long.

"Here we are," the waitress said, placing two fishbowls on the table beside me. "Call these Life-Changers. You'll thank me tomorrow. If you wake up tomorrow."

"If I wake up?"

"Hahaha. Enjoy!"

"These ours?"

"Uh … Yup. Life-Changers."

"Nice. Lucky she was working."

We sat and drank. We closed our eyes and drank, got brain freeze, got more drinks, got buzzed, got drunk. We drank without talking, as if we had been waiting for the drinks just so we could stop talking. And I guess we had been. She somehow finished her last drink a lot faster than me, sat staring out at the restaurant. She'd blink every so often, leaving her eyes closed for a little too long before opening them. "Do you ever dream about real life?" she said.

"This could happen to you, bitches!" a woman yelled, leaning toward a couple of girls at the end of the bar.

"Wooo-hooo. You tell 'em, Tina!" my new friend yelled.

"You know her too?" I asked.

"I used to," she said. "She stole my boyfriend." Then she started laughing until she stopped breathing. Her face turned red and she clutched her chest, all the time still laughing. She laughed so hard that I couldn't help laughing at her. And the two of us sat there laughing, her out of control and losing her mind, me looking around the place at the people eating quietly, sipping their sodas, talking about work and kids and mortgages, living boring, lonely lives. And we laughed harder and harder until I was sweating and she was flopped down in the booth, her wild eyes looking up at me.

The rest of the night flits through my mind in broken images that hardly seem to fit together. They flutter in front of me in a blur. I pick them out of the air, these images, and hold them in my mind, adding details to them, taking things away, not really knowing which bits are real and which bits are stuck there from years of trying to connect them, trying to piece them back together. To make them make sense.

We walked. I see snow, but I'm pretty sure it was early spring. Maybe rain. I remember laughing, falling on the sidewalk laughing. Spitting over the Main Street Bridge. The water ripples when I think of this, farther and farther away, into a summer day when I'm ten. My parents are taking me and my sister for a picnic in the country. There's no bridge, and we don't spit but we throw rocks, which makes the water ripple. So then I feel like the sun is shining on us as we stumble around Main Street under the humming streetlights. I wish I could remember where we walked, but then I thought we were walking aimlessly at the time.

It still feels like an adventure in my head. There was an owl, I think, on the roof of a house, at the peak, staring at us. I want it to be real. I want to keep this alive in my mind, eyes darting between us, wisdom flowing through this bird, offering a little blessing to the perfect little couple. Though when I think about it outside of my little daydream, I'm sure it was plastic, dumb as an ox. I remember blinds closing as we walked by. I'm sure no one was bothered by us, but I remember thinking they must know our secret, and it pushed me closer to her.

They could exclude us if they like. We could walk aimlessly through this life, together.

Then she stopped in front of this tiny apartment building. The picture of it in my head is so vivid—grey siding, four windows, geometric white curtains, red shudders framing each window, flowerless flower beds on either side of the door, black cat smiling from the corner of the north bed, four doorbells in a row. Still, I can't find it. No matter how many times I look. Every time I feel like I'm getting close it's as if the whole thing moves, hides.

"Here we are," she said. Then, "My apartment," when I just stood there, staring.

"What were you doing on Grandview?"

"I spend a lot of time on Grandview," she said, which seemed to answer the question. "Wanna come up? I'm gonna grab a sweater."

"Yes," I said, and I followed her up. I know this is true. It's so clear in my mind. I can almost feel the excitement rise inside of me when I think of it. I can see her face as we sit on her couch, in that moment before—when you each have to decide: this is going to happen, I want this to happen. I meet her eyes with a vulnerability I haven't felt since that day at thirteen when the bottle actually landed on me after Miranda's perfect spin.

Miranda, whom I had watched from afar for so long, whom I'd daydreamed about, who distracted me from my teenage life with her long legs and long lashes, with her rolled-up paperbacks in her pocket, with her different coloured scrunchies for each day of the week, with her sly wit and undeniable confidence. She had seemed an unattainable, supernatural sort of being to me, until the rumour mill started turning out little bits about her fending off Jack, the virtual king of elementary school, by telling him that I, timid and shy little me, was her boyfriend. So I convinced her to come to my buddy's party, where we inevitably sat in the circle and spun the bottle.

Miranda spun first. She spun the bottle and it spun and spun and slowed and stopped and pointed at me. She was across the circle, but I could see that she wanted this, that our wills together had stopped the bottle in the perfect place. As we stared, the laughs and cheers of the other kids, of the entire world, faded into a white fog pushing us closer and closer together. And the seconds—as we crawled toward each other, as we blushed, as we looked from each other's eyes to lips to eyes to lips, as we connected (still on all fours) in a perfect little kiss with just a millisecond of touching tongues, colour bursting forth from our lips and into the world, making it a place worth living in, as we smiled and wiped our lips and she ran her beautiful fingers through her hair and the crowd roared and we blushed even more, stealing looks at each other for the rest of the night, until eventually we snuck outside to walk alone hand in hand under the light of the stars—the seconds slowed. And I wished they would stop altogether, that the moment would last and last and last until we couldn't handle it anymore.

These memories mix because I can't remember past that look on Miranda's face as we skipped out the door. I can see something of the same look on this woman's face as she sits on her couch. But then I wake up in my own bed with no actual proof of her existence, except for one of the worst hangovers I've ever had and a sense of having lost something important. The news didn't even run the story of the bike wreck. No sign of it out my window. I can feel the neighbours talking about it, asking who it was, why he was there, who cleaned him up, but none of them mention me, none mention the girl, the woman.

I do not even know her name. I can't think of when she would have said it, of when I would have said mine. We were strangers. We are strangers. I look for her. I search for her, try to find her apartment, her waitress friend, Tina who stole her boyfriend. Sometimes, I wake from my dreams calling her, calling out to her, her name unspoken, always hidden in the echo, in the silence of my loneliness.

My friend called me one night before a late summer storm. "I know this is crazy," he said, "but would you wanna come by my place tonight?"

"I don't know, man. Pretty tired from work. Just turned the TV on."

"Okay... okay, that's fine. I'll be okay. I'm just sorta freaking out."

"It might not even storm. Hasn't even started raining."

"I can feel it. You can feel it. It sneaks up on you like a goddamn fuckin' panther. You can't get away and it's got you in its claws and it's ripping at your chest and biting your neck and your whole body feels like it's being torn apart but you're just lying there screaming and scratching at your arms to make it stop and you wanna die but you just won't... die. And it just won't st—"

"Okay, okay, man. I'll be right over."

It was quiet as hell outside. I stood on the step to look up at the clouds—thick, dark, rolling over each other, jostling for position. Close your eyes for one second and look back at them, you'd think you were in a whole different world. Static on the radio, inaudible voices mumbling under the crackle of white noise. I fiddled with it as I backed out onto Grandview, searching for anything to block out the silence. And then, just as I landed on a semi-clear station, I felt this crack that shook me so hard as if I'd been zapped to life by some four-thousand-pound defibrillator. The truck stalled.

I sat shaking, wondering if my heart was going to stop. I looked around, eventually, to see what kind of damage a lightning strike would offer, when I saw the car, a sinister black Buick, that had smashed into my truck. There was glass and bits of Buick strewn everywhere. I ran to the car. It was empty. The car was empty and all I could think of was the woman.

Here was another wreck, a scrunched-up bundle of mess outside my house—and all I would have to do was wait for her. What this guy was doing on Grandview, I haven't the slightest, but he had to have been going fast, 'cause I found him half a block down the street. There was nothing anyone coulda done for him. He just lay there, skin torn off his face, eyes wide open, not wanting to miss any of the cloud dance, teeth utterly gone, yet somehow still smiling up at me.

I waited. You'd think the whole street would've heard and come running, but it was just me standing there, waiting. Until this woman, this girl, came running out of the house straight across from mine. I saw her running toward me, her hair wild in the wind, and I could feel my heart slow, the excitement bubbling up in me.

But then as she got closer, a man came running out of the house after her. He gained on her fast and by the time she got to the body and took it all in—gasping slightly, yet still studying it, as if inspired by some kinda prehistoric cave painting—I could see she was young, fifteen maybe, and the man was her father. "Delaney. Oh my God. Delaney, get away from there," and he slung her over his shoulder and carried her off into their house.

I sat on the sidewalk. I tried to imagine what could have gone through this man's head as he sailed over my truck and down the road. But what I thought, what I couldn't stop thinking, is Where is the girl, the woman? Until the man, the father, came out and said, "Are you all right?"

"Yes," I said.

"Have you called 9-1-1?"

"No."

"Okay. All right. I'll do that. What a fucking mess. Do you know the guy?"

"No."

"Okay. All right. I think he looks familiar to me. Vaguely. I have never…"

He kept talking. And talking. And the thunder roared. Lightning flickered, lit up the sky. Clouds settled into each other. One dark cloud. Winds stopped. Birds whispered. Me, I lay down on the ground, and I let the first of the evening's raindrops land on my face, roll down my cheeks, water the grass, seep into the dirt beneath me.

THE ONES REALLY LOOKING

And after all, she would have stopped if she had taken him literally. "You could make a person commit murder with that rattle-clatter," the man had said to his wife from behind his mystery novel. She would have stopped if she had realized, over the years, that he was only a nickel short of the loony bin… She would have. She thought he was only grumpy because he hadn't guessed the killer. She thought he was upset she wasn't painting. She hadn't gone into their third bedroom—the one he had made into a miniature studio—in years, she hadn't created anything of value, anything enjoyable, since before they were married, since before they met.

Her father, when Anne was much younger, took her to the art gallery just west of Main Street because he wanted to see the Group of Seven exhibit housed within. Almost as soon as they got there, he instructed her to stop following him around. "Art is solitary," he told her. "To one person it means something totally different than to anyone else," he said. "And I don't want to hear what it means to you until I figure out what it means to me," he said. He left her there in front of *Odds and Ends* while he sauntered around being solitary.

She stood looking at the tree stumps, the mountains, the strange blue sky. The tall trees in the middle were the worst, stripped of all their branches but for the very tips at the top that looked like funny little toques. She wondered how this painting could mean anything to anyone besides what it was—a bunch of dead trees among other dead trees.

She went to find her father. Even from a distance, through the crowd of people hustling around the gallery, she could she him swaying from his heels to his toes and back to his heels, his hands in his pockets. She could see his eyes scrunched, the corner of his mouth raised just a little, a serene look on his face that she would never forget, ever. She looked at the painting he was looking at and could hardly see why it was in the gallery, the way it just hung there like the painting that hung in her old Sunday schoolroom, the same rigid beams of sunlight shining through some clouds.

She watched her father, though, and began to watch the others too. The ones looking, really looking, instead of rushing through so they could get to dinner on time, had the same look, similar looks, as if they were being drawn into something, or the art was drawing something out of them and they were growing larger than they used to be. Their sweet, peaceful half smiles were reaching out to Anne, making her anxious, in a good way, as if she'd let out a scream if she wasn't careful.

Her father—on the way to drop her at her mother's, who lived all the way south instead of in the centre of town where he lived—said he could tell she had enjoyed it, said she had the look of someone inspired. And she knew what he meant because he was looking at her that way, as if she were that painting, her face shining in the sunlight on the lake—she was worth his time. She said she was inspired, she'd like to start painting, so they stopped at a tiny art supply store she never knew existed where she bought a canvas and some washable paints.

Anne thought she could feel the man on the bench watching her paint. She noticed him reading, pretending to read, and was certain he was only sitting there in order to watch her. She was painting the lake with the trees reflecting in it, the dirt path winding around it, the birds flitting about, but mostly she was painting the people who stopped to look at the lake, the little boys pointing to the sky where they spotted sparrows, or the girls sniffing the flowers, the way they looked desperate to take part in this nature, in something outside themselves.

The man slowed her process so much, sitting there watching with his shifty eyes popping up from his book every few seconds to spy on her. She'd jerk her head to catch him, but it was as if he knew when she was going to look. His nose was sure to be hiding in his book each time she checked, yet she could feel him staring. And she couldn't concentrate with him sitting there. She needed to be alone while she painted, alone with the canvas, the colours, with her subject right there in front of her, nothing else. Solitary.

She found herself painting for the man on the bench. The strokes became wild, a flutter to show off, a little dance he would be sure to notice from his bench. When she'd look at her work later—after he had slipped his bookmark back into his book, untied and retied his shoes, nodding slightly as he left down the path for work—she wouldn't even recognize it, as if someone else entirely had painted it. She'd paint the whole canvas white and start over.

She thought of painting him, but his look reminded her of something she couldn't place, and the way his lips curled at the corners just a little when he looked at her made her nervous. She would go to the park every morning, and every morning he'd be there sitting, reading, spying. Each day it was worse feeling his eyes burning into her painting. Finally, she'd had enough, and tossed her paintbrush into the air and let out a little scream, the tiniest little scream, collapsing on the grass beside her easel.

"No, I'm not alright," she said when the man came running, sliding on his knees beside her, dropping his book in the dirt, leaving the bookmark on the bench, asking if she was alright. "Look at my painting," she said. "Just look at it," she said. "It's disgusting."

He stood and stared at the painting. After way too long he scratched his earlobe and said, "I think it's beautiful." Whatever that means.

"It's amateur. Like I just started yesterday. Like I'm nervous. Someone's got a gun to my head."

He looked at her then, studied her, as if she were the painting and he just couldn't figure out what the artist had been trying to do. "I don't see that at all," he said. "I think it's stunning," he said, and then he turned back to the painting.

Anne sat and began pulling out grass, tossing it in the air, as if worried the wind would pick up.

"Well, I should be off," he said. "If you're alright. I'll see you tomorrow?"

"See you," she said, and she decided she wouldn't go back there at all. What girl—in her right mind, at least—plans to meet a shifty-eyed stranger at the park?

❂

At their wedding, the man told the guests he wasn't convinced he would fall in love with her until they'd actually planned to meet in the park and she'd disappeared for three months. He said he'd thought he'd known who she was—a bit of a drama queen, cute as hell, but somewhat predictable, didn't take herself too seriously—"but then she up and disappears the day after we make plans!" The crowd laughed. All through those three months he would search for her in passing buses, at the grocery market, in darkened alleyways, all through the park. On Canada Day, he went to the park at noon and walked around until after the fireworks were over just to try to find her. The crowd sighed and looked all slobbery at the two of them.

Anne hadn't thought of him, not one single time, during those three months. She had "been glad to be rid of those slippery eyes," she'd told her mother more than once. She hated the way he had spied on her, then lied about her painting the first chance he got. And she would never have even gone back to that spot in the park if her mother hadn't made her.

"Would you please stop complaining about it?" her mother had said. "It's not like those are the only trees in Macleod."

"Mom. Don't do that. You know an artist can't help her muse," she said.

"I know nothing of the sort. Do you think your precious Seven sat around waiting for inspiration to kick them in the ass? This muse or inspiration or 'the zone,' whatever you call it, is bullshit. It's amateur," she said. "If you want to be an artist, girlie, you go be an artist."

So she went back to her spot in the park, though she was shaking so much as she walked that she dropped her brushes all over the path. A bottle of red splattered in the grass.

After forty-three years of marriage, Anne decided she could feel the hate oozing out of the man. He hated that she liked to knit now, loved it. He hated all her broderie anglaise. "It's lovely," he'd say when she held it up for him. He'd smile and say it's lovely, but for the next day or two she thought his face looked vexed. She could see him brooding, wondering why she wasn't painting. His eyes would start flitting around, and Anne would just keep on knitting, or she'd get up and throw the whole piece into the trash and crawl into bed.

It was him who stifled the artist in her anyway. For their honeymoon, he took her out to a secluded cabin on the East Coast, said if the drive across the country didn't inspire her, the ocean—once they got there—would. He said she could paint for days without anyone there to bother her, just the maples and the blue jays and the ocean waves.

She didn't even take her paints out of her suitcase. In the morning—a calm morning, the songbirds singing so loud you could lose your mind—the man woke up before her to set up her easel on the deck facing the sunrise. He then sat right behind the easel like he would at the park, and she already knew his eyes would never stay in his book; they'd be watching her, all greedy and eager to see her ocean water crashing on the rocks.

She told him she'd like to go for a solitary walk instead. He asked her what's wrong, said he could leave her alone if she wanted, said she could paint all day if she liked, said he wouldn't bother her at all, made up all sorts of lies.

She did love him though, she really did. She wouldn't have married him if she didn't. She would sometimes sit and try to remember their wedding day, how he had stopped the priest just after they were asked to repeat the wedding vows, how she could feel the crowd wondering what in hell was going on as he whispered to the priest, how the priest said, It seems the groom has prepared his own vows. He pulled out a crumpled old paper but quoted his poem from memory. What it said she could never remember, but his eyes were nearly still, she remembers that. They were filling with tears that wouldn't quite fall, and the blue of them was pulling and stretching her out, and she couldn't wait for the vows to finish so he could kiss the bride.

In their first house, in the basement, he built a room without telling her. He said he was trying to strengthen the foundation. One day he told her to come downstairs to see his progress. The basement was dusty and the floor had spidery cracks trying to escape under the stairs and the washing machine; in the corner, there was an ugly wooden frame filled in with Gyproc, forming a little room inside the room. He stood there in the doorway with his arms out, the bright lights of the little room shining behind him. Inside, the walls were ice white—the lighting would be all right, considering.

He even said she could paint a mural on the walls if she wanted. She was overwhelmed by it all. Nearly crying, she kissed him and kept kissing him, making love with him there in his secret room. Because she loved him. It's obvious she loved him.

The other men, when they looked at her, would inspire her. Her husband, from behind his book or in the car while driving or lying in bed, would wince as if in pain, as if someone had stabbed him with some memory. Anne understood from these winces that he blamed her for her unfaithfulness, as if she went out to find these men in order to punish him, as if she were taking bits of her love for him and offering them to these men. But she never sought them out, never meant for them to fall in love with her.

She would meet them accidentally—at a going-away party for a friend of a friend; in line for popcorn, her third time seeing *Pride and Prejudice*; at a wedding. Excuse me, do you know if this movie is worth seeing? she'd say, or, So how long have you known the couple? She'd smile her beautiful smile, and she would watch them rearrange the order of their lives in their heads. When she'd tell them she was married, they'd say it couldn't possibly be the same passionate love they shared, or they'd say that a love this true happens only once, or they'd say that her husband is the luckiest man on earth—they'd say any number of artless clichés to which she'd smile a less beautiful, more apologetic smile, and she'd blow them a kiss and walk home or take the bus, drive.

She would imagine herself lying on a bed of black lilies, sleeping, or daydreaming into the clouds. These men would be there, watching her, longing for her, worshipping her. It was the look on their faces, desperation, that would inspire her. By the time she would pull into the driveway, she'd be unable to keep herself from running to the house, into the studio, to paint.

Her husband liked these paintings even less than her not painting at all. The first time it happened—if you could count it as a first time—he seemed pleased. He came rushing downstairs to watch her paint with his firm, intense smile, so he could ogle her while she painted, no doubt. His eyes were practically popping out of his head, she thought to herself. What happened? he asked her.

She stood for a long time, staring at the canvas, ignoring the man, but she could never get started with him standing there. She quickly brushed a few simple strokes across her canvas, strokes without any thought behind them besides the wish for him to leave her alone. The inspiration has been sucked out of me, she would say, and she'd imagine the disappointment clouding his face.

Well what inspired you in the first place? he asked her, and she told him. Because it was completely innocent, that first time. She told him she had met a man at the grocery store who had almost certainly fallen in love with her during their short time together discussing which fruit was in season. It was his broken look of desire when she told him she was married that had inspired her.

He smiled then. "Well who wouldn't fall in love with that tiny nose of yours?" he said. "Poor guy. You'll have to try not to be so sweet."

She stood watching him speak as if he were a stranger in the park whispering at pigeons. She could picture his patchy trench coat, his bristly beard, his balding head, his missing teeth, could smell him as he whispered, as the pigeons landed on his shoulder and started pecking at his cheeks, his eyes.

He stood looking back at her, then, his shoulders hunched, as if she had taken a quilt, soaked it and thrown it dripping onto his back. "You okay?" he said. "Do you know his name?" he said. She told him she didn't. But she wouldn't tell him if she did, she said. He was making a bigger deal out of everything than he needed to.

The next time she came home with that radiance, he didn't follow her downstairs. He just looked at her with his downtrodden eyes which, she thought, seemed to be darting around all over the place, accusing her. So you met another man did you, made him fall in love? his eyes said. And even the idea of him sitting in the living room above her, muttering to himself, shaking his head, kept her from painting anything useful.

Each time she came home feeling as if the top of her head would pop off if she didn't paint her latest conquest, he'd be waiting there, brooding, pretending to read his stupid book. And she'd feel suffocated, unable to do anything but sit next to him and smile and squeeze his hand in her own.

"You'll drive a person to their death with that clickety-clacking," her husband said without looking up from his book. He'd said it so many times. He said it every evening after shutting off the TV and picking up his airport novel, huffing and puffing through the chapters. But tonight she looked up at him and she could see that his eyes were crazy, darting so quickly all around her face, and his lips were pressed so tight, and the outsides of his eyebrows were flying higher and higher until he looked like a madman, possessed.

She felt a terror rise up inside her before either of them had even moved, a terror that brought every memory of their life together into her mind—his stalking her in the park, his confused looks when she spoke of the men she'd met, his refusing to show any anger toward her, his repressing any emotion he felt, never letting her see inside of himself—and she knew, somehow, that all of it had been leading to this very point. Sitting there, she could see every moment of her life had been rushing forward, eager to crash into her in this second. And she resolved in her mind that she was ready for what was to happen.

She slid the white wool off her needles and stood up.

"What do you think?" she said, wrapping the scarf around her neck.

A look came over her husband's face, greedy and desperate, she thought, as if she were the very last piece of steak on earth.

"It looks fine, sweety," he said. He rolled his demonic eyes and curled his eyebrows around and around, he snarled. She could feel him ready himself to lunge at her.

"I think I'll be off to bed after this chapter," he said, and he pried his eyes from her, slipping them down into his book. He licked his finger to turn the page.

This momentary relief, as he looked away, caused Anne's heart to beat even faster. She could feel it inside of her, growing and reaching through her, trying to get control. She was certain he could hear the beat as it rose inside, louder and louder. But she was glad for it. She was glad for him to hear that which was going to save her. Yes, it was going to save her. It would set her free from the hate and oppression, make her beautiful and lovable, powerful. It would rid her of him, and of everything. He would be punished. Everything.

She let it, this thing, her heart, stretch through her every molecule. She surrendered herself to it, gave herself to it, embraced it, and when those devil eyes looked up once more, threatened her, she shot forward and pierced the left one straight through with her knitting needle.

The man threw his head back and grabbed his eye with his hands and let out a terrifying cry so loud it made her step back. He stood, his one eye spewing blood over the recliner, the carpet, the wall, the other eye rolling back, as if it were searching for its brother, leaving only the white of it to stare out at Anne.

The man's breathless cry continued for longer than seemed natural, a pathetic cry, not intent on understanding anything, Anne thought, just glad to be freed. He flailed around the living room, crashing into end tables, scratching at his eye with his hands until he tripped on the coffee table and flew into the solid oak TV stand. The needle found the stand immovable and was shoved deep into the temporal lobe of his brain. He flopped on the floor, seizing and shaking all over on the carpet.

Anne felt the blood spray across her chest, her face, as she watched him twitch. And his right eye rolled back down from inside his head to look up at her, perfectly still.

She sat down on her sofa and watched the eye watching her. The look on his face, under the blood, was not cruelly vengeful as she remembered it, but mysterious, enchanting, loving even, and as she sat, relief flooding through her, she thought of how vibrant the red on her scarf was against the white of it, how beautiful her husband's face looked, how she really ought to hide away in the studio to paint it.

THE WORLD IN A MINOR

"Grandma, what's rage?" I asked, six years old and just beginning to read. I was looking at some old sheet music, a long title I couldn't understand, *Rage Over a Lost Penny* in parentheses underneath.

"Rage?" She looked up at the ceiling fan, fiddled with that whisker on her chin. "Rage is when you're very, very angry," she said.

"Why'd he get so mad over a penny?"

"It's Beethoven," she said. "He was deaf." As if this answered everything.

"I think it looks colourful," I said. Blues and greens and purples, a smidgen of yellow in my head. It reminded me of the other kids—the big kids—chasing each other through a windy meadow, rolling in the weeds and getting itchy.

"Colourful?" she said, and she took the score and held it out in front of her, confused. "Well, it sounds angry. Would you like me to play it?"

"Yes, thank you," I said.

It had been years since she'd played it, she told me, then she sat and pounded on the keys as if she thought they were broken. She'd stop every few seconds to study the sheet, then would keep going, slower and slower. The colours came in sharp blasts, then faded in flashes of misery.

"Are you playing it right?" I said. I wanted the colours to run into each other, velvet, eternal.

"I'm trying my best, Fletcher," she said. She sat up straight and pushed her glasses to the top of her nose, started over. I crawled up beside her on the bench, put my hands on the keys and started playing along with her. I wasn't playing Beethoven, of course, but I was rolling those steep notes through my righthand fingers as fast as I could, a rainbow of gumballs somersaulting just over my head. With my left hand I kept a quick, solid beat just above high C, cherries dripping off their stems into the azure below.

Grandma stopped playing, finally. I closed my eyes and watched the colours meld together. I slid down an octave and they ripened. I played softly and they huddled together, whispering. Loud, and they filled the room. I'm not sure how long I played until Grandma reached around and squeezed me into her side.

"Who taught you that, sweetest?" she said.

"No one."

"No one? You just did it all on your own?"

"I could see it," I said.

"Come. We're getting you a piano."

"You bought her a freakin' piano?" my mom said when she came to pick me up. Then, "Don't say freakin'," to me with a pointed finger. "Where am I supposed to keep it?"

"You have to listen to her play," Grandma said. "Just listen."

I had always heard it, the music, in my head. I just never knew I could get it to come out. The morning had its own sound. The sun, the dew, the bugs lolling in the warmth, people bustling down the streets to work. The afternoon was quiet, whispering secrets. The evening, excited, staccato. To me, the world was a piano concerto in C major. When I sat at my piano, I could shut my eyes and pluck each note out of the air.

Back then, before I lost it, when I still thought music could change the world, the literal definition of happiness. I remember butterflies wrestling out of their cocoons, fluttering away into spring, the first time I played Chopin's Piano Sonata No. 2. My own compositions were sky-blue and played in puddles, took sunny afternoon naps in hammocks. When I'd write my music down, I'd use neon highlighters to scribble words over the notes: *frolic, snicker, floating leaves, yellow daisies, magic.* When I wasn't practising—from 5 a.m. until school, then straight after school until my lesson—I'd think about music, how everything I encountered had its own. Even music theory was music: lines, clefs—treble and bass—the crotchet, the quaver, caesura, scales—whole step, whole step, half. Whole, whole, whole step. Half.

Mom wanted me to do exercises for my fingers. Her million-dollar fingers, she called them. She forbade me to crack my knuckles. She hired a drama coach to watch me play, to get my emotions right. She made me watch Lang Lang and Trifonov on YouTube, tried to get me to mimic them. She did my school homework for me so I could practise. She wrote to Anne Larson, to Derek Wang, Yulia Chaplina, to whomever she thought might offer to apprentice me, give me masterclasses.

I told her the music was a part of me. She didn't need to worry.

At recitals and competitions, while the other kids were sweating and nervous and bobbing their knees up and down, I would close my eyes and watch the music. I'd watch little black spaces whiz past when they made their mistakes. I'd smile and cheer them on as they curtsied or bowed. I would know I had won before I had even started playing. I'd bask in the applause, their standing ovations, as flocks of starlings danced through the air in their spring ballets.

After the competitions, when the other kids took time off to go ride their horses or play with their friends, I'd find a work I'd never heard before and play it all day. Or I'd compose something new.

I received a formal invitation to the International Tchaikovsky Competition for Young Musicians when I was only twelve, after I had given my debut performance with the Montréal Symphony Orchestra. I was ecstatic. I was going to become the first Canadian to win the award. I was going to go on tour, record albums, one day win the real Tchaikovsky competition.

The competition was to be held in New York City that year, the first time in North America. There had been a recent surge of American prodigies, they called them. And I secretly thought they were trying to attract me to the competition as well, but who was I kidding? Emily Shie tied for the win twenty-five years earlier, at the first competition, and there hadn't been an American winner since.

There were kids from all over the world. Russia, obviously, China, Japan, South Korea, Germany even. They were all sweating and straightening their ties and scratching their legs under their leotards, the same as the kids at any competition. The buzz was that I was the frontrunner. I cruised through the first round, a solo round in which I chose "Romance" by Franz Liszt, because it was a budding Rembrandt tulip in my brain.

The hardest part, the part that makes the competition, is round two, when you have to play a piece specifically commissioned for the event. I was excited because it was a piece by Kimberly Choi, but the piece was boring. In practice, just when I could see it was supposed to flutter into reds and oranges, blasting off over the hills, it softened and fell down into an ugly brown, shushing the crowd to sleep. Each time I went through it, I stumbled over the notes. I would slam my forehead on the keys by the end of it.

I decided I'd play it as best as I could. I would try to make up for it in round three, when I could choose my own song, accompanied by the New York Philharmonic. But for the first time in my life, I felt nervous. My hands were sweating, and I could barely see any music in my mind. It was all grey, muted, blended into grotesque sludge. When it was my turn, I almost tripped up the stairs.

I started in, playing the dull red, trying to add a bit of orange as I went—but then it was like no one was there. I was six years old again and I was composing my first piece, splashing into colours I had seen but never touched. I closed my eyes and played the flaming crescendo that I knew was supposed to be there. I finished with a jerk of my head, my hands popping off the keys. There was silence, like the few seconds of a crow's funeral before they all fly off, then a rupture of applause, and I knew I had nailed it.

When they were announcing the Jury Discretionary Awards— awards that said, "Good work, but you aren't through to the next round"—I was smiling, whispering to my mom, not really listening. She was beaming and crying, asking if the song was supposed to sound that way. I could feel the other kids watching me.

When they called my name, I laughed. Hadn't they just heard me? Hadn't they seen what I'd done? I just sat there, laughing, shaking my head, clapping along with the crowd. Until the clapping slowed, then stopped, and I was the only one left clapping. Mom was pushing me out of my chair. My world was silent. For the first time, I couldn't see or hear any music. I was only aware of my hands shaking as I walked. This must be how Beethoven felt, I thought.

"Thank you," the head judge said as he shook my hand. "You were marvelous. A real treat."

I ripped my hand from his and ran over to the piano. I slammed my fists onto the keys, over and over, a baby tossing pots down the stairs. When they asked me to stop, I kicked the stool over. When they tried to grab me, I kicked at them, hard, and as I struggled, I saw my right foot connect with one of their faces. I watched the blood spew out of his nose.

They tackled me and held me to the ground until I stopped shaking. They banned me from the competition, from ever competing again. They said musical prodigies were often mentally unstable. They said it was all very horrifying. Rather devastating. They said it's a shame, to have such talent wasted.

The music hasn't been the same since. Now, when I play "Rondo Alla Ingharese Quasi un Capriccio in G Major," I have this picture: Beethoven screaming, unable to hear himself, crashing into things, pulling out his neck hair. Rage. Over a single penny.

TINA SLINN

Her dresses were all over the floor. All of them. Jeans and dress pants crumpled in one corner. Sweatpants hanging out of a drawer. She lay on her bed in panties and a sweatshirt, grey, Rosie the Riveter flexing at you on the front. She rolled over onto her side, curling her legs up when Earl knocked lightly on the door.

"Should I see if I can push the reservation back?" he said through the door. She had heard him, but who wants to deal with that shit?

"What?" she said, and Earl opened the door a crack.

"Are we gonna go or what?" he said, looking at the mess.

"I don't care." She kicked one leg out.

"You obviously care. Just put something on and let's go."

"I've got nothing to wear."

"Oh my God, Tina."

"Fuck off."

He sighed, which was worse than anything, then he started picking up her clothes and putting them back on their hangers, which was worse than sighing.

"Fuck off, Earl. Just leave it."

He picked up another dress, slipped it onto a hanger, and hung the few in his hands up in the closet.

"Well, I'm just going—" he started, when she turned to look at his little face and he stopped. He smiled, the dumb little smile she hated, but actually loved the second after it was gone.

"What?" she said.

He flopped on the bed beside her, on his stomach, and threw one arm over her belly. She put her hand on his, scratching it lightly with her nails. "We don't have to go," he said.

"No," she said. "It's stupid. I'll just wear my black jeans."

"I don't care what you wear."

"Ugh. Fuck, Earl," she said, and she threw his arm off and got up, digging in the corner for her jeans. He lay on his side, holding his head on his hand to watch her. She did that little shimmy to get the jeans over her ass, took a deep breath into her lungs to get the button done up. She looked at him and stuck her bottom lip out.

He lay on his back and stuck both of his arms out toward her.

"I'm not gonna cuddle with you," she said.

He wiggled his fingers for her to come here, which always got her. She climbed onto the bed and lay on top of him, her head on his shoulder. He wrapped his arms around her, kissed the top of her head.

"I hate you," she said, and he rolled her over so he was on top, looking into her eyes just a little too hard, then kissed her. Her mouth, her neck. His hand was under her shirt before she knew anything. That dumb smile she could never hate.

"Let's go eat," he said.

Tina had been at her thinnest when they first met—but he never ever mentioned her weight, not once. He was behind her in line at the Starbucks on Main, and when they asked her name so they could scribble it on the cup, he looked at her like he had guessed the name in his head before she had said it. She was on her way to her sister's, but for some stupid reason she decided to sit in the corner and sip her latte for a bit.

He ordered his drink and went to the bathroom while they made it. She almost left. When he came out, he put the smallest bit of cream into his coffee, then went straight to her table. "Tina?" he said, and she looked at him. He was a creep, for sure, but he just stood there waiting for her to say something. "Sorry," he said. "I heard you tell the girl."

"The woman?" she said.

"Yeah, the barista."

She didn't know what she was going to say. She turned the cup in her hand so she could read her name on the front. The woman who wrote it was probably not even out of high school. She had dotted the *i* with a heart, as usual.

"Well," he said, and he looked at the door. "I was gonna... Would you mind if I sat here?" He motioned to the chair across from her. He started to sit before she could say anything, but she was never going to tell him no anyway. "I've always..." he hesitated, sipped his coffee. It was hot and he burnt his lip a little, spilt coffee down his chin. She held out a napkin. He dabbed his chin and smiled at himself, not quite as creepy as she had thought. "I've always liked the name Tina," he said.

"Weird."

He laughed. She liked this little laugh, though she never really heard it again after their first meeting. "I guess so," he said. "Is it short for anything? Christina?"

"Nope. Just Tina."

"Interesting."

"Is it?"

"I don't know," he said, and he sipped his coffee. "Jesus, this is hot." He dabbed his lip with the napkin again.

She smiled at him. She had no idea what she was thinking, what he was thinking.

"Anyway," he said. "I guess this was kind of weird."

"What was weird?" she said, though she knew the whole thing was weird.

"I dunno. Just sitting with you for no reason." He looked over at the barista.

"Little bit."

"Well. I like your name," he said, and he laughed, sort of, though he seemed to know he probably shouldn't have. He cheersed her cup with his before standing up, held the door open for a tall man as he left, then turned and walked past the shop, off to wherever he was going. She wondered what she was supposed to do, as he walked by the window. They made eye contact and he just stopped. She probably should have looked away, but she didn't, so he turned around and came back into the shop, over to her table.

"Can I give you my number?" he said, just standing there. She started looking through her purse, who knows what for, when he reached over and took her other napkin, pulled a pen from his pocket and wrote his number. He scribbled his name underneath it. "Text if you want," he said. "Don't if you don't want." And he stuck the pen back in his pocket. He looked back at her. "But you should text."

❂

Her sister got it out of her somehow. Tina knocked on the door, then walked in, slipped her shoes off. The baby was crying from the room down the hall. Then Angel came out holding him on her hip.

"I was trying to put him down, but I don't think he'll go," she said.

"Hi Doyle," said Tina.

"You look good," Angel said, which is a dumb thing she always said. "I'm just making coffee if you want some."

Tina held up her latte.

"Why do you always do that?" Angel said, and she handed Tina the baby and scurried off to the kitchen. "He's got some toys in his basket," she yelled.

Tina could barely imagine living like this, couches littered with throw pillows, an afghan folded neatly on the back of one, toys in the basket, some kind of painting on the wall beside a clock. "Is he tired?" she said.

"I thought so," Angel said, blowing on her coffee. "I'll try to feed him." She took the baby from Tina and sat on the couch, way more comfortable there than Tina could ever be. "Want me to cover up?"

"I don't care."

But she pulled the afghan down and placed it over her shoulders. She kept looking underneath at the baby. "So I guess Mom's coming for August Long."

"What? Why?"

"I don't know. Well. She should meet Doyle, don't you think?"

"I guess so."

"Plus Aaron's mom said they wanted to stay here that weekend, and now I can say there's no room."

"Oh my God, she's staying here?"

"Where else is she gonna stay, Tina?" she said, and she looked under the afghan. "Screw it." She tossed the afghan to the side of the couch. "She's not gonna pay for a hotel."

"I guess so," Tina said, and she watched the second hand tick around the clock.

"You work today?"

"Not till six." She actually looked at the clock now. Then she just said it. She wasn't going to, but she did. "Some guy gave me his number."

"What? When?"

"Just now. At Starbucks."

"Lookit you, Tina. Was he cute?"

"I don't know."

"What does that mean?"

"He's probably a creep."

"Not every guy is a creep, Tina."

"He just came—"

"I really hate Mikey. Will you ever forget that guy?"

"It has nothing to do with Mikey."

"It has something to do with Mikey."

"I don't give a shit about him. I sure as hell don't want to talk about him anymore."

"Okay. Okay fine, but you should talk to someone about it. How long has it been now?"

"Since I left? Fuck. Two years."

"Has it been that long?"

"I don't even think about it."

"Does he still try to contact you?"

"Fuck, Angel. I don't want to talk about Mikey."

"Well call that guy then."

"He told me to text."

"Well text that guy then. What's his name?"

"Earl."

"Earl? How old is he?"

"I dunno. My age."

"Weird."

"Nice smile."

"See? Told you you look good."

When she told Earl about Mikey, three or six weeks into the whole thing, she regretted it immediately. He was angry, but mostly confused, and obviously had no idea what to say. "Why are people so fucked up?" he said.

"I don't know," she said. She was going to cry, and she hated herself for it. "He's a good person, he's just—"

"I don't think he is," he said, and he took off his hat, put it on the table, same table where they had met.

"He's an addict. And yeah, he's fucked, but who isn't—"

"He's an asshole."

"He is. He fucked me up for sure, but he's—"

"Why defend him?"

"I don't know," she said, but she couldn't look at him. He looked too sad, but maybe the most handsome he'd ever looked.

"I'm sorry," he said. "I guess I don't know the guy."

"No. I stayed with him way too long. And I think he'll always be a dick."

Earl put his hat back on, then took it off again.

"But he made it seem like… He made me believe he was my whole world. Like I was afraid of anything else more than I was afraid of him. Everything else."

"Well I hate him," he said, and she thought he probably meant it. "Will you let me hate him for you?"

She was going to cry now for sure.

"I'm gonna go to the bathroom," she said, and she stood up.

"Tina," he said.

"I have to go to the bathroom."

He rarely asked about Mikey, but once, after they had fucked hard—she wanted him to pull her hair, choke her a little—they were cuddling. He was rubbing her shoulder lightly, which was this weird thing he always did. She was just starting to feel self-conscious about lying there naked, a normal thing after the high of fucking dissipated.

"You like that rough stuff?" he asked her, out of nowhere.

"Mmmm. Kinda?" she said. "How do you feel about it?"

"It's not, like… I dunno. Forget it."

"What?"

"No, it doesn't matter. I had fun."

"What do you mean?"

"Nothing."

"Earl." She pushed herself up so she was looking down at him. He ran his hand through her hair.

"It's not… Isn't it kinda triggering for you?"

"No." She wriggled her legs under the blankets. "What the fuck?"

"Well I dunno. I just mean—"

"What? What do you mean?"

"I don't know what I mean."

"Well, you're obviously trying to say something."

"It's just. I mean you…" he put his hands behind his head. "I mean you experienced that shit in an entirely different context."

"What the hell, Earl? What the hell does that have to do with anything?"

"Forget it. I guess I just don't get it."

"What is there to get? You think I'm the first girl who likes rough sex?"

"Woman."

"What? Oh fuck you, Earl."

"I'm seriously not trying to say anything. I—"

"You fucking are saying something."

"You told me… You said you literally thought you were going to die. That's not—"

"Oh fuck off."

"It's just kind of surprising to me that you get off on that shit."

She got out of the bed. "Don't look at me," she said.

"Tina."

"Turn the fuck around," she said, holding her breasts under her arms.

He put his head back, closed his eyes.

She put on her bra, her underwear, a pair of his sweats, her sweatshirt. She left the bedroom.

"I was just surprised," he called after her. "We should talk about it."

She was going to leave, but instead she just sat on his stupid futon in the living room. He came out in his jeans and just stood there looking at her. She wanted to punch him in the throat. "I'm fucked up, okay?"

"You're not fucked up." He came to sit beside her on the futon, rubbed her back, her shoulder. "I wouldn't be here if I didn't want to be, Tina."

"It's your fucking place."

"You know what I mean. I have never for one second thought you were fucked up."

"Well you're stupid."

"I'm kind of having a hard time not saying I—"

She whipped her head around to look at him and he stopped. He looked so stupid and kind. "Don't do that," she said.

"Do what?"

"Just don't. You know I'm crazy. Why can't we just enjoy this while it lasts?"

"You always say that. I don't even know what it means."

"It doesn't have to mean anything," she said. She knew she should have left. "Why does everything have to mean something to you? Why can't you just let things happen?"

"I am letting things happen. I'm actually letting myself feel shit. You're the one—"

"You're so fucking naïve, Earl."

"I just—"

"You are. You think people can just... You really think I'd be good for you? Like, long-term?"

"I know that I feel good when I'm sitting across from you. I feel, I dunno, I feel fucking happy. And yeah, I think that's good for me."

"Fuck you. You feel happy and good, whatever, but sooner or later Crazy Tina's gonna come out and you'll want out, or honestly, I'll want out."

"Are you kidding me?"

"Oh my God, Earl, can we just stop?"

"What's the—"

"Seriously. Please. Let's just have a good time and not over-fucking-analyze everything."

"Okay," he said. He put his head back on the couch, looked up at the ceiling. "Fine. I like this. I like hanging out with you. I like being with you. I like fucking you." She could feel him laughing at himself. "And I'm not going anywhere," he said.

"Okay stop now."

"It's fun. Let's have fun. Until it's not fun, I guess."

"Exactly. Until Crazy Tina comes out."

"Fuck Crazy Tina," he said, and she thought he probably really meant he'd fuck Crazy Tina, and she didn't know what was happening anymore. He pulled her to him and kissed her, and she let him do it. Then she kissed him back hard, as if maybe she really meant it. She fucked him there on the futon.

❂

"Hey Tina," Aaron said as he opened the door. "Nice sweater."

She looked down at it. "Oh right," she said. "Thanks. Angel said you found it."

"Just one of those dumb Facebook ads."

Even Aaron seemed impossible.

"She's just getting Doyle," he said, and he swept the air in front of them as if he were welcoming her into a grand ballroom, his little fucking bungalow. Angel came out with the baby on her hip as Tina slipped her shoes off.

"Oh, it fits perfectly!" she said.

"Yeah. Thanks," said Tina. "Basically the only thing that fits these days."

"Oh shut up, Tina. You look good."

"I'm just kidding."

"You say it every time you're here."

"I don't actually care."

"You shouldn't. You look better than you have in ages. Tell her she looks good."

Aaron smiled at her, which was the literal worst.

"Jesus, Angel."

"You always look lovely to me," he said.

"Oh my God. I don't care. Thank you for the sweatshirt," she said, and flexed her arm.

"You still going to the gym?" Angel asked.

Aaron snuck off to the kitchen.

"Sometimes," said Tina. "Not so much these days."

"Why not?"

"I dunno. Don't think about it."

"You were going every day, weren't you?"

"I don't know. Quite a bit."

"I—"

"Earl doesn't ever want to go."

"How is he so thin?"

"I don't fuckin' know. All we do is eat."

"Well good for him, I guess. He doesn't mention it?"

"Not at all. He's so oblivious."

"It's probably nice though?"

"I don't know."

"Well it's better than harping on you about it."

"I guess."

"That was the worst part about Mikey."

"Oh fuck, Angel. Why do you always bring him up?"

"I'm just saying— Earl seems nice. He obviously likes you."

"I dunno."

"You don't think he does?"

"He does. He fucking does. But it's like…" She looked at the clock up there. "He's fine."

Angel looked at her as if she was looking at a stray cat she didn't want to rescue but felt obligated to.

"He's nice. He's good," said Tina. "He's like so stupid and nice, I don't get it."

"He likes you. Boys always like you…"

"He's just… Fuck. I don't know."

"Well what? You like him too, right?"

"I do. I really do. He makes me feel…"

Angel seemed to think maybe saving the cat wasn't the worst idea.

"I feel like he's too nice. Like I'm sure—"

"What does too nice mean?"

"Like. I'm pretty sure I'll cheat on him if we're any sort of long-term thing."

Angel decided no, the cat could fend for itself. It wasn't not worth the hassle. "Well that's shitty," she said.

"Right? It's so shitty."

"So, like what? You're gonna break up with him?"

"There's literally no reason to. Other than, you know, I'm probably going to cheat on him. But how do you fuckin' say that to someone?"

"I don't get it. Are you bored?"

"No. That's what I mean. He's nice. Like outrageously nice. He likes me. For some fucking reason he basically worships me. He, like, I dunno. He notices me."

"What do you mean?"

"Like he just notices me. Different than any guy I've ever been with. He notices when I have a shit day at work or whatever. Anything. He bought a new candle. Like the exact one I use, 'cause mine was almost done in the bathroom. All of a sudden there's just a new candle in the bathroom."

"Dreamboat."

"Yeah he's a fuckin' dreamboat. And I'm just…" She shrugged her shoulders, felt more sad than she meant to.

"You're fucked up."

"I'm fucked right up."

"But who isn't?"

Tina looked around the living room, Doyle kicking around in his little rubber chair, Angel sitting under the afghan, Aaron finally bringing the damn coffee out.

"He's probably just as fucked up," Angel said.

"Yeah." Tina laid her head back on the couch. "Well. I asked him to come on Friday."

"Seriously?"

"You basically made me."

"No, it's good. I think it's good. Just don't leave him alone with Mom."

"Yeah, fuck that noise."

They all laughed.

"Fuck. What am I doing?" she said, and she really had no idea.

Work was pretty quiet until about nine, when a group of guys she'd never seen came into the bar. They were nothing special, but one was obviously the leader. Broad shoulders, tattoos sticking out of his T-shirt sleeves, dirty blond hair all over the place, eyes that picked Tina out right away. He smiled at her as if he were calling her over to them.

"Hey guys, what are we drinking?" she said, and she could feel him watching her.

"Not even an introduction?" he said.

She blushed, which she hadn't planned to do. "I'm Tina," she said. "What brings you to Macleod?"

They all looked at Blondie but he would have said it anyway. "Work."

"Oh yeah? What do you do?"

"I'm an electrician."

It was stupid how it had turned into a private conversation that quickly, how his eyes were the only place to look, how the others were just bit players on the sides.

"All of you?"

They all said whatever they said.

"Cool," she said. "So what we drinking?"

Blondie let the others order first, then ordered a schooner of Kokanee. "And it's Ben," he said. "You didn't even ask." He laughed too hard. The table laughed along with him.

"I'm Tina," she said, again, and she tilted her head from side to side, which was seriously the worst. She didn't see him grin at her as she spun around to go put their orders in.

The bar filled up a bit and she settled into the night. The guys were drinking a lot, taking turns ordering shots, tequila or Jameson, typical as fuck. Until Ben ordered. She knew he'd say something stupid as soon as he waved her over. "We're gonna do a whole round of Wet Pussy," he said with that big dumb grin. The guys laughed away.

"Sounds a little fruity for a buncha dudes," she said.

"Have one with us," he said.

"I'm good," she said. "I'm actually at work right now." She motioned wildly to her apron. Blinked a bunch of times.

"You can't have one shot?"

"I can. Sometimes. Just not gonna do a Wet Pussy with you."

"Oh, I promise you'll have a Wet Pussy by the end of the night."

"I doubt that," she said, and she was pretty sure she meant it.

They stayed right till last call at eleven thirty, the rest of the bar already clearing out. Ben waved her over once more, and the guy beside him—dark hair, balding slightly, kind eyes she hadn't noticed before—said they'd do a shot of tequila gold. "Do one with us," he said.

"Last shot," Ben said.

"Fine," she said. "But I'm putting it on his tab." She nodded at Ben.

"Put the whole thing on my tab," Ben said.

"No," she said, confused, and she looked at the other guys.

"Seriously. Watch. These bitches will let me pay the whole tab."

The guys looked at her like it was some kind of stupid inside joke.

Baldy said, "It's his money," and shrugged at her.

"Damn right it's my money, bitches."

"Alright," she said, and went to get the shots. When she printed the bill the first time she scribbled the seven digits of her number under her name. Halfway to the table, though, she spun around, went behind the bar and tossed it in the trash, reprinted it.

At the table, she squeezed onto the chair with Baldy so he was between her and Ben.

"To this shithole town," Ben said before they all cheersed and took the shot. She cleared the shot glasses and took them back to the bar.

But Ben followed her.

"I'm gonna pay now," he told her.

"Sure," she said, and she typed it all into the pad. "So you'll be in town a while?" she said while it loaded.

"I will be," he said, his whole dumb face smiling at her. "I'll be seeing you around," he said.

"Well, I'll be here." She looked over at the table.

He gave the machine back. She tore off the receipt.

"Need a copy?" she said.

"Nope. All I need is your number."

"Um. I don't think so." She tore the second copy off and crumpled it.

"I do think so."

"No. No fuckin' way. I'm not that kinda girl."

"Not that kinda … Are you kidding me? Of course you are."

"Think so, huh?"

"I know so. Knew it before I sat down."

She laughed at him, though she couldn't figure out why. "Okay," she said. "I'm gonna say it once."

"What? For real?"

She said her number.

"Wait," he said. Then he tried to repeat it back. He said the first three numbers, then paused. "What's the rest."

"Nope. I said it once."

"You fucking serious?"

"I told you."

He slapped the bar counter. "Look. I didn't tip you two hundred dollars for no damn reason."

"Excuse me?"

"You heard me. What was all that over there?" He looked back at the table.

"That was literally nothing," she said.

"You fucking slut."

"Um. It is literally my job to be fucking nice to you."

"Ya know what? It doesn't even matter. You're a fuckin' slob anyway."

"You can fuck off now, Tito."

"Tito? The fuck?"

"Whatever your name is."

"You know what? Girls like you are a dime a fuckin' dozen."

"Women."

"Oh fuck that shit." He laughed so crazy she wondered why no one came over. "You think you're a fuckin' woman. That's hilarious," he said.

Baldy finally came over and grabbed him.

"Best part of my night," Ben said. "Woman." But he scrunched up his face and made his voice all high and gross. Baldy mouthed "Sorry" as he pulled Ben away, and Tina went straight to the kitchen at the back.

She leaned against the wall and tried to stop shaking. She grabbed her phone from her bag. She texted Earl. *Come over.*

By the time he got the text and made it to her place, she was three beers in. He didn't knock, which was a weird thing he had started doing.

"Take your shoes off," she said.

"What's up? What happened?" he said.

"You need to catch up." She got off her stool and got him a beer out of the fridge.

He smiled, that one she liked. "I can't get too wild," he said. "I've gotta work tomorrow."

"Call in."

"Seriously?"

"Let's get drunk and spend tomorrow hungover together."

He accepted the beer and sat across from her at the kitchen table. "We'll see," he said, and she followed him to his chair and kissed him on the mouth. "How was work?" he asked, gathering himself. He chugged some of his beer.

"Made more than three hundred in tips," she said.

"Nice. Pretty busy then?"

"Steady."

"So you just felt like celebrating?"

"I wanted to see you," which was true. She kissed him again. She could sit in her kitchen laughing and talking with him for hours.

She made him chug a few more beers before he slipped off his stool and around the table to kiss her again. He had this dumb hesitant way of kissing her, even when he was drunk, as if he was never sure she would kiss him back. But she did, and then he'd lose control of himself for a second, bite her lip, or her earlobe.

She put her hand on his chest and he pulled away a bit. "Some douche was hitting on me," she said, and he scrunched up his eyebrows.

"What'd he do?"

"Nothing. Nothing really. A lot of dudes think servers are flirting when we're just being nice."

He kissed her neck. "Did he touch you?"

"No. Nothing like that." She took a deep breath. "He just thought he deserved my number."

He kept kissing her. "You give it to him?"

"No. What the fuck?"

"I'm just kidding." He was grabbing her ass now. "I'm drunk," he said. She put her head back so he could kiss her neck better.

"How many beers have we had?"

"I don't even know." He pulled her closer to him. Was he hot?" he whispered.

"Hmm?"

"Nothing."

"It doesn't matter."

"No," he said. "It doesn't matter." He looked her in the eye and for whatever reason, she blushed. "Kiss me," he said, and she ran her hands through his hair, pulled his head toward her, guided his lips to hers. He scooped her up by the ass and she wrapped her arms and legs around him as he carried her to bed.

"Can't be that drunk," she said, though she knew they were both too drunk.

He took her shirt off, and everything else, then took his own shirt off and started kissing her everywhere. He made his way down to her pussy, and she draped her legs over his shoulders, letting herself relax. She played with his hair and wished the room wasn't spinning, glad she was here with Earl. But she was never going to cum like this anyway, so she let herself drift off toward sleep.

"You're so nice," she said, after a minute.

He started humming.

"Why are you so nice?" She held the sharp C out for a second, like a hiss. She squeezed her thighs together and he kissed her stomach, then her neck again. She thought she said, "Don't stop," but then wasn't sure if she had said it out loud. She was trying to figure out if she should say it again when he said, "You asleep?" And she just rolled over a little bit.

☙

She was surprised he was there in the morning, clunking around in the kitchen making coffee. "We have fun last night?" she asked.

"I think we did." Big smile. "I did."

"We fuck?" she said, and she wished she hadn't. His face, for a second, looked like she had forgotten his name, but then he smiled again.

"Yeah. We fucked."

"Good."

They spent the day lying on the couch, cuddling, falling asleep, watching TV. They ordered pizza for lunch somewhere around two. She said she was going to shower. "You don't have to come tonight," she said. "If you don't want."

"I do want."

"You sure? We could both skip."

"Tina . . ." he said, and he started cleaning up their paper plates.

"I'm just saying. My mom isn't any kind of fun."

"It's going to be fine."

"If I actually had any money I'd bet against it," she said.

"You've got three hundy."

She laughed. "This is true," she said and skipped off to the shower.

Twenty minutes in, he brought her little speaker into the bathroom to blast some music. He climbed in with her and held her while they showered.

They were late for supper, but not too late. Angel didn't even mention it.

"We're in here," she called from the kitchen. She was pulling things out of the oven, waving her oven mitt at the vegetables. Their mom was sitting at the table bouncing Doyle on her knee.

"Where's Aaron?" Tina said.

"Hello to you too," their mom said.

"Hey Mom."

"He ran to get buns. I forgot buns," Angel said, and she blew a bit of sweaty hair off her forehead.

"I don't even get a hug?"

Tina hugged her mom. "This is Earl," she said, and she motioned to him. "Earl. Mom."

"Rhonda," her mom said.

He shook her hand. "How was the drive?" he said. The women looked at each other.

"She took the bus," Angel said.

"Of course she did," Tina said.

But Earl seemed determined. "Oh, how long did that take?" he said.

"Oh my God. Almost four hours with stops."

"From Mount Pleasant?"

"Yes," Rhonda said, but she raised her eyebrows at Tina.

"Sorry," he said. "Tina told me."

"Well. Chris hasn't told me anything about you."

"Chris?"

"Stop it, Mom. Nobody calls me Chris," Tina said. Then, "Mom doesn't even call me Chris," to Earl.

"I do so call you Chris."

"Whatever. She hasn't called me Chris since I was like four."

"It doesn't matter," said Angel. "Honestly, I forget you're even named Christina."

Earl put his arm around her, but she wasn't ever going to kiss him in front of her mom.

"I've never thought she suited Tina," Rhonda said. "Tina's such a small name. But Christina's always been a little... rotund, shall we say."

"Jesus, Mom," Angel said.

"Yeah, Mom thinks I'm fat," Tina said to Earl. He squeezed her into him. "Might as well get that out of the way."

"You're not fat." She smiled at Earl. "I've never called her fat." She tried to laugh. "She does like her sweets though."

"Oh my God, where's Aaron?" Tina said, and she huffed off to the living room.

"So they must make a lot of stops if it takes four hours..." Earl said.

Tina came back and grabbed his arm to pull him into the living room.

"I'm not gonna eat him, Tina," Rhonda said.

"Fucking hell. Do you wanna leave?" Tina whispered to Earl.

Earl tried to kiss her.

"Don't."

"I don't want to leave. We'll be fine."

"I need a smoke," she called. "Angel, do you have smokes?"

"Bedside table."

"I thought you quit," Rhonda said.

"I did. I'm going to," Angel said.

Tina grabbed the cigarettes and took Earl out to smoke. "You should never have come," she said.

Aaron pulled up with the buns. "Smoking already, huh?"

"Fuck," said Tina, and she really thought she might cry.

"Let me have one," Earl said.

"Don't be stupid. Don't smoke," she said, but she pulled one out for him.

"Sneak out for some wine later?" Aaron said before he opened the door and left them alone.

"Seriously. Fuck."

Angel had dinner on the table when they came back in. Aaron was buttering the buns. Doyle was playing with rice in his highchair.

Tina and Earl sat across from Rhonda. Earl tried to ask about Mount Pleasant again.

"We can butter our own buns," Angel said, and Aaron brought the buns to the table.

"No wine?" said Rhonda.

"No, Mom," said Angel. "We're not having wine."

"You guys can drink wine. It's been three months almost."

"We don't need wine."

"I'm fine, you guys."

"We don't even have wine."

"Roll?" said Aaron and he held the basket out to the middle of the table. Earl took one, and they all started dishing themselves.

"So what's this?" Rhonda said after a few bites. "Are you two a real couple?"

Earl looked at Tina.

"We're just getting to know each other," Tina said.

"We've been together five months," said Earl.

"You like her, don't you?"

"Very much," he said, and he squeezed her knee under the table.

"Want my advice?"

"No he doesn't want your advice, Mom."

"Has she told you she's married?"

"Mom."

"Yeah, she's told me a bit."

"Have you seen Mikey lately?"

"Jesus. We are not talking about Mikey."

"Well you'll have to divorce him eventually."

"Will you pass the rice please?"

"I don't know how I feel about this, Earl. You're probably what? Some kind of banker?"

"Mom," said Angel.

"I'm actually an administrative assistant at the university."

"Yeah," she laughed. "You don't want to stick around long."

"Mom. You have to stop."

"I'd like to stick around I think," he said, and he smiled at Tina. It's this ridiculous little smile she'll remember, even years later, when her sons are grown and she's helping the oldest move that dumb futon into his place.

"I don't know," Rhonda said. "I've always thought Tina and Mikey were perfect for each other."

"Jesus. Fucking. Christ. Mother. Will you shut up?"

"He was good for you, Tina."

"He was—"

"I'm sorry," Earl said. "I think Mikey is a shithole, and—"

"Well you don't even know him."

"And. I think it's frankly a whole bunch of bullshit for you to say that."

"Earl. Shut up," Tina said.

Rhonda took a bite of her chicken. "Mikey would never talk to me like that for one," she said with her mouth still full.

"This conversation is over," Tina said.

"Mom," Angel said. "Will you please stop?"

"I'm getting to know my daughter's boyfriend."

"He's not … Fuck. We're leaving."

"Tina, you're not leaving," said Angel.

"You're not gonna tell me anything about him?"

"I don't tell you anything about anything," Tina said. Earl squeezed her knee again. She grabbed his hand. "Because you're a fucking ass about everything," she said.

"Someone's gotta speak some sense to you."

"And you're gonna speak some sense? My fucking alcoholic mother who can't even keep a licence? Or a fucking job?"

"Well—"

"Who fucked off before my fifth fucking birthday? 'Cause she thought a bottle of wine was more—"

"Tina, shut the fuck up," Angel said, and she stood up.

"You sure you should eat all that, sweetie?"

"Fuck you," Tina said, and she got up and left the house.

"We all have our addictions," Rhonda said before Earl could follow Tina out. "You don't want to be with a Slinn, Earl," she called out from the kitchen.

"Fucking bullshit," he muttered, though it was loud enough.

"We can go to Rufus, Earl."

"I don't care."

"You made the reservation."

"Well, do you want to go to Rufus?"

"It doesn't matter."

"Exactly."

"Exactly what. We can go wherever."

"Where would you actually like to go?"

"It literally does not matter to me."

"Okay. I'm going to Rufus."

"I should have worn something nicer."

Earl drove to Bubba's anyway. They held hands as they walked in. It was busy but not packed, and the little sign that said *Wait to be seated*—or *Please seat yourself*, depending on the day—wasn't anywhere. Tina felt lost in a way that she would never be able to explain. She needed the subtle telepathy of architecture telling her what to do, though she would never have noticed this about herself, and certainly would never have said it out loud if she had noticed. She wanted the room to show her—sit here; look at this thing; follow this aisle; wait to be seated.

"Where do you wanna sit?" Earl said.

"I dunno. Are we supposed to seat ourselves?"

"I don't think it matters."

"It usually tells us what to do."

"You want a booth?"

"I don't know."

"Those people are leaving," he said, and he pulled her over there as if she were a balloon tied to his wrist. "This okay?" he said. She slid into the booth, taking a minute to settle in and relax.

"Hey guys. Can I grab you drinks?" the server said.

"I don't know. Are you drinking?" she asked Earl.

"Yeah, I'll have a beer. A pint of Canadian?"

"Absolutely. And for yourself?"

"Should I get a Caesar?"

"Do you want a Caesar?"

"I don't know. I don't know what I feel like."

"I can give you a minute."

"Fuck it. I'll get a Canadian."

"Two Canadian? Absolutely."

"What does she mean absolutely?"

"I don't know," Earl said. He watched the server strut away. He seemed nervous, which was the worst. "You know what day it is?"

"Tuesday. Like the date?"

"The date."

"Twenty-sixth?"

"The twenty-sixth." He just watched her.

"Is it … Should I know something about the twenty-sixth?"

"No."

"Annnnd two Canadian for ya," the server said, setting their beer on the table. "You ready to order?"

"Not even close," Tina said, and she grabbed a menu.

"Okay. I'll give you a minute."

Earl started flipping through the menu. "We met six months ago on the twenty-sixth," he said.

"Oh my God are you serious?"

He shrugged, smiled, maybe blushed.

"I should probably have known that," she said, and she grimaced, but she didn't know anything. She was never going to remember that.

"It's not a big deal."

"Shit. Is that why you made reservations?"

"No. Not really. Maybe."

"Of course you would remember that."

He blushed for real now, which really was the worst.

"It's been a good six months."

"It has," she said, and she could have meant it, if she had actually thought about it. She tried hard to read the menu. She looked out at all the people eating, talking, arguing maybe. Probably not. Earl stared at his menu as if it held the secret to the universe.

"What're you gonna get?" he said, finally, still looking at the thing.

"I dunno," she said, flipping the middle page back and forth over and over.

"Not the chicken fingers?"

"I dunno. I always get them."

"Their grilled cheese sandwiches are awesome."

"Grilled cheese."

"They have like five different types."

She sighed, closed the menu, shoved it to the side.

"What?"

"Nothing," she said. "I'm not hungry."

Earl took a big sip of his beer, wiped his mouth with the back of his hand. "Just get the strips," he said. "You know you like them."

"I hate doing that though."

"Eating food you like?"

"Shut up. I hate getting the same thing every time."

"Since when?"

"Since always."

"You always get the same thing."

"Exactly. Imagine all I've missed out on."

"Like what?"

"Like the fucking grilled cheese. Five different grilled cheeses. How could you fucking pick?"

They laughed at that. She found the list. "Grilled cheese and bacon," she said. "Fried pear grilled cheese. Apple and gouda grilled cheese. Four cheese. Fuck. I could never eat a grilled cheese here."

"I bet they're all tasty."

"Yeah, but that's the point. If I choose one, I'm instantly missing out on four of them." She sipped her beer. "And I'll never ever experience them."

"Okay, that's a little dramatic, no? Just get a different one next time."

"But then I'm still missing out on all four the next time. No matter what you choose, you're actually choosing to miss everything else. You literally do not experience, like, 99.9 percent of everything you could experience." She stopped when she noticed how Earl was taking her all in.

"What are we talking about right now, Tina?"

"What do you mean?"

"I don't know… Look. I know you don't want to label this thing, or whatever. I wasn't tryin' to—"

"Oh my God, Earl. I am literally just talking about food. I even think about the food I don't get to eat I guess."

Earl rolled his eyes, which was a weird thing to start doing all of sudden.

"I'm not speaking in code, Earl. What could you possibly think I'm saying?"

"Be my girlfriend."

"What the fuck?" she leaned back, threw her arms up, though she kind of wished she hadn't.

"Why is that so hard?"

"Why does it even matter?"

"It does matter. It's—"

"It doesn't. It does not matter. We're always together…"

"I think it matters. Things matter, Tina. I don't understand what you're worried about."

"I'm not worried about anything. I'm literally just a fat girl talking about food."

"I'm not talking about food even a little bit."

"We're not fucking other people. We practically live together. We—"

"It matters. It matters that you fucking deny it every time some-one calls me your boyfriend."

"I—"

"What am I supposed to feel about that?"

"Stop overthinking everything. Why can't you just... Like, I'm surprised it's even lasted six months..."

He took his hat off, put his head down on his hands, then ran his fingers through his hair, eyes closed.

"Earl..."

"Have we decided?" the server said.

"I don't think we're going to eat," Earl said before Tina could say anything.

"I'm gonna have the grilled cheese," she said. "One of each."

"We actually have five varieties."

"I know."

"Tina."

"Oh. Okay. Well we're actually out of the gouda right now."

"Oh for fuck sakes."

"Tina."

"I'm so sorry," said the server.

"It's fine. I'm sorry." Earl said. "I'll just pay for the beer and we're going."

"I don't want to go."

Earl slumped down into his seat.

"I'll give you a minute," the server said, and she took off out of there.

"We'll share four grilled cheese?" he said to her.

She pulled her purse onto her lap and made sure she had every-thing, then slid out of the booth. "I'll make grilled cheese at home," she said.

Years later, she remembers him with all the fondness she can muster.

"I could have loved you," he had told her, not all that long after Bubba's, this little phrase filling her with so much hope and feeling throughout all these years. "But I think you're afraid to hear that."

"I don't even know what that means," she had said. She was tired, back then, and wouldn't ever fight with him to stay anyway.

"It means I know you care about me. Or whatever. I can feel it when you look at me. But you're afraid to stand up and fucking say it—"

"I—"

"And I think you're afraid to—just—afraid."

She couldn't look at him, just stared at the floor of the car.

"I feel like you think you don't deserve to be loved."

"I do," she said to the floor, though when she said it, she could feel a thousand reasons squeezing in on her why that was never going to be true. She would have been surprised if he had even heard her say it.

BABY, OH BABY

It's later than I'd like. Some lady on the TV—red-eyed and smiling like she's getting away with something—is confessing that since her husband died, she's been carrying his ashes around with her, holding him, smelling him, tasting what's left of him. Each day, she takes a pinch of him, slips it into her mouth and lets her saliva and the pressure of her tongue pressing against her cheeks, her teeth, the roof of her mouth, transform him into a semi-solid ball, a pill she can swallow to rid herself, for a moment, of her relentless sorrow.

"It's disgusting," the daughter—who has just discovered that her mother eats her father—is saying. "I understand she's grieving, but she could take up painting, or gardening. She could take flowers to his cemetery every day if she wanted, build a goddamn greenhouse over his grave and live in it. It's just—gross."

The TV therapist straightens his tie and tells the camera it's not abnormal to experience these types of quirks while grieving. He's just glad she is seeking the proper help. But I'm watching this lady eat her husband. Again and again they're showing her pinch, press, taste, masticate, smile—her little eyes half-closed—swallow. And I'm thinking she doesn't want any help, they should leave her alone, let her finish the rest of it, of him.

My own daughter was a go-getter. She had an ambition I couldn't understand. Even her labour lasted a mere two and half hours. She could speak in sentences and sing the alphabet before she was two. She could read her own bedtime stories before she started kindergarten. In second grade, when Miss Garrison asked, What would you like to be when you grow up? she said she wants to be like Forrest Gump. Like Forrest Gump, but not retarded (you'll forgive her use of the R-word, I hope. She was only six when she said it). She had been so taken with the movie. How come he walks like that? How come she makes that noise? How come he talks like that? Why's she naked?

She skipped first grade, then third grade, graduated at fifteen. I'll take a year off, she said when people asked her what she would do next. I'll take a year off to see the world, to run a marathon. Yes, I said, but what will you really do? And she looked at me funny, as if I should have known she was going to do exactly as she said. Run, Mommy, run, she said, and she ran in the Boston Marathon, in the New York City Marathon. She set a world record for the most official marathons run in a single year.

I think I'll go back to school, she said after running. She finished a liberal arts degree, double major—philosophy and history—in three years. Playing any ping-pong? I asked her on the phone during her third year. Table tennis, she said, for anyone who's serious about it. And Yes, she said, I am. She was the NCAA champion two years in a row. I just hope you don't enlist in the army, I told her.

What's that supposed to mean? she said.

Forrest Gump, I said. And she enlisted in the Marines the week following her convocation.

She climbed the ranks and was sent to Iraq, where she was wounded saving civilians from Islamic extremists, for which she was awarded the Victoria Cross, the first Canadian to receive the honour. She did not show the governor general her ass when they placed it around her neck. She wrote about her experiences in a memoir, which was deeper than anything I could have imagined. The great thinkers of the world declared it "a scary realization of the world around us. This book, if taken seriously, *will start a revolution*" (italics theirs!). It was a *New York Times* #1 bestseller by the time she stood for her reading at the Barnes & Noble on the Avenue of the Americas in New York City, three and a half weeks into her tour, which was cut short—before I was even able to attend a single reading—due to her unfortunate assassination. The revolution would follow swiftly.

"She donated her organs for scientific research via the micro-document she kept folded in her wallet, signed. The rest of her body, they cremated. She sits on the mantel under the TV."

I tell this story to strangers over coffee, after my yoga classes, to my bus drivers who nod politely and shake their heads and say, "That's crazy." I tell pieces of it during my Thursday night cribbage club, at my Wednesday evening support group for parents who have lost children. I tell this story so often, I know just when to slow down, to elaborate, to get people to really listen.

To the yoga class, I slip into details of her training, how she would run ten to fourteen miles before I'd even get out of bed each morning, how she would eat fish and chicken and grains and vegetables, but the night before races, she'd eat a huge bowl of spaghetti—with just a smidgen of butter, though this is not recommended—how she seemed happiest with a breeze in her face and the asphalt thumping along under her sneakers. I tell them how, as a teenager, she placed in the top ten in two races, unheard of for a sixteen-year-old.

I save the details of her assassination for the bus drivers—who no doubt tire of the usual stories they hear from the regulars about the bargains they've found on fingerless gloves—whose eyes widen at that word. Assassinated. They look at me in the mirror, anxious to hear how the crowds gathered, how the bookstore—all three levels— was packed wall-to-wall with eager spectators. "It's a wonder no one else was killed in the stampede," I tell them. I lower my voice—"the stampede after the man who did it, tattoos on his forearms and neck, a single faded teardrop under one eye, the hint of black ink under his thinning hair, ripped black jeans, chip in his front tooth"—I pause to let the image sit there in front of us... "He jumped onto the stage, shoved over the podium and plunged a knife deep into her neck while her fans went screaming for the door."

To the support group, I tell how she would write home every week she was away at college, twice a week from Iraq, with extra post-cards here and there. How she would never write to complain, only with some uplifting tidbit of information that would provide a simple epiphany of sorts. I tell them how the day before she died (I would never use *assassinate* here), she wrote a letter that said, *I feel like something big is coming, something that could bring about real change, finally. I'm only glad to do my own little part.*

I tell them how she ended the letter so perfectly: *I feel as if something is urging me to tell you just how much I love you, I've tried writing a poem, but have found nothing conveys my feelings better than, I Love You. You must pretend, Mother, that this is the first time I've said it, for I feel a new adoration for you with each day I am away.*

I quote this from memory and watch their tears well up.

I tell this story—these stories—because I'm always shocked when I realize nobody else is ever thinking of her, no one else will acknowledge this sorrow. I tell it because I like the stunned look on people's faces when they find out how wonderful she was, how much she was able to do, the life she lead. I tell it because I like the way they shake their heads and rub my shoulder or give me a hug, how they cry along with me and say, "It's not your fault." I tell it so that for a moment she is real, to offer proof she has not been imagined.

I tell it because I can't bear to tell them I didn't even realize I was pregnant. I met her father at the scene of a horrific traffic accident. We both ran to see a man, already dead, lying in the street. He seemed—my daughter's father seemed—so calm and unaffected by the bloody mess. I was uncontrollably drawn to him. Terrified of him, but unable to leave his side. He said we had to get away; he asked me to go for coffee, but we walked to Bubba's and got drunk instead. We slept at my apartment, slept together at my apartment. I remember being scared of how he was looking down at me. Like he had just found something he had lost a long time ago. We were still drunk when we woke up, and I made him leave, or he left me there. There was some kind of awkward kiss at the door and I never saw him again. Never even exchanged numbers. Not sure we even exchanged names.

I don't tell people this. I don't tell people I just kept on drinking, living life as usual. I didn't notice anything. Nothing new. Nothing wrong. When it happened, I thought, I didn't know period cramps could hurt so bad. I didn't know those period cramps were actually my little daughter rushing out of my toxic womb—in a mere two and a half hours of labour.

She was two pounds, six ounces. She was a fighter. "A go-getter," the doctor called her. "She knew she needed to get out, and she got out," he said. "You're lucky. She seems as if she'll be perfectly fine. Perhaps a slight retardation." (You'll forgive his use of the R-word, I hope. It is still a clinical term, he told me).

"Like Forrest Gump?" I asked, crying.

"Hmm," the doctor said. "Not sure, exactly."

I don't tell people how the doctor tried to comfort me, how he set his hand on my shoulder, how I slapped his hand, his face, how the IV popped out of my arm. I don't tell them how she—my little daughter—thrived for three and a half weeks, how the doctor said she's doing so well, he's never seen a little one with so much spunk. How she suddenly had an attack of gastrointestinal perforation, how she screamed and screamed and flailed around and was rushed to surgery. I don't tell anyone how her little eyes pleaded with me, how they still plead, so afraid of missing out on the future. I don't tell them how my love for her has begun to feel pathetic, a morbid little secret I will not let go of. Time heals, they say, but it does not change what is. She will forever have lived, but will in fact never live.

The doctors tried and tried, but couldn't do anything, in the end. Her little body, they cremated. She sits on the mantel above the fire.

The reality TV show is wrapping up. The woman has seen all the therapists and is saying that she will try to stop eating her husband. The credits roll over her slow-motion face as she tastes just one last little bit with that same strange little smile. The following program has four contestants feeding cupcakes to four judges for the chance to win money and fame. But as I'm watching, I can't stop looking at my daughter, in her urn—just barely less than a pound of white ash. I can't stop wondering how she would taste, how she would feel under my tongue, against my cheeks, my teeth. I reach up, take her off the mantel, hold her close to my chest. I lie on the couch and place her gently on the cushion beside me. I wrap my arm around her so she doesn't fall. I check the seal, fondle it as I lie there. Crying, whispering. "My baby, oh baby, dear baby, sweet baby."

DELANEY WATERS

Delaney Waters asked me if I ever think how easy it is for someone to change your life. At the time I thought it was one of the silliest questions I'd ever heard. I was thinking a religious conversion, or some love-at-first-sight nonsense. She was talking more subtle changes. Like the way you'd make your twos with a loop instead of a point. Or how you'd start looking at thrift stores for a certain type of shoe, turn up the volume when you'd hear a certain tune, take one street instead of another. These things don't change you for others, but they change you all the same.

I met her on the first day of sixth grade, which is hardly unordinary, but I'll never forget how she claimed her desk, just waltzed through the classroom to the desk closest to the window, unpacked her things. She sat down and stared out the window as if somehow she belonged out there, somewhere else. While the rest of us were running around, screeching about our vacations, judging each other's outfits, counting our pencils, she was sitting, staring confidently out the window, unbothered by any of us. Then she flipped the cover of her sketchbook open and started writing something, or drawing, probably drawing. And when Miss Hilsden started her welcome-to-the-class spiel, she stopped midsentence to wait for Delaney to finish drawing. "We usually put our books away when the teacher starts talking," Miss Hilsden told her.

"Okay," Delaney said, but she kept drawing for a few more seconds before looking up at her and flipping the book closed.

"Do you remember your first day of sixth grade?" I asked her once. This was not long before the day I left her on the swings.

"I remember I was the most popular girl in the whole school," she said. And she laughed as if she were being ridiculous. "People remember whatever they want. It's all just made up." But I'll never forget watching her that first day. The other girls were watching her out of the corners of their eyes too, wondering how a girl could be so unworried. I remember hoping I would be her friend, looking around at the other girls and finding them hoping the same. The boys too, I might as well say it. None of us talked to her that first day, so I get her joke. But really she remembers it the same as I do.

As hard as I try, I can't remember the first time we spoke to each other. I remember *a* time—it had to be pretty soon after that first day, because I feel nervous when I think of it. There's nothing I should be nervous about now, obviously, but it's as if I can feel my eleven-year-old nerves rising up as I sit here. I was slipping my knapsack into my locker when I noticed Delaney coming toward me with the same knapsack. I'm not sure how I hadn't noticed it before then. Every day I could feel her walking behind me to her locker—she walked with the same confidence with which she looked out the window. As if nothing outside of herself even registered. I stood there mentally wrestling with whether I should or shouldn't make the joke, then finally decided. "Nice knapsack," I said.

"Oh, thanks." She held it out in front of her to look at it, then looked at mine, and the joke was there. "Same to you," she said. No wait. She said, "Great minds..." Just like that. She left the end off, like I knew what was coming. And I guess I did, 'cause we laughed like we were getting away with something as she touched my shoulder with her hand. Then I remember the other girls looking at us with those darts that said, *I hate you for leaving me out of it.*

There's that time we played four square at recess. It must have been early in the craze 'cause there were only the four players in the box, plus a line of eight or ten other kids waiting to get in. I remember I was king—some of us tried to call it queen when a girl was there, but it never stuck. Delaney was kitty-corner from me and Jack Benson was three or four back in line, throwing little stones at Delaney every time the ball was kicked to her. One time he hit her head with a stone and she missed the ball, so she went after him in line, kicking him in the knee. "Why you gotta be such a dweeb?" she said.

"You're out," he screamed. "You missed it. You missed."

"She's not out you jerk," I said. "Stop being such a dweeb or I'll kick you out." The king could do things like this, in extreme cases. When I said it, the rest of the kids cheered and I got a little embarrassed, not used to being so bold. But Jack got even more embarrassed, while Delaney had this proud little smirk, so I said, "He's such a nerd sometimes," and we laughed and I kicked the ball to her. I think this was a first time too, but then I don't know where the confidence would have come from. I was never the go-getter in any relationship. I always waited until I was sure they wanted it before I declared my loyalty.

We had arranged, a bunch of us girls, to meet at the downtown Famous Players to watch some movie or other. I can't remember the movie. It wasn't the point. The point was that we were old enough to say our sisters would be there to watch us—or in my case, Delaney's sister would be there—and our parents would say, "Oh alright, but stick together." Looking back I'm sure my mother doubted our truthfulness, but I think she felt comforted by the lie, telling herself there was an older sibling there to watch us. Most times, though, we'd split from them as soon as possible. We'd choose a different movie, or just walk around the mall instead, try on shoes we thought we'd never be able to afford, suck on jawbreakers till our jaws hurt.

I remember Jenna was coming this time. And Shayna. April and Rebecca. Probably a few others. But when I got there, it was only Delaney waiting. There's still a nervousness that lingers with this memory, but excitement too. I was always wondering what she thought of me, what the other girls thought too, and if I was as important to Delaney as she was to me. I liked having the other girls there, to show off for, but felt a certain privilege when I got to spend time alone with Delaney. Though this was pretty early on. The feeling dwindled the more we hung out.

Anyway, we stood there waiting, just chatting and giggling and looking for the others until probably ten minutes after the movie had started. "Let's just ditch 'em," Delaney said. "I'm not missing the movie just 'cause these girls can't get here on time." We went in, sat in the front row and laughed till we just about peed ourselves in our seats. We stayed until the credits rolled up and the film ran out and the guys came in with their brooms and asked us to leave so they could clean up the popcorn.

On our way out Delaney said, "It's kinda nice the others didn't show. Don't have to try so hard." I looked at her to see what she meant, but her mom pulled up and she ran to the car, waving before she crawled into the back seat. Thinking about it now, it's possible she might've said it to any of the girls—if I hadn't shown up and someone else had. But back then it meant she was glad it was just us. She wanted it to be just us. She chose me. Somehow.

After that I wasn't as nervous around Delaney. Whether she had meant to or not, I felt like she had declared me her best friend, and this declaration was enough for me. While the others were showing off, vying for her attention, I'd just sit and relax. She'd catch my eye and I'd smile a little, making a secret joke of the other girls. And when they'd talk about her while she wasn't there—"She totally has to like Jackie Benson. Look at the way she flirts with him"—I'd set them straight—"She doesn't even. She's got a boyfriend from the next district over. She told me." She told me, I'd say, and the other girls would look at me funny, trying to figure out if I was lying, then deciding to believe me, sulking a bit.

It's not that we didn't like each other. I had sleepovers with Jenna or Sam, and we'd stay up half the night laughing so hard we got the hiccups. Or if I was walking home, I'd always walk with Shayna, who lived one block over from me. And we wouldn't even mention Delaney, or boys or grades. All of us liked each other, sure, but at that age we were ruthless. We thought the schoolyard was the entire world, and we were jostling to the top of it with our cute smiles and our new shoes and our cutting remarks. The guys would be wrestling or playing tackle football, and we'd be huddled together, laughing and ripping each other's self-esteem to shreds.

Delaney didn't seem to worry about any of this. Oh, she could cut you down. Better than most. But the other girls would purse their lips, trying to glare holes through you just for a second, then laugh it off—not entirely convincingly—with a little flick of their hair. Delaney, if anyone ever tried to go after her, would just laugh in your face, making you feel small for even having said anything. It was like she knew she was at the top. We all did.

So Delaney being top, and telling me things she didn't tell the others seemed to make me number two without even having to try. I just had to say, "She told me."

And she did tell me. She called me once, not long after the movie night, and said, "Meet me at that little park by the 7-Eleven?" I said sure, and ran over to wait on the swings.

She came riding up on her bike, hopping off while it was still going, letting it roll into the rocks and fall over. She sat in the swing next to mine and pumped her legs until she got the swing going so high it screeched at the top, before she flew back down. The way the rust on the chain rubbed the bar, it screeched. I swung beside her for a few minutes until she jumped off her swing to land in the rocks.

"I broke up with my boyfriend," she said. "He dumped me," she said. "Started going out with my sister."

At the time I had never had a boyfriend. Delaney talked about hers, but in a funny sort of way. Like an imaginary friend almost. But one she made invisible on purpose. We knew about him, but would never see him. And we knew it was supposed to be that way.

"He didn't even say why," she said. "Just showed up and asked, 'Is Abigail home?'"

This turned out to be a regular occurrence. She had a way of making the boys like her. She had this wild blonde hair that seemed to drive them nuts, and she knew how to bring attention to herself, how to give out the right amount of her attention before snatching it away, making them work for it. And they worked for it. Well, at least, worked more for her attention than for mine, that's for sure. The problem was with boys she wasn't ruthless. If they worked hard enough, she'd fall for them. Like legitimately fall for them. Even at twelve—that first time she told me on the swings—I could see she was devastated. She refused to look up from the rocks, no matter how much I wanted her to. I wanted her to look at me, to confide in me, or something. Anything. I wanted to tell her the guy was a joke. He was obviously an idiot. She was perfect.

Instead we just sat there. Until finally she told the rocks the story of how she had met him. I let the swing stop swinging and I let her tell it. Her mom had organized a Tupperware party. One of the other moms—a weirdo her mom should never have invited in the first place—called last minute to say she'd love to come, had been looking forward to it, would hate if she had to miss it, but her sitter cancelled, could she bring her son?

They bounced on the trampoline. Delaney'd double-bounce him so high his eyes would bulge and he would lose control of himself, falling through the mat and getting stuck in the springs. They lay on the tramp while the sun set. Then they went in to watch a movie. But she left him on the couch and went up to her room, waited for him to leave. He stole her number out of his mother's address book as soon as he could without his mother noticing. He called, asked "May I please speak to Delaney?" "Mom thought he was a prince," she said. Then whispered, "Abigail," as if she were making a wish.

This Delaney—the Delaney at the swings—was a completely different girl than the everyday Delaney. I felt invisible, as if she'd be there telling her stories breakup after breakup whether I was sitting there or not. Yet she called me each time. "Meet me at the swings?" So I knew she needed me there. Her wild and confident self who didn't seem worried about anything at school or with the girls would slip away, and instead here was a girl burying bits of her heart under playground rocks while I sat on a swing and listened. Eventually she'd say, "Oh he's just a boy," or "He was kinda weird anyway," and she'd hop on the other swing and swing till it screeched.

Once she said, "You know, it doesn't matter who you are, they'll always get tired of you." I think I said, "What?" or "Hmm?" I'm sure I didn't ask her to explain. But I remember she started speaking at nearly the same time that I did. "If they like you 'cause you're crazy, they'll leave you for someone boring. If you're smart, they'll want stupid. Ditzy, they want brains. They always want the opposite of what they fall in love with." And for a long time after this conversation she didn't have a boyfriend. She just stopped.

I'm sure she was mistaken. Surely there must be men who fall in love with a girl, a woman, and love her forever. But all of a sudden it's forty-some years later, and I can still feel the pressure of that conversation in my stomach. The fear planted in that little girl on those swings—the fear of being found unsatisfactory, of being left behind—has grown into this great big life of solitude. The fear of being left alone has held me firmly in the arms of loneliness for far too long.

I did have my chances, I'm sure I did. Even back then. In the summers, we'd go to Wally's Wacky Waterslides. They set up on the outskirts of town, three slides winding down the old Patterson Hill until they landed in a pool at the bottom. I remember talking about them at school—"Did you see the tunnel slide? That one goes in a full circle. There's like a five-foot drop." We'd beg our parents for the three dollars. Or we'd wait until Saturday to collect our allowance. We'd mow the lawn every day, weed the garden even. It was new back then. We were desperate to race down those slides.

It was guaranteed that Jack Benson and his buddies would be there. I have no idea where they found their three dollars every day, but I never went a single time without seeing them. They'd be there to pull our hair, or smack our ice creams over or throw our sandwiches to the seagulls—that first year at least. They were there to chase us up the stairs, to race us down the slides, to splash us, to pretend to drown us, to lay their towels next to ours, making fun of us for trying to get a tan.

I assumed they were after Delaney, and most of them were. But once, as we lay panting on the grass having just escaped the deep end as they tried to pull us under, Delaney said, "Boy, Jack sure can't get enough of you."

"Yeah right," I said. But a whole new world was opening up. One in which I might be important—to a boy. One wherein the things I did—flicking my hair, wiping water from my eyes with the back of my hand, straightening my bathing suit straps, pulling out a wedgie, or even the way I ate my sandwich, licking the jelly off its sides before it all slopped out into the grass—could be noticed by someone, could be thought about and analyzed, remembered for years to come, talked about, reminisced over. I doubt all this went through my head back then, but for the first time ever I considered that maybe I was number one to somebody. "They're only flirting with me because you're here," I said.

"No, Jackie couldn't keep his hands off you over there."

"Oh please. Jackie Benson? I would never," I said. But when I looked over at him, he was there looking back at me, for a second at least, before he looked away and ran into the pool.

It's almost stupid thinking about it all now. There's certain people in this world who just happen to find the other half of themselves, and step into line next to them for a life of togetherness. The rest of us, the majority I'm sure, spend our lives running ahead and slowing down, never quite able to sync. One of you needs to sit still until the other realizes he just needs to sit down beside you.

Jack spray-painted a section of the tube slide black. At least I think it was him. He said there was a section of the fence over behind the bush he could squeeze through, and he just had to climb the metal structure and sit on the one bar and paint. For me, there was no reason not to believe him. He was always talking about his midnight escapades, and once I even went with him—this was years later, just after we had graduated high school. We went under this bridge on the highway just before leaving town. He took out a bunch of spray paint and painted. I didn't know he even still did stuff like this. Some of it was beautiful. Before then, I'd never noticed graffiti at all. It just seemed like a mess on the side of the road, or wherever. But this was beautiful. I couldn't tell what it was, of course, but it pushed me backwards, opened my eyes just a bit wider, stretched the world out a little. "Whatcha think?" he said when he finished. He looked at me so eagerly, as if he needed my answer to keep going.

Or wait. He must have said, "You like it?" 'Cause I just stood still for a minute, tried to figure out this look on his face, then said, "Yeah." One word. I might have used more if the question were what do you think.

Anyway, he laughed. A weird little laugh, like he was asking me to stop lying to him. Then he pulled out a black can and painted over his handiwork. I don't know what I was thinking at the time, why I just stood and let him cover it up. When I remember it now, I run up to him, I grab his arm before he's even done shaking the can, I tell him I love it, I couldn't bear to live in this world without it, now that it's here.

But I didn't. And for years following, that black rectangle, whenever I drove past it, was like a broken toe that healed up all funny. I'd forget about it all day, until I pulled off my sock, and the strangeness of the toe put the memory of the pain back in my head.

It was a long time later—when I saw the city crew sandblasting the walls under that bridge—that I had the idea that the black section of the slide was actually Jack's artwork, that he had spent his nights pouring his soul out onto public canvases of all sorts, then hiding it under layers of black.

There were four or five sections painted black before Wally must have gotten fed up, and had the whole thing painted black. So then you were alone when you slid down it. It was hot, 'cause of the sun. It was uncomfortable. You were hot and alone and it stretched the slide longer so you wondered if you'd ever reach the bottom. We basically stopped using the tunnel slide. "Do you ever think how easy it is for someone to change your life?" Delaney asked not long after Jack painted the slide black.

"What do you mean?" I said.

"Well Jackie Benson changed our lives just by painting that stupid slide. It's not even fun anymore." And for some reason—I was still young—I thought change must be a good thing. I thought she was saying Jack had changed her life, what a wonderful thing. I thought she was laying claim. I think I'll have him she was saying.

"I still like that slide," I said.

"Yeah, but we used to love it."

We didn't go to Wally's as much after that. When we did go, it was mostly just to lay in the sun and show off our suits. Delaney was careful to turn every fifteen minutes to get an even tan. She'd close her eyes as if she were asleep, but she was still aware of everything around us. "It's pretty dead today," she'd say. Or "What's with these little kids?" Or "Why don't the two of you just go out already?" as I was watching Jack come rushing out of the mouth of the tube slide. She'd turn on her stomach, undo her bikini top if the boys were close.

We were just about sixteen. We would have grown out of the water park anyway, I'm sure. But back then, as I sat beside Delaney, watching the kids laughing and splashing, and forgetting any sort of real world, I blamed the black tunnel slide. I blamed Jack, I guess. And Delaney too. We could have ignored the black, made it into a wild adventure. Why were we just lying there, showing off—as if there was anything for me to show. Sometimes we wouldn't even get into the water, just pay the entrance fee to bake in our bikinis.

I brought a flashlight. I guess it was the last time we went. Delaney pulled up to my house, I was about to go running out, but on the table by the door was an old flashlight. I still couldn't tell you why, but I threw it in my bag and ran out to her. It must have been for the tunnel slide—there's just no other reason to think of, even if I try—but I don't remember having the idea until we got to the park and were sitting down to tan.

"We should take this down the tunnel," I said.

"Why'd you bring that?"

"Don't know. Just grabbed it on the way out."

"You want to go down that bad?"

"No. Who cares. I bet it'd look cool though."

"Totally," she said, and she got up quick, started toward the slide. "Like a shot of sunlight or something."

She was more excited than I was, I think. Well I'm sure she was, but I was taken aback. I watched her practically skip to the stairs, looking all around the park as if she thought everyone would be watching us, congratulating us on our great idea, getting out of the pool to follow us up to watch the experiment. "I totally wanna go first. But it was your idea."

"You can go if you want," I said. 'Cause I was trying to figure out why she was so desperate.

"No. You've got to do it. Just make sure you sit up at the end so you're going slow. So you don't get it wet at the bottom."

She was running up the stairs, talking, talking, talking about the best way to hold the flashlight, or what it would feel like to be a ball of light in the darkness. "We'll be a shooting star," I think she said. I remember I was just about to go down, standing at the top looking into the darkness. A thought was forming in my head—something about our roles reversing, how Delaney must have felt something like this when we all started following her—when I heard her scream, "Jackie!"

I turned around and there was Jack, grabbing the flashlight from me and jumping into the slide, disappearing around the bend before I could really process what was happening. I jumped in after him, but he was always faster than me when we raced, and I knew I wouldn't catch him. The edge of the light was just past my reach, and I started hoping he'd just be able to keep it out of the water.

It seems weird remembering all of this. I was always so aware of Jack. Even when I wasn't looking for him, I seemed to feel him, like I knew where he was at all times, somehow. I used to lie in bed imagining him out on his bike, racing around corners, holding his arms out to let the wind blow his hair back, slowing when he gets to his house, leaning his bike against the garden shed, sneaking in the back door, throwing his sweater on a hook, creeping up the stairs, taking his clothes off, lying down in bed, looking out his window, falling asleep. And I think I believed he was actually doing these things. I'd wait till he fell asleep, in my own imagination, before I could actually fall asleep. And I guess I secretly felt he probably did the same with me, or something similar. Even days we didn't say a word to each other I felt I had spent the day with him.

Then all of a sudden the slide lit up, and there was Jack, sitting up, stopped, twisted around to wait for me. I was going too fast. I slammed into him. He yelled something. My big toe burned and pain shot through my foot. The light flickered off. I rode the rest of the slide in a daze while he screamed as if he'd been shot in the arm. I felt his legs kicking under the water as I splashed into the pool. I surfaced in a cloudy mist of blood.

Jack was holding his nose, still screaming, blood dripping down his hands. The chlorine was sucking up the blood, destroying the evidence. "Everyone out," the lifeguard was yelling. "We're gonna have to shut 'er down for a bit. Give me that flashlight. Why would you take that down a waterslide? Give it here. You kids are ridiculous." Delaney came down the other slide, the open one. We packed up our things and left.

For probably two weeks before school started back up, Delaney and I met at the swings after dinner every night, or if we were already together we'd walk over there and swing, talk, gossip. I wish I could remember more of those conversations. She didn't have a boyfriend then, I remember, so we probably talked about all the boys. She'd talk about Jack. And I would too, I guess. But I could never figure out if she actually liked him or not. She always talked about him in association to me—but she'd remember the smallest little details of him. I remember her saying something like, "Isn't it weird how you can tell he's only fake smiling 'cause he's got a dimple when he's really smiling? Like when he's smiling at you?" As if she never stopped watching him, trying to sort him out.

So I'd steer the conversation elsewhere. I just can't remember where. We'd sit and chat until we were too cold or too tired, then I'd walk her home on the way to my house. But the last day, the day before school was to start, I was shivering and so was she, so I said I was going to head home, which one of us always said. But instead of hopping down off the swing to follow me home, she just sat, then said, "I think I might stay here for a minute."

"Aren't you cold?" I think I asked her. And she just shook her head. "Alright," I said, and went to sit back in the other swing.

"You can go," she said, and I looked at her, "if you want." And something made me think I had to leave.

I don't remember what I thought as I walked away. Certainly nothing about never seeing her again. Probably something about Jack. I feel like there should be something here, some memory of her telling me why, explaining, even complaining about how she'd miss it here or something. But there's nothing. What I do remember is being startled, slightly, as I reached the edge of the park and heard the swing screech. I thought it was a person screaming at first, Delaney maybe, but when I stopped it continued in a slow, steady rhythm. I couldn't see Delaney through the darkness, but I could hear her swinging, high enough so the rust on the chain rubbed the bar and screeched. Screeched. Screeched. On its way down. I still hear it, in dreams, far away in the distance somewhere, Delaney screeching at me from the swings.

Four years I knew Delaney Waters, and the next day at school I felt panicked. At least I feel panicked as I remember it. I remember Jack running up to me with a big goofy smile, trying to get me to notice the dried-grass-green bruises under his eyes, I guess, and me telling him to move outta the way. I remember pretty much running to homeroom, searching the room for her, waiting for her to pop out of the corner with her crazy hair, being confused when she wasn't anywhere. I was forced to sit next to Jenna and one of the boys. I remember snapping at Jenna—"How am I supposed to know?"—when she asked where Delaney was. But I couldn't have known she was gone. I probably figured she was in a different homeroom, which would have been strange, and bothersome, but hardly as shocking as realizing she just wasn't there.

I sulked to myself until lunch, tried to find her in the hall, in my classes. I stood in the lunch line and couldn't believe I hadn't found her. I took my lunch and sat at our table. There was a table that was unofficially saved for Delaney. And me, I guess. Usually I'd wait for her, or she for me, and we'd go sit there in the corner. The other girls would filter in after us. Some would even ask permission, which we would laugh at. We really didn't see ourselves as better than anybody. Though I guess I saw Delaney that way, so I didn't blame them.

I didn't wait this time. Just sat. And after a few minutes, Shayna and Jenna came over with their trays and stood in front of me and said, "You want some company?" Everyone waiting.

My thought process after they asked me this question is so familiar to me now, all these years later, but this must have been the first time it happened. They're treating me like Delaney, I need to answer, how would Delaney answer? "Whatever. If you wanna sit, sit."

And in this way I've lived out my life, forever wondering what Delaney Waters would think of me, as if somehow our minds have been connected all these years, as if she were still there pushing my hand up to give the answer, persuading me to go to talk to random boys at the mall, convincing me ol' Jackie Benson was in love with me, had been pining for me all these years. She pops into my consciousness every so often, bats her eyes a little, says, "This way now."

In truth, I heard from her only two times after she left, with two of the shortest letters ever written. The first was her wedding invitation, sent to my parents' old place on Lone Street. My dad called, said he had run into Mr. Cooper, who had bought our old place off my parents. Cooper told him some official-looking letter had arrived with my name on it. I wasn't too worried about it. Until I got a phone call from Jack Benson.

Jack had gotten out of Macleod a few years before this. Moved to the city to go to school and stuff. Jack and I had hung out in high school, and a bit after we graduated, but it didn't turn into anything. The boys—like the girls—just kind of slid me into Delaney's number one spot. I didn't believe it at first, but the girls would whisper about how the boys looked at me, and I definitely had more boys following me around, asking to sit at my table, even with Delaney gone. And one day, one of them actually asked me out on a date. I wish I could remember who was first. You'd think an old lady would be able to remember who she went on her first date with. But all I remember is it wasn't Jackie.

I remember I was so caught off guard by the question that I just said yes right away. I looked at him and said, "Sure. If that's what you want." Of course he took me to the movies, sat us down in the back, tried to move in for whatever he thought he could move in for. And that's when Delaney pops up and says, "This is why you gotta make 'em work for it." So I said, "Whatcha doing?" and he just slumped back down into his seat and started eating all the popcorn like it was the first time he'd ever tried it. I told him I needed the ladies' room and left him there. And I carried on through high school making the rest of the guys work their tails off for my attention.

I was ruthless. It wasn't like it was a game or anything. I even thought I liked some of them, didn't enjoy leading any of them on, or whatever it was. I was just pretending. Pretending to be Delaney, pretending to know what I was supposed to be doing, to know who I was. And even Delaney hadn't been able to keep a guy interested. I'd let them kiss me sometimes, but I knew when to get out. Before they did. Before I became unsatisfactory.

I think Jack saw through it all, though. At first, I thought he really had liked Delaney, not me. As soon as she wasn't around, he steered clear of me, letting the other boys try me out. But I'd catch him—like I used to—looking at me from across the room. Or I'd turn around and he'd be following me up the stairs, looking up at me. It was these moments on the stairs I liked best, 'cause he wouldn't dart his eyes to the side these times. He'd give a quick smile, as if he had wanted me to catch him, then wipe his nose on his sleeve, or scratch the back of his neck, or make a face like he was picking something out of his teeth with his tongue. I'd turn around to check if he was there even when I knew he wasn't.

When he did talk to me, it was to remind me of some party, or to ask if I was going to the city for the fair. Once he told me not to go out with Jerry Donoghue, said Jerry wouldn't stop if I asked him to. I told him to mind his own business, said I'd go out with whoever I wanted to. Though I didn't ever go out with Jerry when he asked.

After high school, it was pretty much only if we ran into each other that Jack would talk to me. Like after the party at Vanessa's house when he asked if I wanted to see his artwork. "Come on. There's a bunch of us going," he said. And eventually I went with him. Of course there was no one else. We drove around town in the dark listening to some weird jazzy stuff on the radio. Then he pulled over, shook up a spray can and painted, asked me if I liked it, then painted it over in black.

I don't know how many times I've replayed this night in my head, and if I did know, I probably wouldn't tell anyone. I just have no idea what Delaney would have done. I think I've decided she wouldn't have let him cover it up. I just don't know how she would have stopped him, what she would have said. I sometimes think my entire life would be different if I had made him leave it.

✿

So anyway, he calls me up. I'm probably thirty-two, thirty-three. He says, "Hey, how ya been? This is Jack Benson. I was wondering if you got an invitation to Delaney's wedding."

I told him I hadn't, tried to think of something—anything—else to say, but couldn't.

"You still live at your old place?'

"No. We moved."

"Might be there. She sent mine to my parents' house. I was hoping you were going. I gotta cut through Macleod on the way to Woodson. Thought we could go together.'

"She lives in Woodson?"

"The wedding's there at least."

"Well, I'd like to."

· "The invite says I can bring a plus-one," he said, and I stood there holding the phone with my mouth open. "Would you like to be my plus-one?" he said.

"Sure. Yes. I would."

We settled on a time for him to pick me up and I told him how to get to my place. Then I drove to my old house on Lone to see if there was an invitation. I don't know what I was expecting. Probably a thick envelope filled with years of regret, explanations. I wanted an explanation, why she'd left me to be on my own, why she'd moved to Woodson—Woodson, goddammit, it's less than three hundred kilometres away—and didn't bother to visit, or call, or write. Until now.

The envelope was small, greeting-card sized, addressed to *Miss Lucy Frazier*. I took it out to my car, slipped my finger under the seal, and pulled out the card. Just a card. I could bring a plus-one too if I wanted. She was marrying Jeffrey Browne. In the envelope—it must have fallen out of the card—there was a small slip of paper. "You have to come. I'm changing my name to Browne."

I still have it.

Jack picked me up early the day of the wedding. The ceremony was at three. Jack said we should get there early enough to grab lunch. He'd never been to a wedding where the food was good, or if it was good, offered more than minuscule portions.

I only remember bits and pieces of the day. I've made an effort to put it out of my mind. Though now that I'm writing it down, the fog is lifting a little. I remember all my clothing strewn about my bedroom before he got there. I can't for the life of me remember what I ended up wearing. I threw it on when I heard his car pull up, as I heard him knocking on the door.

Woodson looked like the perfect place to get married. Skinny little roads with oversized trees planted a century ago in nice rows so the leaves hung over the streets, old Victorian houses with wrap-around porches, white picket fences, dogs barking. The church, once we found it, was nearly exactly what I had pictured, untouched by the present except for a large ramp with a stainless steel railing added alongside the staircase, the rest of it probably 150 years old, stained glass windows, a steeple stretching, trying to reach higher than the others. No cars in the parking lot, though, except for one. And when we pushed the big wooden doors open, there was a little wet-floor sign in the foyer with a single sheet of paper taped to it. *Browne/Waters wedding cancelled*, it said. Nothing else.

Jack walked straight past it as if it weren't there, saying, "That's a shame," as he pulled open the chapel doors and walked halfway up the aisle. Here, I could invent all kinds of meanings. As I watched him in his black suit, just a little too big for him, as if he hadn't quite grown into it after all. As he turned to look around the chapel. As he pulled a hymnal from the back of one of the pews, flipping through it quickly, his thoughts elsewhere, obviously. As he sat and leaned back, staring at the sloping ceiling, the cedar beams. As he said, "Ever worry about finding that perfect girl? Or guy, I s'pose?" By then I had followed him deeper into the chapel. But he seemed to be inside himself, not really speaking to me. From the pews, he asked the question to the front of the room, to the cross hanging on the wall. "Not just a good person," he said, not worried about my answering. "I'm talking about The One. The One that keeps the wheels spinning, the world turning. Makes you wanna tie your tie in the morning." He turned around then, smiled, though he still seemed far off.

I walked down the aisle and slid in beside him. I believed he was talking about me, I know I did, but as I remember it, I felt guarded, hesitant to slip in under his arm in the pew. But then, there I was, and there was his arm around my shoulder, pulling me into him; there I was letting my head rest against him, thinking this must be why Delaney had brought us here. There he was laying his cheek on top of my head and whispering, "Are you ever afraid you missed it?" I turned my head to look at him, and he was looking straight at me, and I was thinking, *This man is about to cry*, and then I was thinking *I should kiss him, I should've kissed him a long time ago, why haven't I kissed him?*

And he said, "I'm still married, Lucy," and I felt myself blushing all over like I was gonna burn up and away in a brume right there in the chapel.

I don't remember what we said after that. I've made myself forget it, mostly. There was a baby. Or there was supposed to be. His wife might have lied about it, but that's beside the point, isn't it? He was so tired of waiting, couldn't wait forever. They rushed everything. But he's a good man, goddammit… I shouldn't have been so bloody oblivious if I was so in love with him. I was too busy pretending to be Delaney-goddamned-Waters that I couldn't see what was right there in front of me.

On the way home, I asked if he still painted. The question kept turning in my mind, gathering speed, growing larger, until it just crashed out of my mouth: "You still paint?" louder than I expected.

"What? Sometimes. Hardly ever. Not really."

Nothing else. The whole way home.

I drove to Woodson to find Delaney two weeks later. I couldn't believe I hadn't thought of her at all—her in the present moment, the Delaney who invited us to her wedding and then cancelled it. I had thought about her, sure. On the way home, what she would do, say. "He's just a guy," she'd say. "They're all the same," she'd say. But then that girl, the one showing me the proper reaction to things, is fifteen. Not thirty-three, and no doubt devastated.

Woodson seemed older. As if two weeks were all it needed to decompose. The picket fences were greying, the paint chipping off them. The trees had all but died, their gnarled branches trying to reach across, rip a limb off the next one over. There was one dog growling at a man hurrying past on his afternoon jog. The houses were all tan and fading earth tones, trying to blend into oblivion. I went to a little diner on the main drag, ordered some soup, asked them if I could use their phonebook. There weren't any Waters at all. I left before they came back with my soup, drove home.

Mr. Cooper died at 109. Apparently he had outlived his relatives, or anyone who would have missed him, because it wasn't until the neighbours smelled something coming from the house—so strong it kept them awake at night—and called the police, who later called my father when they couldn't find any relatives because there was a stack of junk mail in the kitchen addressed to Thomas Frazier.

I went over to the house to gather up my father's thirty-some years of junk mail, which did happen to include a couple of actual letters. One addressed to me in a pink envelope that had no doubt been sitting there for a long time. No return address. My name, *Lucy*, scrawled above the street number. One sheet of loose-leaf folded inside, one side scribbled over, every second line totally blacked out. A stupid little message on the other side. I read it aloud to myself in Mr. Cooper's kitchen, the same kitchen where I used to answer the phone, wrapped up in its springy cord as I lay on the floor talking to Delaney, making plans to meet at the swings.

I'm sorry I missed you and Jack at the wedding. It ended up that I felt like I was planning it all just so I could see you two. I was relieved when it was called off. Jeffrey was in love with Abigail. I wish I could have seen you again. Goodbye Lucy.

No signature, but a P.S. that said, *You ever think of trying glowsticks?*

I looked around the kitchen, spotless, every dish hidden neatly behind cupboard doors, or thrown out by then I suppose, I didn't look. I tried to remember what it was like living in this house, smaller now, somehow, the walls moving gently forward, squeezing me out the window and into the yard where I had sat in my flowing sundresses, dreaming of what things might be like sometime in the future. Nearly forty-five years ago, was it?

And as I stare out the window, watching my younger self, I can't remember what she wanted, back then, the picture she would have had of the woman today inside watching her. *What do you want to be?* they ask you at every stage of your life. My answer, at this age, is a sigh, a glance at the dust on the floor, and a run of my fingers through my hair to the back of my head.

I started writing that evening. I was writing to remember, to be reminded. I started with Delaney who has kept me company all this time, but who was really only brought along through the years by my own imagination. She grew up. Became a woman. Made her own regrets. Moved on.

Wally's Wacky Waterslides had been closed for years by the time I found Delaney's letter, but some quick internet searching pointed me to a park just outside Mount Pleasant, a city close enough I could make a day trip out of it. I also found Jack. I typed in his name as a joke, a stupid thing I might have done in my twenties had I had the chance. But there he was, only the fifth Jack Benson down the list, a picture of him standing in front of a giant mural, a story about him picking his artwork back up again after an old friend reminded him he loved it. The death of another friend—within weeks of Jack's divorce being finalized—all but forced him back into it, making everything bearable. The story ended with a link to his website, which had a section with his contact information.

I dialled the number in the same sort of joking state, not really believing the phone would ring, that it was his number I was calling, that it would be him picking up the phone, or that I'd have to say something when he did.

"Jack here," he said, which made the joke unlaughable, flipped over onto me.

"Hi," I said, and then, "Hello," as if I needed to make up for the squeaky little hi.

"Hi?" he said, as a question.

"Hi. Uh. This is Lucy. Um…"

"Lucy."

"Yes. Lucy. How are you, Jack?"

"I'm fine. Doing fine. How're you?"

"Yes, fine," I said. I stood there, not knowing what to say. I pictured his face, a mixture of that teenage face with his thirty-something face in the chapel, his face from the internet elbowing in, trying to make room for itself too. The silence must have lasted three or four full seconds, or maybe longer, or shorter, before he said, "How are you?" in a different voice, one that made me feel it might have been okay for me to call him.

"I'm fine," I said. "I'm… I wasn't sure you'd be home."

"Oh. Yeah, I'm pretty nearly always at home these days."

"Yes. Of course. Me too."

"You still in Macleod?"

"Yes. Still here. Though I'm going to Mount Pleasant tomorrow."

"Mount Pleasant? To live?"

"No, no. Just… I got a letter. From Delaney."

"Delaney? Recently?"

"No. Well, not really. It was at my old place the last twenty-some years. It must've been a few weeks after the wedding."

"Oh my God. How'd you find it? What'd it say?"

"Nothing really. Sorry 'bout the wedding. She missed us. Said I oughta use glowsticks."

"Glowsticks?"

"I wasn't sure wha—"

"On the waterslides."

"Yes. I think that's… How'd you know?"

"I'll come with you."

"What?"

"To Mount Pleasant. I'll pick you up and go with you."

"That'd be close to six hours for you. Both ways."

"Doesn't matter. Wouldn't miss it."

He was at my house by eight in the morning. Must've left at 5 a.m. I heard his car door close, and I looked out the window to see him hurrying up the walk. It might as well have been him as a teenager running across the playground, mischievous little smile, wild hair—darker back then, of course—his eyes searching, wondering what'll happen next. I imagined this so many times—Jack walking up my walk to pick me up, take me out—that it hardly seemed strange, but it occurred to me, as I watched him walk all the way up to my door, wiping something off one of his shoulders, preparing to knock, that this was the first time he had ever actually done it.

I smiled when I opened the door. I'm sure I was smiling before I opened it—my perfectly straight smile that always surprised me if I ever caught it in a reflection, how different it was from what I imagined—but I wasn't conscious of it until the moment he smiled back. I think I might have even blushed. Of course I blushed. Forty-five years late.

"Luce," he said, and I told him just a minute and went upstairs to grab my coat from the bedroom.

In the car, we chatted. I felt much more at ease than I should have, than I imagined I would have. I kept thinking of our last drive, thinking that heavy awkwardness would start rising up from the floor mats, suffocating us. I rolled the window down, just a bit, to try to ward it off as long as possible.

Finally he asked if I got a lot of mail from Delaney. I told him I had gotten two letters, and he was quiet. So I said, "Do you?" before my mind started dreaming up all kinds of ideas. About him getting one every week, or something terrible like him writing her again and again, desperate for a response.

He said, "I also got two letters."

"Were they as bleak as mine were?"

"What'd yours say?"

"Well I told you the one. And the other was in the wedding invitation. It said I had to come to the wedding 'cause she was changing her name to Browne. That's it."

And Jack laughed. "Sounds like her. Turning things all dramatic."

"Yeah," I said, not knowing what else to say, and not knowing if I actually agreed.

We sat for a while, looking out the windows.

"Mine said I should be with you," he said, in the moment after I had stopped thinking about the letters, decided we were done talking about it. I kept staring out that window.

"She said bring Lucy. To the wedding. In the invite. She said she had a vision of us two... No. Of the two of us. In a little blue bungalow. I'm standing in the door, asking how I look, and you straighten my tie and say 'There now.' It is Lucy Frazier straightening Jackie Benson's tie that makes me believe true love is even possible in this world. That last bit's word for word," he said. "Memorized it."

I sat. Scratched my head. Thought how grey and wiry I was already. Thought how everything was sagging, into something much different than it once was. Thought I would cry. But decided not to. After all of this I wasn't going to cry. Is this the vision she had? Two old... Too old. Not old the way we thought of people this age back then. But certainly too old to be running off to the waterslides on our first date, if this was even supposed to be a date. Glowsticks, goddammit. Is this what she had wanted? Is it what I wanted? Dust on the window. Tree after tree after tree. Power lines dipping. A crow. A cow, on its own in the shade. Maybe I would. Cry. He was probably waiting for it.

"You wouldn't have to change your name."

"What?"

"If you don't want to."

"I—"

"I wouldn't mind if you did either."

"I—"

"It has got a bit of a bounce to it."

"Jack—"

"It's been a lot of years I know that—"

"It's just—"

"But I think—"

"Jack—"

"Just... Okay. You go."

And as we danced this way, trying to step in line next to each other, I had this memory. I'm young. So young. Walking down the hall in our old elementary school. There must be others in the hall, but now it's just me walking toward Jack. He's still got that preadolescent chub he had. And that one missing tooth. I've got my lopsided pigtails. We could just step aside and go around each other. But instead we lock eyes, and he steps to his right, me to my left. Then I step to my right and he to his left. And we do it again, and again, until we just stop. And my knapsack falls from my shoulder. And it's as if the memory, this whole car ride, the whole trip, is about this knapsack. Because it's green. With little white butterflies all over it. Jackie doesn't do anything, doesn't bend over and pick it up for me, doesn't slam into me, doesn't do anything at all. Just smiles a little, maybe says sorry, but I doubt it. Just walks past. The knapsack, though, was green. It wasn't pink. It wasn't the knapsack Delaney had, the one that brought me to her.

And I'm comforted, as the cool wind blows in from the open window, by this memory from before Delaney Waters walked the hallways of my mind, by this moment that was just me and Jack. Before anything else. Just me and Jack. Jack Benson.

BECEUSE YOU WRITE IT DOWN

I only ever said I love you to two different girls. But that's not what I want this to be about. Not really. I'm just noticing things. And writing them down. Things I never noticed before. Or even thought about. Before. But you have to notice things if they're going to mean anything.

I read my girlfriend's diary. Not all my girlfriends'. Just the one. The second girl I ever told. And that made me think you could notice things. Think about things.

I didn't really love the first girl. I thought maybe I loved her. Even though I pretty much just started hanging out with her. But then I met the second girl. Decided I loved her and decided I didn't love that first girl. At all.

The first girl screamed when I told her I loved her. She just screamed and jumped up and down. Kissed me on the cheek. Then my mouth. For probably a full ten seconds. Maybe longer. She stamped her feet through the whole kiss, so she was wiggling around and bouncing and not really kissing me at all. So then I started to wonder. In the middle of the kiss. Could I really love a girl who stamped her feet and screamed and wiggled around when I told her I loved her? I decided I couldn't. And dumped her. The same day I told her I loved her. Which sounds mean. Now that I'm thinking about it. Writing it down.

My second girlfriend's diary made my life sound interesting. That's why I read it. It made things more interesting than I thought they were. Before that, I lived a pretty mediocre life. The older kids bullied me in high school. But they pretty much stopped when I told the dullest of them to leave me alone. I made second string on the football team. Had decent grades. I had been in college five years. No major. Still. But then her diary made me sound. I don't know. Interesting.

I started reading it by accident. Waiting for her to finish freshening up. She called it that. Not me. She lived in her grandmother's huge house. And she was almost never home. Out trying to figure out what she was supposed to be when she grew up. She said. Once. The diary was sitting on the couch. I didn't know it was a diary. Just picked it up. 'Cause I was bored. Black book. Blue ink. Like bright blue. Not blue pen. I started reading it 'cause I saw my name. Flipped through it. Saw my name. Started reading. And I couldn't stop. Could not get enough of it. Wanted to take it home. Read it all.

> He's so different than Greyson! His eyes are blue, but they're dark, as if he's keeping secrets. His hair is thick, and black, like smoke rising in the night. It hangs in front of his face and makes it impossible for me to tell if he's looking at me. But when he does, when his eyes meet mine, I can hardly sit still.
>
> Oh my God, I'm such a horrible person. I should break up with Greyson. But I like Greyson. He's mostly kind and nice, but when we kiss or cuddle, I'm mostly thinking of ways to get out of it. I need to break up.
>
> With Emerson, oh, with Emerson! I just want to be ravished!!
>
> That's embarrassing. But I think it's true.

There's my name. Right there. I was hooked for sure. Only put it down 'cause I didn't want her to catch me reading it. We went swimming that night. But I couldn't concentrate. Kept thinking about the diary. I wondered what she said about me. What else. I wanted to go back to her apartment. To read it. All night long. I wanted to take it home. Wanted to ravish her. Take her home.

I'd coax her to sleep. On my lap in her living room. Watching movies. And when she slept I read her diary. Her writing was pretty. Messy and pretty. I noticed. Later. Once I started noticing things.

I tore out pages. After she wrote ahead a bit. A week. At least.

I feel incredibly guilty. I can't stop thinking about this guy I met in my English class. I seriously can't stop thinking about him. Professor Shields made us pair up and talk about "The Overcoat." Which was crazy, I'll admit, but all this guy says about it is he thinks it's all bullsh*t. That's it. He just kept tapping his pen on the table and bobbing his knee up and down, up and down, up and down. And I was just thinking, "What if the professor calls on us?!"

And then Shields asks what we thought of it, and the guy just blurts out, "I think it's all bullsh*t," without even putting up his hand. Oh my God, I was so embarrassed. But then the prof asked him to elaborate and he said he couldn't believe the guy would fall in love with a coat, or that he couldn't see anything but words when he walked, or that he didn't even know what to do with his arms at a party. He said it was bullsh*t like four times. I couldn't believe he had the guts to say that. And to a professor! But after he said it, he slumped down in his chair like he was embarrassed. His hair was in his face and he seemed so cute and innocent, like a squirrel who ran out of a tree to grab a peanut, but got scared before he could stuff it in his cheek, or something, even though he seemed so… strong? Passionate. While he was talking.

I just can't stop thinking about him. OMG. I can't ever let Greyson see this.

There was a lot of garbage about Greyson. I couldn't believe the shit he did. The shit she said he did. In the diary. She made him seem like he thought he was some kind of genius. Like she thought he was a genius. Like it was all they did. The two of them. All they did was walk around thinking about him being a goddamn genius.

She met him at some art gallery. She was looking around at everything. But he just stood in front of the same painting the whole time she was there. So she went and stood behind him to see what it was he was looking at. He noticed her. Behind him. Tells her, Isn't it perfect? Which doesn't mean anything. When you think about it. He says, "It just feels right. Looking at it." Says he doesn't think he would be able to live properly without having some art to look at. It tells him how to live. He said. Autymn must have known he was an idiot.

Autymn. That's her name. The second girl I told I love you. Should have said that sooner. It's beautiful. Her name. Red hair. Green eyes. These little brown freckles on her nose. It's like her name told her how she should look. She's beautiful. Which doesn't mean a lot. Now that I wrote it down. But I bet it's the truest thing I ever wrote. So far.

He wrote poems. Greyson. Stupid little poems that rhymed. Autymn kept them stuck between pages in her diary. I had to remember where I found them. So she wouldn't notice if I moved them. Garbage. Pure garbage. Straight out of the weekly top forty kind of stuff.

The guy was an idiot. Any idiot I meet now I usually think, They're not that big an idiot. 'Cause I'm thinking of Greyson. Who was a huge idiot.

He slept with some girl. Cheated on Autymn. At a party. Or after it. Got drunk. High. And slept with some girl. I was there. At the party. Autymn asked me to go to it. For some reason. She said it would be a little get-together. I said, Sure. Because I thought it might be a date. And she said great. All excited. Like she might have thought it was a date too. But then she showed up with Greyson. The party was pretty much what I thought it would be. Mostly. I don't go to a lot of parties. If I'm not seeing a girl I can tell you exactly what I'll be doing. Any day of the week. I'll wake up. Work. Eat. Watch TV. Sleep.

But when I am seeing a girl, things change. I could eat at Applebee's. Walk around the park. Minigolf. I could make out with her. Maybe. I feel weird at parties. If I go. I lean on the wall. Then think, When does anyone really lean on a wall? So I find a chair. Or a couch. And sit. Sometimes I cross my leg. But I don't ever do that at home. Or anywhere. So I put my leg back down. Bob my knee. I make eye contact with people. But look away before they recognize me. It's more awkward than anything. So I don't go. Very often.

Everyone tried really hard. At the party. To be cool. Interesting in some way. It was loud. Like a movie. Like they had all watched a movie about going to parties. And then went to a party. But like they were happy with that. And I was too. Happy with it.

I couldn't tell what Autymn was thinking though. At all. This was before I read her diary. She showed up with Greyson. I saw them walk through the door. He kissed her cheek. Pointed to the kitchen. Left her standing by herself. She looked around until she found me and came to sit on the arm of the sofa beside me. So I had to look up at her. She said, You came. All excited. I said, Yeah. She said, Do you know anyone here? I said, Recognize a couple. She said she'd introduce me to Greyson. He's just getting a drink. She sat. She tapped her foot. She looked at her nails. She opened her mouth. And shut it. She smiled at a couple people. Flipped her hair. I wanted a beer.

She said, There he is. And pointed to Greyson. He was coming out of the kitchen holding two beer. Going up the stairs. Scoping the place out. She said, Wanna go upstairs? I said, Nah, I think I might take off. She said, Awww we just got here. All sad. I thought. So I said, Okay fine. She raised her eyebrows. Leaned forward. Turned her head so I could speak into her little ear. I said, I guess I'll come up. She said, Okay cool. Put her lip stuff on. Wiped her lips on the back of her hand. Wiped her hand on the sofa. Which seemed funny. At the time. I still can't think what that meant. I thought she was flirting. Maybe.

I followed her upstairs. She looked in the rooms. Until she found one with people in it. Lying around. Laughing. Sort of. Drinking. Greyson only had one beer now. Everyone had a beer. Except me.

And Autymn. She moved over to let me go in first. I sat on the floor by the door. Leaned back against the wall. She stood in the doorway. Leaned on the doorpost. Greyson was talking. Kind of like they were all in the room just to listen to him talk. It needs to scare you. He said. It's why I say stand-up comedy is the truest art form. No one laughs until something shocks them. Art isn't art unless it scares you. He said. I'm not talking like shivering scared in the corner. I mean, it startles you into action.

There was a girl sitting beside him. Blonde. Flowery dress. She nodded after everything he said. Said, Yeah totally. More than once. I know what you mean. She said. I'm sure she's the girl. Though it could have been any of them. I guess.

Everything I've ever done I did after being shocked by a piece of art. He said. I coughed. Or laughed. They looked at me. At Autymn. At me again. Greyson said, Who's this? Autymn said, This is Emerson. Emerson this is everybody. Emerson's in my English class. Greyson said Emerson what do you think about art? I said I think art is interesting. Which doesn't mean anything. I knew that. Greyson said, Art is a lie. And looked around. At everybody. A lie that makes you realize the truth. He said. I said, But what does that mean? I looked at Autymn. She stood watching. Looked nervous. Maybe. Greyson said, Emerson are you an artist? I said, No. Not at all. Greyson laughed. The room smiled. Autymn wouldn't look at me.

Everyone started talking again. Laughing. Drinking. I wanted Autymn to sit down. Wished I hadn't. Greyson said, What we need is some weed. And a guy in the corner sat up. I never noticed him before. He dug in his bag. Pulled out a bunch of weed. Greyson said, Now it's a party. Weed reveals your self to yourself. Someone said that once. He said. Then asked me if I wanted any. I said, Nah thanks, I think I'm gonna take off. He said, Autymn? And she said, Greyson. Looked at him. All mad. He said, What? She took her ponytail out. Started putting it back in. Said, You know I don't want any weed. He said, Whatever. Just asking. She took off down the hallway. I followed. Greyson said, See you 'round Emerson. From the room.

He told her about it. About cheating. Like a week later. Tried to sound innocent. Said he was only living in the moment. Doesn't regret it. But he wanted her to know. Didn't want to lose her. Seriously. What an idiot.

I'm just so confused right now. I am SO mad at him, but he made me feel so stupid. I don't even know why I'm with him, or why I started in the first place.

But it hurt. So so hurt.

He was all like, "Hey Sweets, I need to tell you something." And told me to sit down, tucked my hair behind my ear like he was gonna tell me something lovely. So I'm sure I blushed. Of course I blushed! And he was probably thinking how much I loved him or something stupid. And then he just said it. He said, "I slept with Aubrey." Oh my God, I'm even crying right now. It's like he tucked my hair behind my ear so he could have an open cheek to slap. I almost couldn't breathe. But then he was all like, "Oh come on, Autymn. It didn't mean anything."

It didn't mean anything!! He said that to me!! He was just like, "I was drunk and then you know. I got high, and I barely knew what I was doing. Yolo, right?

And I was like, "Yolo, Greyson? You freak. What the hell is wrong with you?"

"Relax, Autymn," he said. "I love you. I don't care about her at all." And he looked all melty and dreamy, and tried to kiss my neck. I pushed him away, but then he was like, "Look at me," and looked right into my eyes, like he was trying to reach inside of me to make me understand. "I love you, Autymn. That's it. That's the whole point." And I was sitting there searching him, thinking, The whole point? The point of you sleeping with Aubrey is that you love me? So then all

I'm thinking is get me away from this guy, I need to get out of here.

But then he was all like, "But hey, I guess you've got Emerson."

So I was like, "WHAT?!" And he's like, "Oh please, Autymn. I see how you look at him. How you talk about him."

"He's just a friend," I said, obviously.

"Come on. I don't buy it. He's an idiot too."

"He is not an idiot."

"Come on. He's clueless. Just a big idiot. I don't think you should see him anymore."

"Oh my gosh, Greyson. You can't tell me who I should or should not see. It's not like I slept with him!"

"No, but you like him. I can see it. If you were the guy, you'd have slept with him already. And he'd sleep with you if he had the chance. Just stay away from him."

So then I freakin' started crying. And it almost looked like he was going to cry too. So I started thinking maybe I really did do something to hurt him. When really it was him who cheated! But then I started thinking how it's true. I do like Emerson. I have no idea if he likes me, but I like him. I think about him all the time. So then maybe I did push Greyson away. Ugh! I should have broken up with him. I'm going to break up with him. I don't know. I'm just SO confused!!

I read this later. After she broke up with Greyson. After we started hanging out. I wished I didn't. Afterwards. I hated reading about Greyson. I hated how she liked him. Even when he was a dick she liked him. I decided I wouldn't read the diary anymore. After that.

But I was hooked. I needed to read about myself. About Autymn. And me. She made life seem interesting. In the diary. Even parts with me. More interesting than when they were actually happening. Different than when they were happening. They were different and the same. At the same time. She noticed things. Made them into something. When I looked at her, I was just looking at her. But in the diary we were talking as we looked. Discussing things. Thinking about each other. About the future. Just from looking at her.

This one time she started wiggling while I was reading so I put the diary on the coffee table. Before she opened her eyes. And when she opened them I told her she was beautiful. 'Cause that's what I felt when she looked at me. She smiled. Kissed my cheek. Said she was tired. I told her I'd see her in the morning. Went home. Dreamt I was walking down a street. But everything was words. The buildings were just words. Typed on top of each other. The cars rolled along on words. I had words typed all on my face. So that all I could see was words. Everywhere. I tried to delete them. And I could. In the way you can fly. In dreams. I could reach out and delete them. And type new ones. If I wanted. Ones that changed the story only a little bit. Made it better.

I woke up and saw the paint on the ceiling. Decided I would try to notice things. The wallpaper in my room. How the pattern repeated again and again. Like it wanted to mean something. But it wasn't sure what. The stuff in my closet. I tried to think of reasons for keeping it all. My cleats. Too small. Baseball cards. Old. Worthless. A box of G.I. Joes. One stuffed dog. Pictures of old classmates. Football teams. I thought it might be worth something. Maybe. Not money. Just something. I stopped calling it junk.

I called Autymn. Told her I missed her. 'Cause I felt like I did. She said, Aw. She held it out so her voice got higher and higher while she said it. I noticed. I miss you too. She said. But I was also thinking of the diary. I told her we should skip class. Hang out at her place. She said we should do lunch. I said I'd bring something over.

I only had a few seconds when she was in the can. To read it. I Flipped till I found my name underlined three times. Then she came out. We watched a movie. She snuggled so close. I couldn't breath without smelling her. Fruity. Watermelon. We fell asleep snuggling. She wanted to go out when we woke up. I read while she was getting ready.

I asked the mystery man his name today!! I know, I'm so bad, but he's always just sitting in the corner looking so cute and lonely. I could barely help myself. I asked him if anyone was sitting in the spot beside him, and he barely even looked at me. He just looked up through his hair and shook his head. I don't even like long hair, but his makes me feel like he's hiding a beautiful secret, like he's just waiting for the right woman to whisper it to. I was so embarrassed just from him shaking his head! I was blushing and gushing all over, and I felt so stupid 'cause half the classroom was empty. But I had to sit there, right? I couldn't just run away after asking him. OMG! I'm even embarrassed talking about it.

Then I was just desperately trying to think of something to ask him, and all I could think of was, "Have you started on this paper yet?" So he pushed his hair out of his eyes to look at me and I was totally shocked to find they were blue! I never would have guessed he'd have blue eyes. They're like dark blue, like navy, but not navy. They're like deep deep ocean water. They're just freaking gorgeous.

But anyway, he looked at me, "Been thinking about it," is all he said, and laughed. At least I think it was a laugh. I hope it was a laugh, 'cause I laughed. I laughed and said, "Yeah me too." Haha. OMG then I said, like I was some chick from *The Great Gatsby,* "So what's your name anyway?" I just blurted it out! He probably thought I was gonna say, "big fella" at the end of it, or "ol' sport!"

But he smiled. A real smile!!!

Emerson. It's just so perfect. Oh, don't you feel like
Emerson is such a noble name? I feel caught up in it
when I say it, like I'm floating in it and it's gonna carry
me off into some fantastic place where nothing makes
sense. Am I falling in love with Emerson?! I wonder if
he's even thought about me at all...

I don't think I did think of her. Back then. I know I didn't. Not until
she asked me to her friend's party. Her friend's get-together. I don't
think I even realized she was the girl I was paired with. I never tried
to fit one day with another. Or one thing with another. Back then. I
just lived a boring life. I'd go with a friend to the bar. I'd have a couple
drinks. I'd give a girl my number. If she called I'd take her for coffee.
I'd take her around the park. I'd take her minigolfing. I'd make out
with her. Maybe.

But now. That I met her and read what she thought about me. I
couldn't stop thinking about her. About her diary. How it made one
thing fit with something else. How she saw things and thought of
something else. How I was kind of like Greyson in it. But not like
Greyson. How Autymn tried to figure out what other people were
thinking. How she felt so many things at once. I only felt bored. All
the time. But her diary made me feel... I don't know what it made me
feel. Different.

I started thinking about everything I did. Everything. Tried to
figure out what Autymn would say. About the way I stood. At a bus
stop. Or waiting in line. The way I ate my eggs. Brushed my teeth.
Tossed before I fell asleep. The way I had to curl up to fall asleep. In
a ball. Every night. I noticed how I chew my pen when I'm studying.
I crack my knuckles. When I'm bored. In class. I talk to myself when
I'm gaming out. I step on the cracks. On the sidewalk. On purpose.
I chew my Slurpee straws. I feel lonely when the lights are off. When
the street light shines in my bedroom.

I noticed things about other people too. About Autymn at least.
How she turns the volume down for the music. Up when the host

starts talking. She flips her hair to the side. Over and over. When she's saying something important. Something she thinks is important. She slurps her coffee. Her ears turn red when she talks in class. When she kisses me. Her eyebrows curl up at the end when she's mad. Frustrated. She clicks her pen. All the time.

These things were boring. Before. But now they were interesting. I felt like I could do anything. Like Autymn could do anything. Not *the sky is the limit* kind of anything. Just capable of anything. Like one thing could mean a million things. And I couldn't tell you which. The things she said I did were true. Sure. But not true totally. I wasn't mysterious. I was shy. I wasn't strong. Gogol just pissed me off. I'm not like Greyson. At all. And I'm not noble.

I could hardly do anything without reading the diary first. It told me what to do. I read what she wanted. Then did it. I was not in control.

Remember forever ago how I'd always say "mysterious" was just another word for "creepy?" Like how a greasy-haired old guy with hairy shoulders sticking out of his dirty wife beater checking out joggers through his sunglasses is just as "mysterious" as a dark and handsome Italian winking at you as he sips on his latte? The only difference is that one is good looking? And remember how I met Emerson and totally changed my mind? How I couldn't stop thinking about him, and was basically in LOVE with him before I even broke up with Greyson, 'cause he WAS mysterious? He IS mysterious. And remember I changed my mind and said "mysterious" is definitely a good thing? It turns me on? OMG I can't believe I said that! It's so embarrassing reading old entries!! I always wonder how I came up with half of it.

But he does turn me on *blush blush.* I just wish he would open up sometimes. I feel like I have to guess what he's thinking all the time. Like I'm pretty sure he likes me. Like, likes me likes me, as in wants to be with me, but he's never once said it. I know everyone hates labels and all of that, but I want us to be official. I want him to look me in the eye and say, "Autymn, I want you!" Oh, that's so girly and stupid. But hey, a girl can wish can't she?

I read this while she was sleeping on my lap. Her eyes were moving. Under her eyelids. And I was freaking out. Losing it. I put her head on a pillow. And left. Sat in my car. With the lights off. Head on the steering wheel. Thought a thousand things. Turned on the car. Turned off the radio. Sat. Waiting. For nothing. Then her light shut off. And I watched her crawl into bed. In my head. I let my car idle down the street. To the end of it. Drove home. Silent. Missed every red light.

I let my hair fall in my face. The next day. Let my hair fall in my face as I walked around staring at the ground. More than usual. I knew it wouldn't stop her from seeing me. Talking to me. But I thought maybe it would.

Every pair of shoes walking by was Autymn. Shoes she wore on our first date. Shoes I helped her pick out. They were all her. All of them. Running up to me. Stamping her feet. Wishing I'd just open up already.

I ran into a guy who was holding the door for some girl. I was looking behind me. Trying to see if it was really Autymn walking past. Trying to see her red hair. Sorry. I told the guy. And I walked through the door. She was at a table reading a book. Not homework. I stopped. Watched her. She licked her finger and turned the page. She uncrossed her legs. Re-crossed them. The opposite way. She took her little finger and scratched the inside of her nose. She looked up. Finally. Said, Emerson. All excited. Her ears turned red. How long were you standing there? She said. I told her, Not long. She said, Have you read this? You probably haven't. I said I haven't. She said, Oh my gosh I just started it last night and I can't put it down. It's so beautiful.

They made a movie out of it. She said. I said, Sweet. She said, What's wrong? I said, Nothing. Looked out the window behind her. Down at her shoes. Back at the door. Out the window. She said, You sure? Turned to see what I was looking at. I said, Yeah. She said, Okay. But looked at me weird. For a second. Well you know what I was thinking? She said.

Yes. I do. I do know what you're thinking. Because you write it down. And I read it. You write down what you're thinking and I read it. You want me. To want you. To come out and say I want you. Jump up and down and scream and wiggle around like the first girl I told I loved. But I want to read your diary. I want to hang out so I can read about it later. I don't know what that means. I thought all this in one second. Didn't say anything.

I was thinking we should skip class. She said. We could go out to the lake and read under a tree or just people watch. We could even stay the weekend if you wanted. I said, I think I better go to class. And she looked sad. Confused. Like I had cheated on her. Like when she told me Greyson had cheated on her. She took her ponytail out. I felt mean. I felt sad. She said, Okay. Yeah. You're probably right. Put her ponytail back in. Put her book in her purse. Rubbed her eye with her finger.

I went home. Didn't go to class. I walked right past my classroom and walked home. I shut my phone off. I skipped school the next day. I went to work. But said I was sick. Left early. I ordered pizza. Played vids. Watched TV. Tried to sleep. I couldn't sleep. I wanted to know what Autymn was thinking. Which was not possible. It was not possible for me to know what she was thinking. Or anyone. Without reading their diaries. And I didn't know what to do if I didn't know what she thought about me.

I figured she would hate me. Probably. She thought I had ditched her. Dumped her. Left town. Was living in the moment. Kissed some girl and slept with her. I shouldn't have read her diary. Never should have started. Mysterious. I'm mysterious. I don't worry what anyone thinks. Don't even think about what anyone thinks. It's too stressful.

Too weird. It's impossible anyway. Even when she was right she was wrong. She wrote down my thoughts. Thoughts she thought I thought. And I thought them. But not till after she wrote them. So what does that mean. She was a mind reader. Mind writer. But then she thought I was too. Emerson is so wonderful. She said. In her diary. I feel like he just understands me. Knows what I'm thinking before I do. I can practically see him reading my mind. She said.

Red ears. Embarrassed. Or excited. Flipping hair. Nervous. Excited. Crooked smile. Flirting. Looking at her nails. Flattered. Embarrassed. Chewing on her pencil. Not listening. Concentrating. Head on headrest. With a smile. Having fun. Without a smile. Tired. Turning the music down. Remembered something. Turning it off. Headache. Taking her ponytail out. Putting it back in. Take me home. Putting a movie on. We should cuddle. On the couch. Taking her socks off. Going to sleep.

I figured these things out. But even if I was right, I was wrong. Sometimes she'd take her socks off and start talking. Past the end of the movie. So the screen was blue. And she would just keep talking. Or whatever. She was a mystery. Mysterious. She told me everything. But still. She could be thinking anything. Anything at all. And I'd never know.

She knocked on my door. It scared me. Three little taps. I put some pants on. Put some plates away. I opened the door. She said, Emerson. Flipped her hair. Scratched her earlobe. Looked at the door post. At the mess behind me. At her nails. Said I didn't know who else to talk to. She talked and talked. Kept talking. And flipping her hair. She stood in my doorway and flipped her hair and talked. And I started thinking could I love someone who comes to my door and just talks and flips her hair. And I thought, Am I in love with this girl? Or with her diary?

I think I'm in love with you. I said. She stopped. She said, What? I said, I do. I do love you. She said, What the hell Emerson? Stomped her little foot. Said, Were you listening to anything I just said. I said, Uh. Or something stupid. She said, Oh my gosh Emerson. The guy died. On my street. After I told him to get lost. You can't just open the door and—plus you disappeared. After I asked you to go away with me. You can't just open the door and say I love you. When have you ever said anything like I love you? She said, I never know what the... Stopped. Took her ponytail out. Shit. She said. All embarrassed. ...is going through your head. I never know what the shit is going through your head. She said. Can you tell me what the shit is going through your head? Put her ponytail back in. I looked at her. Tried to figure this out. Wanted to laugh. Decided I shouldn't. She wanted me to say I want you. I read that. But now I said it. And now she's mad. Swearing.

She said, Whatever Emerson. I'm going home. Walked down the hall. I said, Wait. She kept walking. I said, Wait. Louder. She said, I can't. Walked through the door. Down the stairs. And I stood there wondering if I should shut the door. Sit on the couch. Order some pizza. Go back to my boring life. My predictable life. I could go to the bar. Give some girl my number. And if she called I could take her minigolfing. Or through the park. I turned and looked at my living room. At my spot on the couch. And I could see her get on her bike. In my head. See her ride home. Run inside. Flop on the couch. Grab her diary. Write in it. All fast. *OMG He just stood there. I left and he stood there. Like a. Like a stupid. Like. Like an idiot. A big fucking idiot.*

I ran after her. I turned around and ran after her. In my socks. My one sock was too big and hung off my foot. Flopped as I ran. I could feel it slapping the top of my foot. Slipping off my heal. Every step. And I started thinking, What does this mean? That I'm running down the stairs. Jumping down the last flight. With one of my socks falling off my foot. Decided I would write it down. Later. I would write things down. Things like my sock. Slapping my foot and slipping off my heel as I run down the street.

MUMBLE MUMBLE

I am a man who sits in his house, alone, a man who could not wait to finish his day at work so he could rush home to his house where his wife was cooking dinner, or feeding his daughter. He looked forward to being in his house and relaxing in the comfort of his chair. And now, I am a man who writes, alone in his house, without even a pair of pants to keep him company, though I would never show what I write to any sort of person. I write, and read, if I ever hit a wall. I have written I-don't-know-how-many novels and so many stories I have stopped keeping track, and am in the middle—nearing the end—of my autobiography. I don't show what I've written to people, because there is this thing inside my own head who reads everything I write. The Ideal Reader, I've seen them call it, on the Internet. It looks like me, this thing, and thinks like me, and so obviously enjoys all that it reads, while I write. I am only certain a story has hit its mark once this reader takes over and begins to write it.

I am a man who walks his dog every day, as anyone else would. But the reason this man is walking his dog, the reason he even rescued the dog in the first place, is so he could walk the eight blocks north and three blocks west to the little park, fenced off, with little signs demanding dog owners keep their dogs on a leash—but were ignored by dog owners due to the perfect little fence that kept the dogs safe from buses or cars or cats that wish to lure them away and scratch holes in their ears. At the park he waits, this man, for the woman he saw, once—before he ever thought a dog might be something he wanted—bending over to pull a slobbery tennis ball from the mouth of a giant Saint Bernard. She threw it with, what seemed to the man, everything she had. The dog trotted after the ball, obviously thinking far less of the game than the woman had been.

By the time she had arrived at the park—sometime around nine thirty each morning—all the courage he had felt as he had leashed his dog and walked the eleven blocks to the park had vanished. He stood, a fair distance from the woman, and watched her put everything she had into throwing a ball. He threw his own ball, for Mr. Scruffs, in the opposite direction of the woman. Mr. Scruffs loved this game, and would play until he couldn't anymore. Then I would sit—the man would sit—and Scruffs would flop his head in the man's lap before lying down to catch his breath.

I change tenses when I write, which I believe is purposeful, though I was never quite aware of it until my daughter pointed it out after reading a story. Past, present, future perfect, whichever I need. She is—my daughter is—sometimes the only person I will allow to read my work. "I don't like how you can never tell when a thing is happening," she said to me, after shutting the notebook and slipping it onto the coffee table. "Is it happening right now or has it happened already?" she said. And I said, "Both, of course. And it will no doubt happen again," and she looked at me like she thought her father might actually be out of his mind.

Of course she is doing this all the time too, shifting tenses. Brian was all like… And so Sheri's like… And then I'm like… And so Brian was like… Time shifts. Live in the moment, they say, but the time it takes to think a thought, such as this, moves you beyond the moment, into the future, which is only the future for so long. There is future. There is past. And we here in the present don't know what we ought to be working toward.

I am a man who has tattooed a portrait of every woman he has ever made love with on his body, in places invisible if he is wearing a shirt. He keeps them as permanent secrets, attached to his heart, his shoulder blades, his abdomen, his rib cage. He takes photographs of the women, on dates, before they've ever made love, before they've even decided they are in love. He takes photographs of them at a moment in time in which he believes they are falling in love with him.

The first time, the first photograph, was not planned. He believed, as he was shooting it, and as he was shooting each one after that, that it would be the last photograph he would ever take of a woman falling in love with him, for he believed his love to be eternal. Having very little room left under his shirt, he is now afraid to fall in love again, though he longs to shoot one more photograph, the last photograph.

I miss my wife, who was a liar, even as she was leaving me. She left a note saying, *There's spaghetti in the fridge, you can heat it up, or wait for me and I'll do it. I'll be home after the gym.* There was spaghetti in the fridge, but she did not come home after the gym. I spent three days inventing stories about her disappearance, and so it was easy, when my daughter arrived asking why her mother wouldn't answer the phone, to simply choose one of the stories, to slump in my chair while she stood—my daughter stood—in front of me, shocked. I decided not to tell her how her mother had been agitated for months, for weeks, pleading with me to put down my pen, to get outside for once, to live, in the real world. Goddammit. My wife was once the only person I allowed to read my work. And now she is gone.

I am a man whose face was just too good looking to be slumped behind a desk, according to the woman I was with at the time. She said this face—my face—was one of those faces you couldn't help but fall in love with. "Who actually has black hair and grey eyes?" she'd ask me. "It just isn't a real thing," she'd say. "When I went up to you—when you sucked me in like a magnet," she said—"I was certain you'd say you were an astronaut or, you know, something outrageous. An actor researching a role," she said. "I should have known the minute you said accountant," she said. "A person with that face has got to be damaged if he chooses to hide it in a crummy little cubicle," she said.

"I can change," I told her, though I did have my doubts.

"No, I'm not talking about going out on Fridays instead of ordering in," she said. "I'm talking flipping everything on end. Flying to China. Or, I don't know, Guatemala, for God's sake. I'm talking something that'll turn your undies over, something just plain old weird, so crazy it'll give your mother another heart attack."

It was a stroke.

"You know what I mean. You're nice," she said. "Kind as hell. And hot, obviously. But you're just not the kind of man I can see myself buying a bungalow with."

She apologized and left, and I went into the bathroom and stared into my own grey eyes, which I had always considered to be a dull blue, in the mirror. They blinked—these eyes blinked—as anyone's would have, and for a moment I believed they were tearing up, but then I thought, They do have a certain spark. And I decided I wasn't the kind of man who wanted to sit at a desk counting, but rather one who should do as he pleased. He could wear blue jeans on Tuesdays, leave the house without combing his hair. He'd stop ironing his clothes, any of them. He'd spend a little money with a little frivolity. He'd walk downtown to the local theatre which had been holding an open audition for a short play written by one of its very own amateur actors.

This man, who was no longer an accountant and so hardly felt like myself at all, bumbled through the script in a way that made his face burn up, his upper lip sweat. Any confidence he had found in his beautiful face was washed away in a flutter of regret. Until the man watching, taking notes, said, "Have you done much acting previous to this?"

"No. Not a lot, no."

"Well, you'll need to work at it a bit. Are you free for practice on Thursday evenings?"

"Yes. Any evening is fine... Wait. Am I to understand I've earned a role in the play?"

"You could have belched the alphabet, I'd have given you a part. Would never pass on a face like that."

The director on Thursday was less concerned with the man's face. "You're a vagrant," he said. "I hardly think you'd be walking straight up with fists clenched like you're seconds away from shitting your pants. Become the part," he said, which the man had heard before. "Become the vagabond. If you need to shit, take a squat and shit. You are not the man who walked through those doors. You are a goddamn bum."

He spent—the man spent—the night before the opening show sleeping under a bench at the bus stop across the street from the theatre. He made a sign out of cardboard that said *Will dance for lunch money* and was forced to imitate an old black-and-white tap-dance routine he found somewhere in the back of his memory. He was taken to Bubba's on Fourth Street for a grilled cheese and bacon sandwich. "I don't normally do this," the woman who took him there said. "But there's a spark in your eye what makes me think you won't be on these streets for long."

The audience went wild on opening night and the rest of the week was sold out. The papers wrote of an unknown actor who had stolen the show, and who had allegedly been approached by a talent agent.

If I were speaking factually, I'd say I have loved the same woman for the whole of my life, though I'd never write this in any story. "No one would believe your story," my wife would often say when she was here, when she would read my autobiography, when she was the only person I would allow to read my work. "You're one big cliché," she'd say, and I'd say, "Life invents cliché. A thing becomes cliché," I'd say, "not because it is written about too often, but because it has happened too often."

"One reads literature," I told her, "to escape from one's life, if only for a moment, and so I've an aversion to cliché, having found it earlier in the day walking down Main Street. One reads autobiography, my dear, to be offered an example of one who has manoeuvred the way through all of it unharmed, able to write it in a book, and so one doesn't mind a bit of cliché in autobiography."

"I don't think that's true," she'd say. "I think people want to read about the weirdest sons-of-bitches out there. I would."

"That's only because cliché has left you alone all these years," I said, trying to be flirtatious, though I did believe the statement to be true.

"Oh please," she said, and she stood with her eyes dancing around the study, as if she were worried one or the other of us was losing our minds.

I am a man—with grey hair now, white some would probably say, with arthritis so bad he can't even scratch his own earlobes. He has to write with a recorder attached to his computer that writes down his words, spoken to himself aloud—writing of himself as a boy, athletic in a second-string sort of way, smart in reads-the-signs-at-museums sort of way, good-looking. One thing I can say about my own life, the man writes, is I've lived without regrets. Though if I could do a thing differently, it would be this: I would get down off my high horse and roll around in the mud. It is hard for me to admit it was a high horse, for I was never too stubborn and self-important to tell a woman—a girl, I suppose—how I felt. It wasn't anything like pride that held me in the saddle. It was that itchy feeling I got, under my chin, the backs of my ears, that tormented me, made me feel as if I might break out in shingles, whenever a certain girl came floating into a room.

The feeling came before I even saw her sometimes. I'd be reading a book and my nose would burn up so red I could see it there in front of the page, so then I'd look up and she'd be tiptoeing toward me, the smell of her hair already wafting through me. And in all those books I read back then of sleuths and adventurers and unlikely heroes, there was no one who showed you how to actually speak to a woman—a girl. Saving the world, or even just the county bank, was enough to send them scurrying into your arms. I couldn't imagine myself doing anything heroic at all, so I'd close my book and hustle out of the library, ignoring the screeching at the door that told everyone I hadn't checked the book out.

This girl snuck up on me once. In high school. She tapped me on the shoulder as I was finishing up a chapter, in the hall, halfway inside my locker, about to slip the bookmark inside, toss the book on the locker shelf, run off to class. I turned and saw her there, and watched my brain erase everything I had just read, everything I had ever read or listened to or seen or heard, until my entire existence was a white room with no exits, no corners, just a polished-up bubble with this one girl sparkling in the centre of it.

"What's going on with you?" she was saying. "I thought we were supposed to be friends. Oh. You're just gonna stand there? Oh my God, we have one conversation. An actual conversation that actually means something, and now you won't talk to me? Whatever, jackass. Come see me when you get off your high horse. Or ya know what, don't even bother. I hate you."

It wasn't a high horse, I told you that. It was an inability to speak around a girl—a woman, whichever. So yes, if I could do one thing over, I'd just say something to this specific girl. I'd just blurt it out, the first thing that came to mind. Watermelons. The smell of her shampoo. "We are friends," I could have said.

Every story I have ever written has been in first person, which is unwise according to a critic I read long ago. He said, "Sooner or later I'd eventually feel as if I've read this story before, I've heard this voice, when reviewing some collection or another." He said, "You get the idea, he—the author, I can't remember his name—is trying to tell his own story again and again." This is almost exactly what my daughter said when she asked me why all these stories are about me. I told her she was being childish and that just because the story says *I*, it doesn't mean it is the author speaking. That is ridiculous.

"I know that," she said, "but it sounds like you."

"Oh really," I said. "It sounds like me? It sounds like I tried to cut my own heart out after I finished a twelve-ounce steak, prepared to perfection? It sounds like I haven't said a single word out loud for more than thirty years? It sounds like I'm going to—"

"No, Dad. I just mean—"

"No. You listen to me. Everything is in first person. Every story, every critique, everything written down is autobiography."

"Dad—"

"Which does not mean it is about me, about my life, about me in any way."

"Okay—"

"Shut up. A story is a response to something. A reaction. All those writers with their third-person pretentious narrators who act like they know what he's thinking, or she's thinking, as if anyone knows what she's thinking. They're just telling their own story. They're choosing. They choose what to say, when to jump from his mind to hers to the goddamn dog's. It's all a joke. A nuisance. A distraction from what they want to say. Just say it. I, I, I. Just man up and say it, goddammit."

"Okay, Dad. So what is it you wanna say? What do you have to say that's so fucking important?"

"It's not me that says it."

"Oooh, so it's not you."

"It's the story. The characters."

"Oh my God. You're such a joke. Mom said—"

"I am—" I said loud, almost as if it wasn't me who said it—"a ruffian." She looked as if she couldn't recognize me, couldn't quite remember how she knew me. "I am an amanuensis," I said. "I am the vessel through which they speak. I am my characters, as any writer is. They speak. I'm just here with a pen and ink." I could feel the blood pulsating in my temples, my eyes blurring. Her face changed into her mother's. "Oh don't look at me like that," I said, and I scratched my neck under my chin, noticed I had snapped my pen in half somehow.

"Whatever Dad," she said, and she packed up her things and walked to the door. "Try going for a walk sometime," she said as she slipped her little shoes on. "Fresh air might keep out the crazy."

I have always considered myself to be more capable than I actually am. That is to say there are instances I would imagine myself in, and when they actually occurred in my own life, I behaved in ways I never could have thought. I have mentioned my wife's leaving, which I had imagined a thousand times before she actually did it, mostly because she had said often enough that she would leave me if I didn't give her a reason to stay, and while I knew her to be a liar, I did believe there was truth to these threats. I imagined her with new jobs in foreign countries, or casting directors pulling her out of crowds—other men.

Each time, when she would tell me she was leaving, I would go over to her, take her in my arms, and tell her she couldn't leave, I wouldn't let her. And if she tried to leave, I'd pull up my socks and run, confident, certain of things, out the door, after her. But instead, when I found the note, I just put the spaghetti in the microwave, sat there eating on my own.

She came back a few weeks later—day twenty-seven—which I haven't told to anyone. She said she needed to grab her clothes and decided she didn't need to hide from me, she was too good to hide from me, which was, no doubt, a lie, the whole thing made up just so she could come check up on me.

"What are you doing?" I said.

"I just told you."

"No. What are you doing that you need more clothes?"

"Oh God. You are so… insane. You are insane. Not everyone wears the same shirt every day without even thinking about it. What am I doing? I'm living, you idiot. Going out. Meeting people. Paying four dollars for a coffee for God's sake. Good coffee. So yeah, I need to change every now and then. So here I am."

"I can change."

"That's not what I meant."

"I know," I said, because I believed what I said, at first, and wanted her to know that.

"Oh really," she said. "Prove it."

"Prove it?"

"Put on some pants and let's walk to Starbucks."

"Starbucks?"

"We have a Starbucks now. On Main. I bet you didn't even know that."

"I… uh…"

"Stop rummaging through your shit. Just put on your pants and let's go for coffee."

"I gotta…"

"If you go for coffee, I'll move back in," she said.

But I was in the middle of a sentence when she came pounding through the door, and it was impossible for me to leave just then, something she had never been able to comprehend. She left without any of her clothes, which is not surprising.

There was a man who wrecked his motorcycle in front of my house one day while my daughter was visiting, which, I will say, I had never imagined before. It is a useful thing, one's imagination. I am able to invent what I might have thought, had I imagined a wrecked motorcycle in front of my house before it was there. It would have gone as any story goes. We would have been sitting, as we were, discussing my writing, as we were, and we would have heard the roar of the bike as it somersaulted along, as we did. I would have jumped from my sofa, gotten to the window before my daughter could have. I would have closed the curtains, leaving only a slice to look through. I would have said, "Oh it's nothing," or, "Imagine that, everyone is safe and sound." She would have sighed, she would have asked, "Is there more tea?" She would have said this story—the story she had been reading—was her new favourite. She might have apologized for not coming to read it sooner.

Instead, we heard the roar, she jumped up and ran to the window and said, "Holy shit, that guy just crashed his bike," and she ran out the door. And I was strapped into my chair, chained there, wrapped up in twine, bound and gagged, shivering, sweating, unable to even pick up the phone to dial 9-1-1. My daughter didn't come back, has not come back.

I am a man who told himself he should think of one thing he has always believed to be impossible, and then set out to do it. I decided— he did—I did—the man decided he would drive down to the hospital and tell the woman he loved that he loved her, had always loved her. He strutted down the walk to his car, turned the ignition and took off. He decided, last second, to drive past the turn taking him to the city bypass, and instead drive through the city, taking his time, following the speed limit. He found the hospital, where it had always been, and drove around the block maybe a hundred times until the gas light came on, scared him a little with its ding. He parked, finally, and went in without plugging the meter. Inside, he stumbled around, looking for the woman, trying to remember what it was she did at the hospital. He believed she was a nurse, but now he was in there he thought she might be anything. She might look after the used-book cart, she might take the brake off the motorized wheelchairs so the occupants could wheel off to lunch, she might be a doctor.

Now that he thought of it, it seemed very likely she had spent the last ten to twelve years becoming a doctor, she was doing surgery, she was chief of the entire staff at the hospital, she ran the whole damn place, she was somewhere watching him walk through the halls on the security cameras. As he walked his head hurt, it squeezed in on itself so he couldn't breathe, and the world all around him was white-washed and blurred and each face he looked at was a version of his own, squinting, grimacing, snarling, lapping at the blood dripping from his temples which had—he was certain—just burst open.

He sat down on the floor, stretched himself out, laid his head gently on the tiles and went off to sleep. Until someone was wiping his face with a warm cloth, saying, "My God, what happened to you?"

"What?"

"How long have you been here?"

"What. Uh..."

"Shit. I'm getting a doctor."

He got up and walked down to the emergency room, where the doors open automatically and usher you into the reception desk, where the woman he loves is sitting, waiting for him.

"Oh my... What happened? Are you okay?"

"I came to see you."

"Seriously? You shoulda called."

"I needed to see you."

"I could have just come over after work."

"I meant to be here sooner."

"Well what happened? You look awful."

"My head hurts."

"I'll get you some Advil."

And when she came back with the two little red pills in her palm, the earth opened into a bright and shocking place. I was here under the fluorescent lights, sitting in a stiff plastic chair, her hand rubbing my back as she sits next to me, and I felt the future revealing itself in a big bright museum of things to come. Here on your right is the day you'll ask her to marry you, rolling dice on the floor in her basement while playing Monopoly, watching her try to stifle her laugh as you land on Marvin Gardens loaded with a bright red hotel, looking down at your stack of ones, your one pink five, St. Charles, St. James and all of the others face down on the floor, saying you haven't got the money but would she take your heart instead, watching her erupt in laughter, toss her piles of money in the air, jump across the board, tackle you, kiss you, roll around laughing and kissing you until you say, "Marry me," with a confidence that shocks you, makes you believe it will be impossible for her to say no.

Just up on your left is the day—you'll remember it well—that you carry her across the threshold of your tiny blue bungalow, which really was tiny, but was yours, finally, after three years of living squished together with her brother in his apartment which might have actually been bigger than this bungalow, but which was not yours in any way. Here is your living room, which will feel like a dream as you snuggle close on the neat little used sofa you'll find for next to nothing at a garage sale at the end of your block.

Here is your bedroom, your bath, your kitchen where you'll conceive your daughter unexpectedly, just after eating your Cheerios, before your love leaves for work, catching her watching you with a look that makes you feel as if you've never made a single mistake in your entire life, taking her hand and kissing her fingers one by one, seeing her unbutton her blouse with her other hand, ignoring the smash of the bowl on the ground, the glasses, the jug of milk spilling out onto the floor. Here is your backyard with leftover plants from the last owner that you will never be able to salvage, that you will ignore, letting them take over on their own.

And down there at the end of the hall is an exhibit labelled *Your Daughter.* The day she's born, four weeks early but still healthy, able to breathe on her own after only three days, giving you a sense she is close to indestructible, though you know this isn't quite true. Here's the day you'll wake up excited for her fifth birthday, and you'll go to her room to wake her up. You'll lift her above your head and drop her back down on the bed, which she'll love and laugh about and ask you to do again. You'll do it again, this time tickling her, making her wiggle and giggle and making you lose hold for a millisecond before you toss her onto the bed in a funny way that bends her arm wrong and fractures her radius. She won't cry, so you won't believe it's broken until the doctor is actually wrapping it in a cast.

And here's her first day of school, all the more memorable with a bright pink cast on her arm. Here's another day, unremarkable but for the drawing she, in her little red dress, brings home, her mother with red lips and big blue eyeballs, you with unnaturally large muscles covering all of your body, all three of you standing beside a blue bungalow that is taller than the girls, shorter than you.

Here she is graduating from eighth grade. Here she is in the passenger seat of her friend's car, driving into a parked car causing very little damage but causing the airbags to ignite, slamming into her face, breaking her nose. Here she is walking through the door, black-eyed and bloody. Here she is asking you to be her prom date, saying the only thing she wants is her father at her graduation ceremony. Here she is laughing when a bird, a goose, shits on your shoulder—she's grabbing your arm now, pulling you into the car, before you can get back inside to clean it off, put your favourite shirt back on, sit in your chair—holding your hand all the way to the school, looking at you as if taking your daughter to graduation is the best decision you'll ever make. Here she is moving out. Here she is visiting. Here she is trying to make you laugh. Reading your stories. Calling you crazy. Running out the door to help some guy who wrecked his bike.

The man in the waiting room took the Advil, smiled at the woman, said he was going home, would she like to come over after work. She kissed his cheek, said she would love to.

I am a man who is forced to make every decision he ever makes with the future, all its beauty and devastation, stretching out in front of him, an ocean never finding its coast. If he decides to talk to the girl, the woman with the dog in the park, he must watch the conversation in its entirety, how he—the man—begins to sweat before the woman reaches the park, as the minute hand reaches the six, as he sees her—a speck on the sidewalk forever away—how she unleashes her dog and he his, how he throws a tennis ball toward her so hard she jumps when she sees it coming and has to do a two-step to dodge it, how she looks scared when his dog goes bounding after it, how he apologizes, bumbles over the words, how she says, "Sorry what was that?" twice before she understands: he's sorry, his name is mumble mumble.

"What?"

"Mumble mumble."

"Oh. Yes. Nice to meet you."

How he explains that he's seen her before, how she looks nervous, maybe even scared, how she asks about his dog, just as he'd planned when he'd rescued it, how she tells him she's gotta go, she's meeting her fiancé for lunch, how he throws the ball once more and leaves as the dog is chasing it in the opposite direction, how the dog follows him home and he starts to think maybe a dog will be a nice companion after all, how he starts talking to the dog as if it could understand, starts walking it in the direction opposite the park, the woman.

If he decides to say something to a certain girl in the hallway—"Watermelons," for instance—there is her reaction—"Excuse me!"—right in front of him. "What is that supposed to mean?" she says, and she wraps her cardigan around herself, tight. "You're so weird. You're just gonna stand there? After that? You're such a jackass. Ya know what, don't even bother. Forget I ever said anything to you. And you can sure as hell forget about watermelons."

If he decides to write a story, finally, in third person, he sees his pen floating away, unable to control itself, moving from his own mind, to hers, where it finds all sorts of fascinating yet startling things about the way he moves, the way he scratches his chin or his ears more than anyone she has ever met, and he'll find himself moving from her to some man she makes eye contact with as she stops, turns left at a four-way stop, who considers turning around to follow the woman home, but decides that it would be pathetic and moves on to daydreaming about his future life after he wins the lotto all the way to his apartment where he nods, smiles at the woman in 2B who thinks, Why will he not even say hello? She wonders does he know her name, even, after all these seven years of living next to each other, and she curls up on her sofa and scratches the underside of her dog's belly, who can't stop wondering why he is somehow incapable of making the love of his life happy...

If he beats his daughter to the window, says, "Oh everything's fine," he's forced to watch her follow him up to the window, practically shove him out of the way, say, "Everything's fine, are you serious? That guy just wrecked his bike." He's forced to watch her run out the door, disappear, forced to sit back down in his chair, alone.

If he stands. If he puts on his pants and walks to the door. If he steps outside to take his wife for coffee, he will be forced to breathe the air, to look around, forced to admit he is alone and can't tolerate it, forced to feel what it would be like to say that, to feel a sentence like that wrapping itself around you and squeezing you until your jugular comes jutting out of your neck for the mosquitos to suck on, forced to feel the light of the sun burning up your liver as it searches your insides and pulls out your secrets and offers them for anyone to see, to feel the pain of working at not being alone, sharing yourself with this woman, trusting her—or anyone, the stupid coffee barista— with bits of yourself, hoping she won't dip these bits in her coffee, suck the juice out of them, then spit them into her napkin and scratch at her tongue to get the taste off of it.

So instead of deciding anything, he decides nothing. He sits—the man—me—I sit—here with a pen and ink, and I listen, pantless, and I write, and read sometimes, if I ever run into a wall.

SCRATCH & DRAG

In my drawer, under my underwear, I have nearly a dozen of these hidden away, waiting. They're there, wishing they could get out to sit on my pillow for you, anybody, to read them. Or they're wishing they had never been written. If you were digging, if you were ever interested in digging into any part of my life, then you could look for them—I've hidden them where I hope you will find them, though I'm not surprised you haven't.

I should throw them away. Each time, I try to build the courage to leave them there on my pillow, but I end up rereading them to make sure I haven't misplaced any semicolons or left out any commas, and by the time I'm finished, I'm embarrassed at the melodrama. But I'm shocked at how much of myself I can drop onto the page. I feel as if these notes are a part of me, as much as the ink becomes a part of the page. I feel as if my pen knows my thoughts clearer than I do, as if I could let go of it and watch it write my life away.

I'm amazed at Delaney's courage. I'm sure you'd agree. I doubt she reread her note. You didn't know she left a note. It didn't say much. It said she loved you. You and Dad. But I doubt you've ever doubted that. Other than that, it didn't say a damn thing. That was the problem with her note; after you read it, you'd be more confused than if she hadn't left a note at all. You'd start thinking maybe she really did it because of you, like she was trying to get back at you for something you hardly even knew you were doing. You'd start blaming yourself until you'd realize, finally, if that was her plan— getting back at you—that it had worked better than she ever could have hoped.

That's why I threw it out.

My problem is the opposite. With these notes. I keep rambling on and on until none of it fits together. It's 'cause I never know where to start.

I remember the day Delaney was born. I was only two, but I remember Dad saying we were going to meet my little sister. And I remember walking upstairs holding Dad's hand. Grey stairs that never seemed to end. I remember looking down at them, no thoughts in my head, just stairs.

You didn't believe me, but it's true. I told you once and you told me that's impossible. "I don't think you even came to see her at the hospital," you said. You said I was at Grandma's. And I guess that's how I've felt my entire life since she was born, like you were watching her, smiling at her, bragging about her, happy, or close to it, and I was somewhere else, waiting.

Remember when she was trying on wedding gowns? You probably try to forget, how she tried on fifty-four dresses until she settled on one. We had to sit in those horrible chairs, waiting while she squeezed into each dress. My God, she could have chosen any of them and she would have been beautiful, but you kept smiling, that nice smile you used to save just for her, and you kept dabbing at your eyes with that stupid handkerchief and saying, "Oh I just can't believe my daughter is getting married." As if you were the first mother to ever watch her daughter get married. As if she was your only daughter. As if you had forgotten I was sitting right there next to you.

Tell Mom and Dad I loved them. That's all her entire note said about you. You would have been devastated. The whole thing was written for me. To me. As if she knew I would be the one to find her, her face bloated and blue, her neck red and raw from the ugly grey rope, her eyes already faded to an egg-white haze, her hair wild, perfect, as it always was.

I'm sure you've stopped reading this by now. You probably had a picture of her asleep in her bed with her makeup done and a tiny peaceful smile, patiently awaiting eternity. Certainly, if she had seen herself after, she would have chosen a more romantic way to do it.

She had folded her note neatly, then crumpled it. She must have been holding it when she kicked the laundry basket away, squeezing it tight just before she dropped it beside her, *Abigail* in her frilly handwriting screaming at me from the floor. She must have known I wouldn't let you read it; she didn't even think to tell you herself. *Tell Mom and Dad.* I almost wish you had found it, found her.

Death had always been all over her, you tell people. Ever since that man crashed in front of our house and she ran out to see him sprawled in the middle of the road. She ran out before any of us could stop her, the story goes, but we never tried to stop her. Why would we? Who expects to find death in the road, or in the closet, or anywhere? When Dad finally pulled her away, she was hysterical. You tell people that she was never the same after that.

I let you say it. It's nice to say that death landed on Grandview that day and after that, she could never escape from it. I can see the stress ebbing from your face as you say it—after you've had a few glasses of wine and Delaney is all you can talk about. So I let you say it. It's nice to have something to blame.

But she wasn't even crying when she came back to bed. She told me it was the man from our lemonade stand who'd had a crush on her, tipping her five dollars once. She couldn't recognize him, but she knew it was him, that's what she said. And she thought the man who killed him might have had a crush on her too. He seemed excited to see her running down the sidewalk, she said. Most likely he was. She described the dead man with the same sort of wonder that a young painter describes the work of a master, a newfound inspiration. And I know she never forgot it. She'd bring it up every so often when we still shared a room, after we'd spent the night sipping Slurpees and eating candy, laughing, hysterical, as we were winding down to sleep. "Remember that man?" she'd ask. And I knew she was talking about the dead guy 'cause she looked the same as she did on that night. "I've never seen someone look more at peace," she'd say, "at ease."

Death does have a way of holding you, I won't deny it. That face—I hardly consider it hers anymore—is everywhere. It follows me. I used to have nightmares about it: we'd be kids again. I'd be sitting in class and she'd turn around and her face would be blue, her eyes wild, she'd be scratching at the rope, breaking her fingernails on the skin of her bloody neck. But I could never move out of my seat to help her. I could only watch her eyes plead with me. I'd wake up in a sweat. I'd look over at her bed to make sure she was all right—and I'd remember we weren't kids anymore, we didn't share a room anymore, she wasn't in her bed, wasn't anywhere.

And I'd cry. Yes, I did cry, do cry. I've heard you tell countless people I haven't cried, that I'm so strong. You don't know how I can do it, you say. But I see the way you look at me when you say it, as if you've known all along I was heartless.

I just never wanted you to see.

Now I see her everywhere. When I'm trying on sweaters in change rooms—as I slip my head through the neck, she'll appear, right there, in the mirror. I'll be chatting with some guy at the gym and her purple lips will smile at me from the TV on his treadmill. I'll be checking to make sure the eggs aren't cracked in the supermarket. When the refrigerator door shuts, she's standing there behind it. She drives all the cars under the city lights. She walks the dogs and bends over to pick up their shit. She sits behind me at the movies and whispers.

Now when I dream she looks normal. She's skipping rocks at the lake as a child. Her rock skips a dozen times then hits the water funny and flies up, hitting a fish that just happens to be jumping out of the lake, like magic. She's doing my hair in braids that are too loose, and I have to beg you to redo them. She's playing with the neighbours in the front yard. She's trying to read *Mrs. Dalloway*, then tossing it back to me, saying, "I can't get past the second page." She's blowing out candles. She's trying on dresses. She's writing notes.

I see the way Jeff looks at you, she wrote. *I wouldn't doubt if he sleeps with you before you read this.* As if it's up to him and I have no say. As if she's nine years old again—which means that I'm just barely eleven—and she's apologizing to me for making Kayden Leftwhich ask me out. He broke up with her to ask me out.

Do you know I've never gone out with a man who hasn't first gone out with Delaney? I can guess your reaction to that, if you're still reading. You've probably put the note down and gone to the kitchen to pour some wine. You're leaning on the counter, looking up at the ceiling, going through a list of my boyfriends in your head, the ones you remember at least. You're probably thinking, How could she possibly? And I've often wondered the same thing. I've never been able to play it cool enough to make a guy think I'd be any fun. I'm always sweating and nervous, I can see guys skipping over me as they scope out the room. It's easier to be myself when guys are drooling all over Delaney.

She wouldn't do that, not to Delaney, you're saying.

Keep going down the list. Soon you'll realize it's true, and you'll chug that whole glass of wine before pouring another, you'll bring the bottle with you to the living room where you'll start reading again. You might call me a bitch, having found the proof, at last.

"I'm terribly sorry you have to date him," Delaney said to me when Kayden dumped her and asked me out on the same Thursday of our week at summer camp. Kayden was a spry ten-year-old and he had immediately pounced on Delaney—her fluttery giggle, her wild blonde hair, typical eyes, her cute little half smile that she had invented just for him. On the first day, the camp counsellors instructed us to get into groups of three for a game of tag. To get to know each other, they said. Delaney dragged us through the crowd straight to Kayden, as if she had spied him out hours before. She took his hand and giggled and pretended she didn't know how to play tag. They were dating, or whatever you call a relationship between a nine- and a ten-year-old, by supper time. By Thursday he was tired of her.

She felt sorry for me, that I even wanted to date a jackass like that, she said. She closed her eyes, tilted her head back, pinched the bridge of her nose while she said it. Always overdramatic. Always imitating you, dear Mother.

This first time was much like every other time. I never planned on stealing any of them. Most times I wasn't even attracted to them.

Delaney would lure them in, entertain them for a while, then introduce them to me. She'd take me along on a hike, "'cause Abigail does this hike all the time," she'd tell them. Though I never went a single time without her. We'd talk about movies, books sometimes, we'd point to little colourful birds and wonder what kind they were, we'd sit and eat our sandwiches in the dirt.

Afterward she'd ask, "So what do you think? Do you like him? Could you ever see yourself with a guy like that?" I used to think she was digging for proof, that she assumed ever since Kayden that I wanted to steal all of her boyfriends. If I gave the wrong answer, she'd catch me in the act. But now I think she was pushing them to me. You'll say I'm making excuses. Every whore believes she's innocent. Every homewrecker claims only to be following her heart. But why would she invite me along if she thought I'd steal them? She tired of them, the same as they tired of her.

I did sleep with Jeff. Before I read her note. Before she wrote it, I'm sure. Before he proposed.

I was writing at Starbucks on Main, in one of the big chairs by the fireplace. (I should spare you this story. It's just the thing that would make me hide the note under my underwear, if I were to reread it... but I'm going to try not to reread this one.) A guy came up to me and said the rest of the tables were full, did I mind if he sat across from me? I said, "Go ahead." He was the type of guy—handsome, but not stunning—I never would have noticed from across the room, but sitting there right in front of me tapping his finger and sliding it around his iPad, I felt drawn into him. If I believed in love at first sight, I would have held onto him tighter.

You have to believe I didn't know Delaney had anything to do with him. To me, he was a complete stranger. He sat for a while. I caught him looking at me more than once and I'll admit, I let him catch me, though I started to wonder if he was just noticing my sweat. "I'm sorry," he said. He said he just had to ask, "Do you always write in your notebook with a pen?" I told him I liked a pen a lot better than a pencil. His smile when he asked made me think he was flirting.

He smiled wide and ran his fingers through his hair. He said that was interesting. He asked me why I didn't just type it up.

You'll be happy to know, Mother, that even when talking to guys, you're right there with me, telling me what to say. I had a picture of you telling me that you can't even read my chicken scratch, and you think my writing in a notebook is pretentious. So for a second I was lost, I didn't know what to tell him. I told him I didn't know. He tilted his head and squinted his eyes and said, "You've gotta have a reason." And he looked like he might actually be interested. He shut down his iPad and set it on the arm of his chair.

"I guess I just like the scratch and drag of the pen on the paper," I told him. "It gives me an extra second to think. On the laptop, I just start rambling without any thought to what's coming. On the laptop," I told him, "I'm full of clichés and melodrama."

"Well isn't that romantic?" he said, and I thought he was making fun of me. I blushed and looked at my watch.

"No, I'm serious," he said. He said he wished he cared about something passionately, like I did, which surprised me because I was trying really hard to say it nonchalantly, like I didn't care at all. (I'll spare you all the details of the conversation. I'm sure you've tipped the bottle back and you're probably wishing that last drop had landed in your mouth instead of on your chin. You'll be wondering when I'll stop trying to justify my whoredom.) We got onto books, Jeff and I, and it ended with him driving me to that little bookstore at the other end of Main where I helped him pick out an armload of books. You wouldn't care which ones, but you have to see why I might have liked the guy.

He didn't even ask me—though I'm not denying I would have said yes. I would have jumped at the idea. He just drove across Macleod to his condo in one of the new parts of town. He got out and opened my door. We went up to the twelfth floor.

You'll remember the night, Mother. I left my car in the Starbucks parking lot and someone broke the back windshield to get at my laptop. "You can replace it yourself," you said. "Were you drunk?" you

GRANDVIEW DRIVE

said over and over. "Why did you leave it there?" And you were so mad at the smug, defiant, ugly little smirk on my face, you said.

I was happy. Guys, when single, find all the bubbly wonder of a blonde-haired-laughs-too-loud-hysterical-fembot wildly alluring. They see these girls biting their lips and tying up their hair, watch them as they pull out the elastics, shaking their heads as their hair falls back to their shoulders, as if they had decided in the two seconds that their hair was up that maybe the ponytail wasn't a good idea. The single guys imagine sitting in some low-lit restaurant making witty jokes about the poor service, their wannabe babycakes giggling so loud all the other men in the restaurant look over to see the happy couple. The other men nod in common agreement. The single guys smile. The ladies eat their salads.

It's brains they want, really. They just need the beauty out of the way—under their arm, or at work, or at home getting ready for their date—before they notice the brains. I thought I had found a man who had noticed me without first being bored with Delaney. So I was happy. I didn't know anything about the call he just had to take while we were out book shopping, the person he apologized to a thousand times, the person he told, "We'll have to do it tomorrow," before rolling his eyes and hanging up and saying, "Mothers," as he looked at me—I didn't know that was Delaney. I was just agreeing with him about mothers.

It wasn't until a few nights later, a week actually to the day, when I went to a movie—yes, the dreaded "night on my own" you think is so hilarious—that I found out. It was a corny romantic comedy. I was going to pretend it was Jeff and me up on the screen, our worlds comically crashing down around us, but still clinging to our endless love. Roll your eyes if you want, Mother. A night on your own is meant for fantasies.

I saw a couple snuggling a few rows ahead of me. Soon they were kissing, and I shifted my attention to them. Now I was pretending it was Jeff and I making out, so unashamed. But the more I watched, the more he started to look like Jeff, and the more I noticed the wild blonde hair that was so familiar. I snuck out of the movie before I even got to see what the huge misunderstanding would be, before they could sort it all out.

I never returned his calls, Mother, until after. I made myself go to their parties, to their engagement party in particular, so he could see that I knew, but I never answered his calls. He called even more after the engagement. I didn't want to hear his apologies, excuses. I didn't want to believe them.

He was the first person I called, though, when I found Delaney. I thought it was his fault. I wanted him to see how distorted she looked, how he had destroyed her. But when he got there, he just held me. He rubbed my shoulders and kissed the crown of my head and told me it wasn't my fault, as if he knew everyone would blame me. And not him. He helped me get her down and put her on the bed.

You're probably pitching the wine bottle at the wall and trying to pull your hair out, but could you really imagine seeing her hanging there, eyes bulging, one shoe on the floor, the other just barely hanging on to her little pink foot? I know you're glad I moved her.

Jeff wanted us to be together. Not right away, but sooner than I would have thought. Three months. He called me after three months and told me he missed me. His fiancé was dead and he missed me. I agreed to meet him for coffee, at Starbucks on Main. He said he knows he should be mourning Delaney but he feels like he's mourning me.

You have no idea how that made me feel. I felt like maybe I was first. Maybe here was someone who had been waiting for me. Maybe I could forget about Delaney. But then she was all I thought about. All I think about. I kept going over her stupid note, to myself, in my head. *I knew he loved you the minute he saw you,* she said in that damn note. *That night I brought him over for Mom's birthday,* she said. And I just kept thinking of how devastated she would be if she knew we had slept together, already, weeks before. But then she's dead, I'd think, how much more devastated could she be?

I could never have lasted with Jeff. Some nights he'd cry, like weep, harder than I'd ever cried, and I'd ask him what was wrong. He'd say some lunatic bullshit about being happy he had me. Then once he said, "I called it off, Abby." He said he couldn't stop thinking about me and he didn't think that was fair to Delaney. So he called it off. The worst mistake he'd ever made, he said. He thought he had done the right thing. He thought it was better to hurt her now than later. He thought he would call me up and marry me instead, like it was all up to him, I had no say. He didn't know, he said. He didn't know how much it would hurt. How much he would miss her. He thought he was trying to live without regrets, he said. Helpless.

He'd be crying the whole time, looking off into the past somewhere, and I would find myself waiting. Again. Waiting for him to finish crying. To finish blubbering over Delaney. Even when she was dead I was waiting. Waiting for him to remember I was sitting right there next to him.

I sat there watching him and not a bit of me cared. I was so angry, Mom. At Jeff, obviously, for wanting me to comfort him when all he could say was that he wished he had never done it, he wished he had never called it off, he wished he still had Delaney. At Delaney and her stupid note; it was just like her to be all dramatic and go hang herself over a boy. And blame it on me.

But then here I am writing the same note, over the same boy, and blaming her.

I won't leave you the guesswork, Mom. You can blame Delaney if you like, for being so damned perfect and making everyone worship her. You can blame Jeff for making me fall in love with him, for loving Delaney. But if we're being honest, you can blame yourself. All I ever wanted was to feel like Delaney must've felt. But you couldn't even hug me that night when I finally told you I had found her. You went screaming to her bed and said, "This can't happen to me. How could my own daughter want to kill herself," you said, as if she did it to you. As if her suicide was an attack on you. We could have gotten through it. I would have cried if we had hugged. I would have wiped my nose on your shoulder and sobbed in uncontrolled shakes as you held me against you. I would have held you.

Oh, don't be so needy, I can hear you saying. But I'll admit it—I needed you, Mom.

Tell Mom and Dad I loved them, her note said, and I guess I'll say it too, because I did love you Mom. I do. Tell Dad, too, if you ever see him again.

Now I'm going to go sip some angel's trumpet tea and lay in the barley fields, or put on a flowing gown and go float away down a river, fill my pockets with stones and sink to the bottom, or hook up a hose from the exhaust to my Jetta and fall asleep listening to Chopin. Most likely, though, I'll read over the damn thing, scratch half of it out, and slip it in with the rest of them under my pink fucking panties.

THE FORCE OF THIS HAND
PRESSING DOWN UPON ME

I was pacing around the living room practising for the coming Sunday's sermon. I had spent a year as the youth pastor, but this was the third week of an indefinite trial period during which my father was trying to pass his church, Macleod Pentecostal, to me. I remember fumbling over the sentences as if someone else had written them, as if I were trying to explain string theory to a group of twelve-year-olds. I was questioning, as I often had, whether I even believed what I was preaching, or at least, if I was in any way justified in believing it. I remember crumpling my typed notes into a ball and tossing them at the ceiling fan, watching them shoot across the living room to settle down on the sofa, or to hit the window and fall to the ground.

For as vivid as this night is to me, I can't at all remember what I was planning to preach about. I've used this night countless times now, at weddings or Easter or various Sunday services, though the story's been whittled down to almost nothing for these sermons.

I grabbed a glass of water, then sat down at the baby grand piano. I pretended to flick my tails back, linked my fingers together, stretched them out in front of me to crack my knuckles, then pretended to play. I hunched my shoulders over, squeezed my eyes shut and swayed along to the clunking of my fingers on the keys. I still do this sometimes, pretend I'm in front of thousands of people waiting for me to pour myself out before them.

I remember the sudden thud made me jump and slam my fists down on the keys and look around to see what had happened. The room looked different, somehow, as if any one of the paintings on the wall, or any of my mother's funny ornaments on the fireplace mantel,

147

was capable of thudding around the room as I played the piano, had spent its life struggling to break free into our world of living, thriving things. I watched the grandfather clock ticking in the corner, then realized the thud had to have been the window. Now that I was looking at it, I could see it hadn't been washed for a long time, so that you noticed the streaks of filth before you noticed anything past it.

A sparrow lay in the flower bed under the window, panting, eyes so wide, its one wing twitching so softly, trying to get comfortable down there in the dirt. And I needed to find the lesson that was to be learned here, how the reflection of trees in a window could look so enticing—a shade darker than the real trees, flowing just so in the wind, so that anyone would have wished to sit amongst such lovely leaves. How maybe none of God's creatures is satisfied with what is standing blatantly before them, but longs for something more, something reflected in the window, a different version of that tree you're sitting—

A little black car smashed into a half-ton pulling out of its driveway across the street. The blast was different than the thud on the window, filling up the street, the inside of my house, my head, so that I stumbled backwards from my window. I dropped my water glass then stepped on it and floated through the air until I slammed on top of the coffee table. The back of my head smashed the glass tabletop into a thousand little shards, though they stayed tight in the metal frame they were resting in. I sat up, hurried back to the window.

A body lay crumpled and bleeding in the street. If it weren't for the differing colours of the vehicles, you wouldn't be able to tell them apart, the two of them merged together looking like a devil trying to claw his way out of the pavement. I watched from the window as the man in the truck got out, walked over to the body, stood over it as if he were examining a painting on the wall. Then he looked wildly all over the street, back and forth, up at our houses, trying to find out who could have done this. I thought he might see me watching him. I touched my finger to the window and focused my eyes on the stain it left there.

He lay down in the grass at the side of the road just as a girl—twelve maybe, or seventeen, or nine—from next door ran up to the body, her wild hair a striking dirty-blonde wave flying after her. A man—it must have been her father—chased behind. He grabbed her up in his arms and held her in a tight hug, staring down wide-eyed at the body, his one hand holding her head into his shoulder so she couldn't look back around at it. She flailed her arms and kicked at him and screamed so I could hear her through my dirty window, as if the body were hers, she had loved it the whole of her young life. Her father turned and carried her back to their house as she stretched out her little finger to point back at the body. The man in the grass held his hand to his forehead. The body sat still in the street. The father returned a minute later, daughterless. He said something to the others. Then pulled out his phone.

I stood watching it all as if it were happening to me. As if I smashed into the truck and flew out of my car to bowl down the middle of Grandview Drive. As if someone smashed into my truck and flew over the bed and slid down Grandview until they couldn't slide any longer. As if I were a little girl uncontrollably drawn to the gore. As if I were chasing my own little daughter as she ran out of the house to try to keep her from seeing this. None of us knew what we were to do in the face of this death. We were frozen with fear. Only the responsibility of a life not our own, one outside of ourselves, our daughter's, drove us to act.

This fear was creeping down into me, holding me in place at the window. I felt small and embarrassed and I made myself go outside. To help, I guess, but to say I refused to let fear take hold. I remember the grass on my socked feet felt strange, as if it might open up and pull me under if I didn't hurry. I could count each blade as it scraped against my foot. The raindrops—I hadn't noticed the rain from behind the window—surprised me, pricked my skin like someone was sprinkling little bits of fibreglass down on top of me. Then they started to massage my skin, to hold on to me and seep into me all at once, to calm me down, to help me breathe.

My feet slapped onto the sidewalk then onto the street and I could reach out and touch the black car if I wanted, or the truck. The hole in the windshield was too small. The glass splintered all the way through to the end, so that without the hole you wouldn't be able to see through it. But the hole was so small. A man shouldn't have fit through there. He should have thought to put his belt on, settled for deep bruises across his chest, a dislocated shoulder, shattered shin bones and torn tendons, maybe a broken nose from the airbag. The car wasn't as small as I first thought, squished up as it was. He must have loved that car. Napkins fluttering in the breeze through the hole in the windshield.

I walked past the car without touching it. The man in the grass was whispering something, still holding his forehead. I couldn't make any of it out, now that I noticed it, as if he was reciting some sort of poem into someone's ear, or praying, one of those prayers you're not sure of, you make out of habit more than out of any real belief that it will be answered. I wanted to lie down beside him, for a second, to try to understand what another human being could possibly pray for after finding a little black Buick crushed up against your truck. Or maybe he was—

"Reverend," the father said. The relief on his face was obvious, as if this man's only prayer his whole life had been that when two of his neighbours crash their cars into each other and one of them is dead, please God let there be a religious man, or any other man besides me, there to deal with it. I could feel the rain picking up, falling in rhythm onto the hood of the truck, in through the hole in the windshield onto the dashboard, the leather seats, pushing me forward, forcing me to move, as if the spirit of God was descending upon us.

"Johnny," I said.

"My God. I just called the ambulance. I hope they can do something I'm so glad you're here I don't know what the hell I'm supposed to do here. I don't think they'll be able to save this guy have you seen him before? I don't even recognize him I mean even if you could recognize him, I don't think I recognize him. I think the other guy's in shock or something. Oh my God who the hell goes this fast down Grandview—"

"My name is Johnny," I said.

"What's that?"

"I'm not a reverend." The man didn't know what to say to that, and I didn't know what I wanted him to say, but I wasn't there to talk about if or why I would ever decide to become a minister anyway. I was there to see about the body, which I had been avoiding, I could see now, talking to this guy.

It lay there waiting. And when I looked at it—stepped around the devil's claw and really looked at it—I knew it was there for me, that even now we were connected to each other in a way no one else had ever been connected. I had known it all my life, had waited to come upon every minute since I could think, and now here it was in the middle of my street, two houses past the house I had grown up in. I walked toward it like I might have been drifting toward a bright white light, stepping gently, embracing the glass and the pebbles through my socks, not wanting any of them to miss this encounter with the living spirit of this one true thing. It lay there bleeding, one arm bent under its back, the other stretched out past its head, the skin on its face scraped through to the cheekbone on one side, the eyelid above it torn partway through, its bloodshot eye staring up. The other eye closed tight. Teeth were missing. Its nose pushed up between its eyes. An earlobe hung loose.

"Reverend?" the father asked, and I looked at him, but he wasn't there. Or he was outside of what was happening right there with us. He was staring back at me like he had just seen a ghost and wasn't sure if I would believe he had. "You gonna be okay?" he said.

"Johnny," I told him. And I sat down beside the body's head, its one eye still looking up at me.

"What a mess," the father said, staring at the eye now.

I found a rock and placed it on the one open eye as the rain beat down upon the body's skin, splashing into smaller drops here and there. At the first youth retreat I'd ever been to—I was thirteen—the preacher asked us if we would come forward to the front of the sanctuary, offering ourselves at the altar of the Lord as an act of surrender. I rushed forward, eager to show my devotion to my father and everyone else who was there. The preacher had us line up along the front of the stage so he could pray for us each in our time. He said the Spirit of the Lord was present, it would show itself to you if you were willing to see it. He lay his hand on our foreheads and screamed into his microphone: "Power"—or—"Holy Spirit Come"—or just— "Come"—and as he said these words, the kids would fall over, some of them shooting back so the adults behind them could barely catch their weight.

When he arrived at me, he placed his hand on my forehead, as he had for all the others, and said "In the name of Jesus, come…" but nothing really happened. I was glad to be up there, and was happy to be prayed for, but no driving force pushed me backward. The preacher bent his elbow, pulled his hand back to his face, then shot it back to my forehead, "Come!" and I started crying, believing myself to be in the presence of the Spirit. He pulled back again, then pushed his hand hard at my forehead, "Power!" He left his hand there, put his microphone on the ground, hopped off the stage, came in real close, started praying in tongues so neither of us could understand.

Then he started pushing against my forehead, gently at first, then harder, until I took a step back with one foot, and opened my eyes to look up at him before stepping closer again. He closed his eyes quick and whispered, "Jesus," and moved on to the next kid, but it was the force of this hand I could feel pressing down upon me as I sat next to the body watching the rain streak down its forehead.

And the whole earth sang out before me. The trees stood at attention as if they too had been waiting for me to open my eyes and listen to them for all but a minute. Here I am, they were saying. Tell me, they said. Where were you when we were seedlings sucking light from the soil until we could sprout out and grow? Where were you when we fed from the waters that fell down from the Heavens? Show me the path to light's dwelling place of old. Show me where darkness inhabits the land. Tell me, they said. From where does the east wind begin to blow? All that you see in this world is the Word of the Most High, so that nothing consists of anything visible.

The trees stood still, then, and the leaves hung down. And birds of every size and song flew by with my name on their breath. And the clouds bundled together, rumbled their applause, and sent the rain pouring down around me in sheets. I found myself desperate for this life—this body's life—to mean something wonderful and whole even as it lay there in front of me. How foolish I had been to seek the lesson life will teach me, when this day would come, when all of life and death would be, for now and for always, right in front of me—

"Reverend?"

"Yes?" I said to the father, and he motioned to the man beside him.

"Would you excuse me, sir?" said a police officer holding a yellow tarp. "We'll need to cover the body." The man in the grass was gone.

"Yes," I said, and I stood and stepped back. And I knew, as the body knew, that it was time to set out on our separate paths with the uncompromising hope of things to come. The officer spread the tarp over the body. In the darkness, under the clouds, the blue and red lights on the car swirled around, reflecting off the houses, the white headlights shone forward, away from the body, the unbridled beauty of it all screaming, Something is right in the world. I needed to preserve it. I ran to get the camera from my father's house.

"Did you ever want to be anything other than the pastor of Macleod Pentecostal?" I asked my father once.

"Are you kidding me. I'd never have chosen this myself," he'd said, and I dropped out of seminary the next day, halfway through my senior year, feeling as if I were an ant, as if someone had pried up one of the patio bricks and found me below. Only instead of scurrying under the next block with the rest of them, I looked up, saw the thing, five hundred times my size, lifting its foot to bring it down upon my head. But here on the street I had been offered a choice. I had seen life in the face of death and felt I could fly away on spirit's wings right then.

As I took the first step up the walk I saw the sparrow hopping around in the flower bed. But as I stepped forward to thank him, his little eyes looked right at me, and he flew away down the street. How majestic is the tiny sparrow as it flies, not longing for any reflection in the window after all, but sacrificing its earthly body so another might look up and see.

PARKING SPACE

"I need to see you in my office."

"Sure. Just give me a second." He holds up a finger.

"Mmm, no I think right now would be perfect."

"I'm on the phone, Steve. Just give me a minute." Palm over the receiver.

"That is precisely why I want you in my office."

"I'll be right there."

"Hang up. Right now. Or I'll do it for you."

"Steve—"

Steve presses his finger down on the hang up.

"You..." says Henry. "Hello? Hello?" He throws the handset at the wall. Its cord is too short, so it pulls the phone off the desk. The bit of plastic on the top of the phone snaps off.

Steve says, "Take it easy," as Henry bends to pick up the phone.

"Just give me a good goddamn minute." He slams the handset against his desk once for each of the last three words, clenching his teeth, looking right at Steve, hair slightly dishevelled.

"You can go ahead and leave, Hank. Go make all the personal calls you'd like."

"Steve, wait. That was... I couldn't ignore that one."

"You know I've waited too long to do it, Hank. You just need to pack your trinkets and leave."

"Steve."

"It's been a bloody slice."

"Fuck you, Steve." Henry takes his stapler and his three-hole punch and leaves the office. Walks around the back of the build-ing. Throws the hole punch at Steve's Mini Cooper. It flips end over end before sticking into the windshield like a stake through a heart. Slowly, it slides through the glass and sits still on the driver's seat.

Henry hangs the stapler so one side is in his pocket, the other out. He pushes a staple into his pants. It doesn't stick, just falls to the ground. He throws the stapler at the Mini Cooper. It glances off the windshield and flies over to the parking lot behind the car. He walks over to the stapler. Bends over. Pounds eight or ten staples out of it then walks away. Throws his tie over his shoulder and walks away from the lot, toward his own car. Four blocks down. Saves him two hundred dollars a month, not being in the lot.

A woman stands in front of his car, filling out a parking ticket.

"Oh my God. What the hell?" says Henry.

"You can't park here."

"I park here every day."

"No you don't."

"You bet your balls I do."

"Ohhhkay."

"Oh, I bet you think you're just the shit."

"I do not think I am the shit,"—she raises her eyebrows, bobs her head on her neck—"I am only doing my job."

"And how do you feel about your job?"

"I feel fine, sir."

"Do you feel like a complete ass?" Leans up on his tiptoes.

"I do not. Here is your ticket."

"Oh that's great."

"Have a good day," she says. Turns to walk away.

"I bet you feel so good right now. Making everyone miserable."

"I feel fine."

"Oh." He sticks his hands out to either side, looks around the street. "She feels fine. You feel fine. Now that you've just shit all over my shitty day, you feel fine."

The woman turns around then. Walks toward him. Quick. Eyebrows scrunched in. Henry shuffles backwards slightly. She stops a foot in front of him and stares at him for a second without speaking. Looks down at his lip, or chin.

"I feel pretty darn good," she says.

"Oh reall—"

"I am only doing my job. Diligently doing my job, and you're out here having a grown-ass tantrum right in the middle of downtown Macleod. Over a thirty-five dollar ticket."

"I—"

"Compared to this," she waves her fingers in front of Henry's face, "I feel pretty damn good about myself."

Henry stands there. Pushes his hair out of his eyes. "You have no cl—"

"Please," she says. "Have a nice day."

Henry spends two days watching TV, falls asleep on the couch during a third loop through SportsCentre the second night. He wakes up, tries to straighten his hair in the mirror that hangs behind his toilet as he pisses, goes to his room to change.

He searches online but gets frustrated having to write new cover letters for each position, having to fill out the same information for each application. He prints a dozen resumes and makes a list of twelve offices where he'll drop them. He taps the pile on his counter, trying to straighten them out, then slips them into the trash can. Goes to his room. Puts on jeans nearly worn through in the knees. Rummages through his closet until he finds an old T-shirt, grey with a little sailboat sailing off toward his left armpit. He leaves his phone, his keys, on the kitchen table and takes the bus downtown. Leaves the door unlocked.

Downtown, he sits on a bench in the park. Pulls his right foot up to rest on his left knee. Switches his left foot over to his right knee. Crosses his leg all the way over till it hangs and bounces. Puts his arms up on the bench. Looks up at the trees. Watches people singing to themselves in the cars as they speed past. There's an old man cracking peanuts open and dropping the nuts on the ground for a squirrel to munch on. The squirrel stuffs each nut into its cheeks, then looks up at the man to wait for the next one. The man is still dropping peanuts when Henry walks away through the park.

At the other end there's a man tap dancing without any music on a flattened refrigerator box. His tie is arranged in a circle on the concrete. He looks down at his feet mostly, but when he looks up at the crowd gathering around him, he smiles. He smiles with his whole face, with these wide eyes. And Henry pulls out his wallet as the rest of the crowd pulls out their wallets. Henry has a ten-dollar bill and some small change. He drops the bill silently into the middle of the argyle tie.

After the dance, a woman—older than the man, pantsuit, long strap on a little round purse—presses through the crowd to put her arm around the man. Smiles, trying to make her eyes open as wide as they can. "Are you hungry?" she asks the man in a kind way, neither condescending nor flirting.

Henry, after hearing the question, walks to the food court in the mall for lunch. He stands in line at three different places. Takes his watch off and slips it into his pocket while he eats. He sits back and watches people rushing around when he's finished, waits for a mall employee to clear his tray.

When he leaves the mall, the tap dancer is gone and so is his crowd. But his cardboard is still there on the ground. The woman who issued Henry's ticket is standing between two cars, typing licence plate numbers into her little grey computer. She wipes her forehead with her shirt sleeve, looks up at the sun, squints, then rolls her sleeves up past her elbows.

"You done shitting on this guy's day?" says Henry.

"What? Oh my gosh, you have got to be kidding me." She tears the little ticket off the computer, slips it under the wiper. "What do you want?"

"No, I'm… I was kidding you. I am kidding you."

"Ah."

"Pretty nice car, huh?"

"I am very busy right now, sir."

"Right. You probably see all kinds of cars, huh?"

"Like I said."

"Right. Busy. Hey, so do you work for the city?"

"Uh. Yes."

"So you just applied at City Hall?"

"You want a job?"

"Need one."

"Just apply online."

"Online. Right."

"Then call every day till they hire you."

"Okay. Thanks."

"The nice cars are always the biggest assholes."

"What? Oh right. Yeah. Sorry."

Henry walks back through the park. Nods at the peanut man, who has two squirrels now, darting back and forth from a tree to his peanuts. On the bus, Henry sits at the back and watches people get on and off, sharing little intimacies of their lives with whomever wants to listen. He stays on the bus all the way around its route and gets off again downtown. Walks home. Two messages on his phone, one of which is Steve. "Okay, Henry. Call me back. Corporate says I should have just written you up. Which to me is… You'll have to do some anger management before you come back. Just call me back."

Henry saves the message. Finds the application to the City online. Fills it out. They call him the next morning as he's sipping coffee out on his balcony. A couple of mourning doves are snuggling into each other on a balcony rail across the parking lot.

He settles into his new job nicely. Walks quickly through the streets. Pleasant smile. Nods to passersby who look down at the sidewalk or check their watches. He lets people—mostly women—out of their tickets sometimes, if they don't come screaming at him from a block away. If they approach him kindly, quietly. He sits at bus stops for breaks. Watches people hop on and off, slipping quarters into the slot, explaining why they ought to be let on even though they've forgotten their change. He watches them walk to the back of the bus as it starts driving off. Two directions at once.

He tickets the same black Buick every single day.

Lone Street is his last before quitting for the evening. More meters are plugged than not on Lone, and often the black Buick is the only car he has to ticket. He often looks for it as he rounds the corner, punches in the licence plate before reading the meter.

"Do you have a favourite car?" he asks the woman who had ticketed him—Bridgette—in the little staff room where they have their lockers.

"Hmmm. A favourite? Not really."

"No?"

"Well, I always joke with my boyfriend about getting one of those Mercedes wagons." She scrunches her hair in her hand, tilts her head off to one side as she looks in her tiny mirror on her locker door. She puts on lip gloss. Presses her lips together. A little pop when they come apart. She smiles into the mirror, practising. "We're actually in the market for a new car. Or he is. I'm trying to get him to look at one with me. I know. Why would we get a wagon?" She opens her eyes extra wide to put eyeliner on. "We're not thinking about kids that's for sure. We're not even officially together. But he's saying strange things lately. Like last week he says..."

Henry watches her talk. She looks deep into her own eyes as she talks, her expressions more pronounced than usual, her motions bigger. She flips her hair more often.

"...He says he hated how his dad would never take him for ice cream." She digs around in her backpack. Pulls out a blusher brush, and smiles at herself, a big fake smile, before sweeping the blush over her cheeks. "And he comes grocery shopping with me now, and last time we were there we ran into his mother..."

Big, brown eyes darting around her own face. From cheek to lips to something on her forehead. Blinking into her own eyes.

"...he said that. To his mother." Eyes shifting to the side to look at Henry. "That's pretty serious, huh?"

"Yeah. Serious."

"Oh my gosh, I'm sorry. I'm totally blabbing. Do you have a girlfriend?"

"Ah. No. Not really. Well, I don't know. No. I guess I don't. I do not have a girlfriend." He bends over to untie his shoes. Ties them back up.

Bridgette turns around. "Sorry," she says. "Well, what's your favourite car then?"

"What? Oh I don't know."

"Well why'd you ask then, silly?"

"I was talking about on route."

"On route?"

"I got this one black Buick that parks in the same spot every day, but never plugs the meter. Ticket every day."

"And that's your favourite?"

"Think so."

Henry likes to take his time meandering down Lone Street, sometimes waiting all the way to 5:30 p.m. before ticketing the Buick. A few times he brings his supper and goes back to Lone to eat it on a bench across the street from the Buick. He brings a book once. Holds it in his lap while he watches people sink into their vehicles, loosen their ties, straighten their hair in their mirrors, rest their heads on their steering wheels, before idling down to the stop sign and driving off down the road.

He slides his book into his back pocket when he notices headlights reflecting off the stop sign into his eyes. He walks across the street. Cups his hands around his face. Bends over to look inside the Buick. A pair of sunglasses on the driver's seat. Stack of Starbucks napkins neatly piled between the seats. Leather seats. He tries to imagine the driver, whether man or woman, the whole way home. He kicks his shoes off when he finally gets home, then pulls off his socks. Another message from Steve. Rubs his feet as he watches SportsCentre.

Henry's walking down Lone, punching in the Buick's licence plate number as he usually does, when he stops.

There's a red Jetta parked in the Buick's spot. A woman, brunette with blonde streaks streaming down both sides of her little face, gets out of the car and clops quickly toward Henry. She smiles at him briefly as he stands staring.

"Oh shit," she says. "Can you please? I'm almost late for this interview. And I already rescheduled once. Please please please? I'll bring change next time. I promise."

She brings her hand up and pushes it through her long hair which flips back, then falls to the same place on either side of her face. She stomps her little foot in her high heel, then says, "Fine. Whatever. I can't be late for this," as Henry stands there looking at her. She walks past him. He leans to the side to let her pass. Some kind of fruity perfume in the air for a second. He digs into his pocket for some change, looks around the street. Plugs the meter for an hour.

Henry shuts his alarm clock off before it can buzz the next morning. Slips through the sliding doors to his balcony and leans on his railing in the sunrise. Closes his eyes. Birds singing from everywhere. Brakes squealing from somewhere. He leaves for work in time to stop at Lizzie's Diner for breakfast.

"Good morning, mister," the waitress sings.

"Yes I think it might be," says Henry. Bacon and eggs. French fries.

The red Jetta is there instead of the black Buick again. Henry stumbles on a crack in the sidewalk as he steps up to it. Time expired.

"I'm here," the blonde-streaked woman is yelling. Running down the sidewalk in bare feet. High heels hanging on her finger, thick file folder clutched to her chest. "I'm here. I'm moving. I'll move," she says.

"It's fine. Don't worry. It's fine."

"Oh thank you so much. I saw you from back there and just ran for it. You guys are bloody relentless."

"Just doing our job."

"Of course. Of course you are. But it's like you can smell a meter running out. Same thing happened at noon. I came running down to replug the thing and some woman was about to give me one."

"Got the job?"

"What? Oh. Yes! That was you last night?"

"It was."

"I fuckin' nailed that interview— Oops," two fingers up to her lips. High heels hanging down. "Sorry," she says.

"It's fine."

She goes around to the driver's door, tosses the folder, the heels onto the passenger seat. "I always thought you guys would be assholes," she says, standing. Car between them. She reaches behind her seat, pulls out some yellow sneakers, faded, almost white, lifts each leg behind her to slip them on one at a time. Examines her fingernails. Hand through her hair.

"I know," says Henry. "Everyone does."

"Well honestly!"

"I know."

"Well, thanks for not being an asshole."

"No problem. Have a good night. Good luck with the new job."

"You too," she says. "I mean. Good night. Old job."

❖

"Jerry bought a Mercedes wagon!" says Bridgette as soon as he walks into the locker room.

"Seriously?"

"Seriously! He said they're fuel efficient, reliable, blah blah blah and then he asked me to move in with him."

"Wow."

"Eeeeeeeeeeee."

"Aaaaahhhh."

"Oh stop it."

"No that's great."

"I feel like I'm being a big dumb girl."

"It's exciting."

"Woooooooooooo." Eyes wide, bouncing on her toes. "Hahaha. Oh my gosh, I'm sorry. How 'bout you? You seem a lot happier these days." Whips her towel at him.

"Really?"

"Oh my goodness are you kidding? You totally seem happier. You got a girl on the go?" Head tilted.

"What? No. Not really. Well, no. I don't."

"Haha. Sounds like a fib to me."

"No it's nothing. It really is nothing."

People downtown start walking slower at around four in the afternoon. Henry sometimes steps on the heels of people's shoes. Apologizes. Skips around them as they fix their shoes. He sometimes doesn't even apologize, it happens so much. One woman—short, round—takes her shoe all the way off. Tries to hit him with it. "Slowpokes get stepped on," says Henry. Then, "Just kidding. Sorry. In a rush."

"Asshole," says the lady. Limps over to a bench. Puts the shoe back on and sits. Henry can see her watching him as he turns down Lone.

If he doesn't get to the spot before five o'clock, ten to some days, the woman and her red Jetta will be gone already. Often he will be strolling up and down the opposite side of the street when she comes around the corner, always with her shoes on her fingers. He then makes his way over to the Jetta. Nods as she gets in. Says hello sometimes. She says thanks and pats the top of the meter. Once, she pretends to strangle it. Sticks out her tongue—long, thin—while she does it.

Henry smiles. Tips an invisible hat.

⚙

"Hey I've decided I have a favourite spot."

"What's that?" says Henry.

"Remember you said you have a favourite car? On route? Well I have a favourite spot. That one on the corner of Lee and Fourth. It looks like a spot but there's no meter. There's a car there every time I go past."

"Same car?"

"No, just a car. Any car. I love that. Maybe this *is* an asshole job." She looks at herself in the little locker mirror. Rubs a finger hard under her eye. Stray mascara.

"Gotta make quota."

"Yeah I guess."

Henry sits for a second. Counts something on his fingers. "I got my favourite spot too," he says.

"Yeah?"

"On Lone. Same red Jetta parks there most days."

"What's special about it?"

"Just the Jetta I guess. It's actually the same spot that black Buick used to park in."

"Black Buick?"

"My old fave."

"I know. I know it just clicked. You see the paper this morning?"

"No."

"Check it out." She pulls a paper out of her locker. Slaps it on the bench beside Henry. "That your Buick?"

Front page. Fuzzy coloured pixels. Blue Toyota Tundra horizontal to the road. Black Buick. Crushed. Half the size. Can't see the start of one or the other. No beginning. No end. Buick's windshield and windows blown out. Cop car in the distance. Blood on the street. Yellow tarp over something. A body. *Tragic wreck on Grandview: second this year*, reads the headline.

"Shit," says Henry. He stands up. Holds the paper in front of him as he paces around the locker room. "Can I keep this?" he says.

"Sure."

Henry pushes the door open with his back.

"Did you know the guy?" she says as he takes off down the hall.

North on Fourth Avenue instead of south. Everyone is walking south so he has to dodge the neckties and leather purses. Paper rolled up in back pocket. Air is warm, strange. He shuts his eyes. Bumps into a small boy. "Sorry mister." Makes his way to the side of the sidewalk. Leans against a bookshop window. Bends his knee to place his foot flat against the glass. Looks up at the eavestrough. Chipped paint. A robin's nest. A knock on the glass. He turns. A woman—old, grey perm in tiny ringlets—wags her finger. Points at his foot. North again. Past each of his regular haunts to the corner of Fourth and Lee. Car in Bridgette's spot. He opens the door to Yang's Garden on the corner. Table for one. Just water to drink, for now. Chugs it all in one go. Pulls out the paper. Stares at the bits of glass and blood all over the road.

He gets up to leave. Tells the waitress he's sorry and leaves. Looks up to watch the bell jingle as he pushes the door open. One block up to Lone. East. No car in his spot. All the way down so the meters stop and the houses get bigger, wraparound porches on most. Trees on either side of the street lean over the middle, wave in the wind. A woman walks past pulling a paper cart full of towels.

"Evening."

"Yes."

Still walking. Slower now. Foot on each crack between the concrete blocks of sidewalk. Across the street a man—no shirt, firm fat belly hulking over his belt buckle, bald—sits on the front step, smoking. Henry crosses the street.

"You got an extra?"

"Sure. Come on over."

"Thanks. Light?"

He holds a lighter straight out. Flicks it open. Henry leans over and pulls the flame in. One deep breath. A small cough.

"I quit a long time ago."

"Me too."

They don't talk. One stands. One sits. They Look out across the street. A squirrel runs around and around the trunk of a tree. Their eyes follow it up into the leaves until it disappears.

"Crazy little shits all over the place."

"Yeah, no kidding."

"You want another?"

"Might as well."

The man lights one for himself, then hands a cig and the lighter to Henry. He lights his. Puts the lighter in his pocket. Pulls it out and sets it on the step.

"You see that accident over here?" says Henry. Grandview Drive, the next street up.

"Nah."

"Heard about it?"

"Oh yeah. Fuck I heard it happen."

"Heard it?"

"Sure. Fuckin' torpedo blast. Scared the shit outta me."

"Jeez."

Gust of wind. Dust in the air. Henry coughs. The man's finishing his second. Lights a third. "One more?"

"No thanks," says Henry. Puts his second out on the railing.

"Whole thing's got me thinkin' though.

"Yeah?"

"Was down to two cigs a day before it happened. Just a huge fuckin' explosion. No screech. Didn't even try to stop."

"Shit."

"Think I'm gonna quit."

Henry kicks a stone off the walk into the grass.

"Tomorrow. For good."

The squirrel jumps to a second tree. They both sense the branches moving and look up. It scampers straight down the trunk and skips through the grass away from them.

"Well. Good luck."

"Fuckin' eh."

Henry walks back down Lone away from Grandview. Gets on the first bus he sees. Rides it down to the bus depot. Transfers to his regular bus. Sits in the back row. Misses his stop by a block. Makes a pot of coffee at home. Deletes the messages from Steve. Drinks the coffee on his balcony. Watches the doves across the lot flirting. Stays up most of the night.

He drives to work the next morning. Takes thirteen minutes to find a parking spot. Plugs the meter.

Everyone's in a hurry, can't wait to get to their cubicles. Turn on their radios. Henry keeps scrunching his shoulders in as he walks down the sidewalk, flinching, looking over his shoulder, then stepping to the side to let waves of people scurry past. He stares into their faces as they pass. "Morning," some say if they notice him staring. Henry just nods, joins the queue behind them.

He finds more illegal parks than he does on a normal day, but after the second ticket, after the third, he goes into iWorld on Eighth Avenue and buys a flip pad of paper. Each time he finds an illegal park, he prints on a page: *At 9:16 a.m.*—or 10:11 or 10:18—*it was noted that you neglected to plug your meter. Please ensure you do so upon visiting downtown Macleod in the future.* Or something like this.

He spends the day handing out warnings. Can't help smiling each time he traps a note beneath a wiper. He adds a skip between steps every so often.

Makes his way to Lone Street by four o'clock. Walks up and down either side of the street. Eyes on the sidewalk. Talking to himself.

Smiling. Issues three or four warnings. Looks through the Jetta's windows each time he walks past it. Cups his hands around his face, once, to look right inside. Kit Kat wrappers scattered in the back seat, on the floor. Backpack on the passenger seat. iPhone charger in the lighter. Cigarette package between the seats. He crosses the street. Palms sweating a bit.

The Jetta's owner comes around the corner. Folders clutched to her chest. Heels hanging from her teeth. Earlier than usual. Four forty.

Henry jumps behind a car. "Shit. Shit." He sits on the sidewalk. Leans against a black Corolla. "Early." Crawls to look over the hood. She's tossing her things into the car. He sits back down. Hears her door shut. "Okay." Deep breath. "Just gotta do it." He stands up. Dusts his knees, his ass. Pretends he'd been walking the whole time. Runs across the street. Around the back of the Jetta. On the sidewalk. Backpack open on the passenger seat. Exhale. Knocks on the window, leaning down.

She screams, loud. Tries to cover herself up. Bright blue bra.

"Oh my God," says Henry. Spins around. "Sorry," he yells as he skips away. Bright blue bra. Tiny little rolls. Pigeons flying overhead. A man hurrying toward him. Bright blue bra. "Shit."

"Hey! Hey wait."

Henry keeps walking.

"Wait. Please wait."

He turns. She's chasing after him. Black sweater, now. Hair bouncing behind her. Blonde streaks, red now. He stops. Waits.

"Hey," a man from behind him says.

Henry turns around to see Steve marching toward him.

"Friggen eh," says Henry.

"Oh my God. Hank? You're the one giving me all these goddamn tickets?"

"Just calm down, Ste—"

"Don't tell me to calm down you son of a—"

The woman stops beside Henry. "I am so sorry," he says.

"Every goddamn time I park down here I get a ticket."

"Just give me a second, Steve." Turns to the girl. "I'm sorry. Should never have knocked."

"No! Seriously. Who changes in the middle of the street? I thought I'd looked around—"

"I'm not paying this ticket, Hank. I bet you just get off seeing my car there all time."

"I have never noticed your car, Steve."

"Oh, come on! I should've fucking known it was you."

"Just doing my job, Steve."

"Fuck you, Hank."

The girl backs up a little, behind Henry.

"It's just a warning. Take it easy." Starts walking away. "I'm so friggen sorry," he says to the girl as they walk.

"Bullshit warning," says Steve. "You bastard."

"Don't be sorry. I never change out here. I'm just supposed to be going to my mom's."

"Don't worry, I didn't see anything."

The girl blushes. Looks down at the street. Flips her hair back. Familiar fruity scent in the air. Then, big hand on his shoulder.

"Remember this?" Steve says as he swings a three-hole punch through the air and cracks Henry across the jaw. Flash of light. Flash of pain that grows and grows. Falling. Slow motion. One tooth flutters gently through the air. Bounces off the right rear tire of a silver Civic. Henry thumps down into a parking space between the Civic and a Fiesta. The three-hole punch falls to the ground beside him.

"What are you doing?" the girl screams. "What the hell are you doing?"

"Stay out of it. This little bitch got me fired."

"So you're just going to assault him? You stupid ass."

"Oh come on. Assault?"

Henry lays on his back. Holds his jaw. Rolls to his side. Rolls to his back. Watches the girl's lips as she speaks.

"Damn right assault," she says, digging in her purse. "I'm calling the cops."

"Fuck that."

"Fuck nothing. I'm calling right now." Cell phone in hand. Dialling.

Henry can hear Steve running away to his car. The thud of his door makes Henry flinch.

"Just hold on," she says, kneeling down so she's looking straight at him. Then asks, "Henry?"

He squeezes his eyes shut.

"You'll be okay, Henry... Mom." She stands. "Hi. Yeah. No, Mom. I can't come."

Henry lays his head on the sidewalk. Watches her run her fingers through her hair, holding it all in a bunch on the top of her head.

"No I didn't meet some guy," she says. "I'll call you later." She lets her hair fall. "I don't know. It's a fucking emergency."

She hangs up. Crouches down beside him. "Can you sit up?"

Henry rolls to his side, pushes himself up. The light fades. A fog is closing in. He groans. The woman sits beside him on the sidewalk. Grabs his arm. Puts it over her shoulder.

"We'll just sit till you can stand," she said. "And I'll take you to the hospital ... or should I call an ambulance?"

"No," he mumbles. "We'll be fine. I'll be fine."

Arm around the girl. Hand on his jaw, feeling the blood pulse through it, swelling. Hard. Empty parking space. His head resting on her shoulder. That fruity smell all over the place.

THAT BRUISED & BLOODY FEELING

by Abigail Waters

Anne Legion pled not guilty to the murder of her husband claiming her mental health as the cause of her actions. The story—the official story (plus some details she's shared)—goes something like this: she had been working on knitting scarves for various friends and family members for months. When she finished the last stitch of an extra-long white number, she lost all sense of who she was or where she was.

She says she remembers nothing but the terror she felt for her life. She believed that her husband was a devil or had been possessed by one—this is never clear—and that he was about to, as she puts it, "dig out my heart and my liver, and eat them." She says these words each time she tells the story, as if they are the most important part.

And perhaps they are. She stabbed him in the eye with her knitting needle to prevent him from eating her organs. She called the police the next morning, and when they arrived, *Bruised and Bloody Carcass* was sitting on an easel beside the body. She was wearing a white scarf, on which significant splatters of the victim's blood had dried.

I've been interested in Legion and her work for a long time. She once lived two doors down from me. I met her for the first time about three months before her husband's death, though as often as we've talked about it, I can't remember the meeting. She remembers it because it was the first time she'd spoken to any of my family since we'd moved in, but I can't even picture the living room when she describes it.

Back then, I was busy taking care of my chronically depressed little sister. And truthfully, I was busy being a melodramatic teenager myself. I had no idea of the genius down the street. She tells me I would go to her house, along with the rest of my family, for the annual block party she threw every November, "before everyone gets busy."

I often wish my sister Delaney were around to compare notes with, and to whisper about this woman who had killed her husband, how we had stood in the very room where it had happened.

That's just the type of thing Delaney would have been giddy for. There were three fatalities on our street that year: Anne's husband and two car wrecks. No one believes me when I say that, until I tell them it's true, my sister became obsessed with death afterward and eventually killed herself. People cover their mouths when I tell them, and they start apologizing, and they say they'd be terrified to go back to Grandview Drive.

And I am. But the truth is, Delaney was obsessed with ghosts and darkness and death even before all of that. At summer camp, she'd tell ghost stories so scary the counsellors would end up praying that the other campers wouldn't have nightmares. In our room, before bed, she'd ask if I'd ever thought of all the people who'd lived in this house before us, how many of them were just gone now—how many of them had died cold and lonely—or in love and happy, their lovers miserable when they left.

She would disappear into herself on those nights, and while I tried to stay awake with her, I knew there was no way I'd be able to keep her company all night. 2002 was a good year for my parents because they were able to blame Delaney's weirdness on all this death so close to us, but they must have known, too, that it had started before.

Suicide runs in my family. Which is, I suppose, another reason I'm writing this essay. "Mental health" is something of a buzzword these days, even used in marketing campaigns, but now that I'm reading and thinking about it, I'm realizing Delaney was my first overt encounter with someone who wasn't mentally healthy. Whatever way we talk about it, it's awkward and uncomfortable for anyone who hasn't experienced "losing" their mental health, losing their mind.

I've always been anxious; my anxieties take turns somersaulting around my brain so that I can't differentiate one from the other. It all makes me believe the world is ending and I have to react, which is usually lashing out at whatever boyfriend I'm with at the time, who sometimes believes the horrible things I say about him. And I end up feeling helpless and breaking up with him, or him with me. I suppose we're lucky, though, that so many are researching mental health and writing books about it now.

But nobody writes a book about a woman who stabbed her husband in the eye with a knitting needle. Anne Legion became more of an obsession for me when I saw *Bruised and Bloody Carcass* at an exhibit in Montreal in late 2019. I was floundering through college, trying to write, trying to be anybody but myself, reading anything but my textbooks—instead I liked to read nature books about how animals are more like humans than we first thought, how animals grieve and worry and obsess over food, how they pace when they're anxious, wearing holes in the earth. So the way Legion called this body—the body of her dead husband!—a carcass, welcomed me in like a long lost friend. I was desperate to find more of her work.

Bruised and Bloody is not her best work, technically speaking, but it does stand alone amongst her dozens of paintings—mostly dead men gazing longingly at an invisible onlooker. In *Bruised and Bloody*, the body is covered in blood; the knitting needle actually sticks out from the left eye. The right eye looks slightly upward, as if it's trying to remember someone's name. The lighting is strange, a whitewashed blur, but the body is distinct, clear and almost three-dimensional, the way it jumps from the canvas. This painting, more than any of her others, seems to take joy in the gore. Most of her work, it might be said, is straight reportage, as if she's simply bearing witness to the bodies she's stumbled across. *Bruised and Bloody* calls out to you in a way that demands you to take note.

The honeysuckle archways and the rhododendrons and the lilac trees did little to calm my nerves the first time I visited Anne. I spent the two-hour drive to Woodson asking myself why I was doing this, going to visit a known murderer to speak with her about art. Why, of all the things I could write about I had chosen Anne Legion.

I lived in Woodson for years, until Delaney killed herself, until I tried to, before I moved back to Macleod on my own, but in all that time I didn't even realize we had a psych ward. I found a half a column written shortly after Mr. Legion's death that said Mrs. Legion would be held at the Woodson Psychiatric Centre. It made me feel dizzy that she had been—that a facility like that had been—so close this entire time.

It was easy enough to find. "Just drive down Main, turn right on Twelfth and follow your nose." I stopped at the gas station to fill up and the attendant was so jovial I just wanted to keep talking to him. Yes, I'd like you to check the oil—even though it's a rental. Yes, I'd like you to wash the windows. Could you tell me why I'm here?

"Could you tell me how to get to the psychiatric centre?" I asked him, finally.

He smiled as if he already knew I was headed there. "Follow your nose," he said, just the sort of thing I wanted him to say. I laughed hard and he laughed along with me. "You'll see," he said, and we both stopped laughing. "Those crazies know how to keep a garden is all."

And I could feel myself getting offended at the word.

Ninth Avenue was lined with poplars that must have been planted fifty years ago, the way they reach so high and out into the middle of the road. It was all quite beautiful, and I would have rolled down my window to see if I really could smell the centre, but for the dust churned up by the gravel road.

For a moment, as my car slowed to a crunch in the centre's parking lot, and especially when I stepped out of the car onto the gravel, I remembered summer camp all those years ago when my sister and I would spend love-filled weeks away from home and I felt, in this moment, I was doing something good, noble. All the flowers, though, crowding the sidewalks and blocking the windows made me feel claustrophobic. The smell could strangle a person, and by the time I got to the door and rang the intercom buzzer, I was wishing I had gotten lost and never found the place.

I had to sign in and show them the contents of my pockets, but once it was clear I wasn't trying to smuggle in anything dangerous (i.e. knitting needles), reception seemed pleasant enough. A nurse told me to follow him, and he took me to Anne's room.

"Shut the door. Shut the door," Anne said as we walked in. I looked at the nurse. He smiled as if nothing was out of sorts and shut me in with Anne.

The room hardly seemed like the sort of place you'd keep a genius. No murals on the walls, no mini-masterpieces on the ceiling tiles. Just neutral colours throughout, a green handrail at hip level all the way around the room. A heavy bathroom door, shut. A small cot, a bedside table with a lamp on it. A short bookshelf, half-empty, half-covered in old books I'd never heard of. Loose-leaf everywhere, covered in scribbled writing.

She lifted her mattress and grabbed a pack of cigarettes from under it, then she went into her bathroom where I could see her digging in one of the drawers. "Gotta keep everything separate," she said, emerging from the bathroom with a lighter, lighting a king size. She inhaled long and hard, then, "Like it's a goddamned shotgun," she said before exhaling. She coughed once, then pulled the window down. She drew in the smoke, eyes closed, as if she were sipping the last glass of water on earth.

I'm not sure what I had thought she would be like, but her actual person erased any of it. She took up the room as if everything else was just furniture for a dollhouse. I felt worried that I was doing something she didn't like from the second I walked in, even though I was just standing, watching her.

"I'm surprised they sent a woman," she said.

"Well, nobody really sent me," I told her.

She told me she used to wish for a man to come interview her. She thought people might care, if it were a man, but eventually she decided no one cared. "If anyone cared about me or my art, I would not…" she said.

But then she stopped, suddenly—there's no other word to describe it—she stopped in the middle of the sentence and just looked at me, the first time I felt she was actually talking to me. "You gonna ask me anything?" she said.

Paul came in just then, the nurse who had made me empty my pockets. "Give 'em here, Annie," he said, and she gave him the lit cigarette and the rest of the pack without even looking at him.

"Where's the lighter?" he said, holding out his hand.

"What lighter?"

"We'll have to remove your door again."

"They think I'm crazy for smoking these," she said, pulling the lighter from somewhere—I couldn't tell where, even though I had been with her the whole time—and handing it to Paul. "But it's the only thing keeping me going."

Paul said they want her around as long as possible, and she stared at him, unimpressed. "The lady's trying to ask me questions," she said.

When I first saw *Bruised and Bloody Carcass*, I was in Montreal to clear my head, to figure out if I should continue my psychology degree. I had just survived a suicide attempt six months before, and my dad thought a trip would be good for me. The plan had been Paris, but the closer the trip got, the more worried he was about me being so far away, without knowing anyone. I tried to convince a bunch of people to come with me, but only Sarah and Chelsea, two of Delaney's old friends, agreed. And they pulled out in the weeks leading up.

We cancelled Paris, but I convinced Dad that a trip close to home would still be good for me. I told myself ten days in Montreal, on my own, would be just what I needed, but once I was there I had no idea what to do. I watched TV in the bed and breakfast on the first day, the French flying over my head, even though I'd taken two full semesters of it. The next morning I took the subway and got off at random stops, then walked to the first coffee shop I saw. I tried to read, but ended up just watching the door for I-don't-know who, staring at random people until they noticed, then burying my nose in my book. A couple of men came over, but we could barely communicate, even if they spoke some English. One, who I'd been staring at, stuck up what I first thought was his middle finger, but which turned out to be his ring finger, the ring on it very prominent.

It was the perfect moment in time for me to come across *Bruised and Bloody*, so desperate to fall into something. I had finally convinced myself to do something unique to Montreal. I packed a bag so I wouldn't have to return midday, and I set out, but nothing at the Museum of Fine Arts kept my attention for all that long. I kept feeling like I should be interested, and I should be awed, but I was more worried about where I was going to eat lunch than any of the wonders in front of me. I left and took the subway back to my bed and breakfast. The owner was there and asked me why I wasn't out exploring. I told him I had just returned from the Montreal Museum of Fine Arts and was tired. He told me to rest, then to go here—and he wrote down an address.

I got lost on the way, and might never have found it, but as I was walking down Rue Jean-Talon, I thought I heard someone call my name. I turned around, but no one was anywhere. Then I saw it, La Belle Vue. I had walked right past it. The gallery was in a very old house, transformed into commercial property, and seemed to be newly set up with an exhibit simply called *Nouveau Canadiana*.

Bruised and Bloody was the first painting I saw. It was at the end of a long hall, hanging on its own, and it pulled me to it. It was as if the world had melted away and my brain had stopped spinning, as if everything I had ever done had been in preparation for this moment. I walked slowly up to it, to the red, red blood, to the off-white of the needle next to the pure white of the eyeball, to the way the other eye couldn't figure anything out.

I stood in front of it for nearly two hours, the fastest and most invigorating two hours of my life. Anne had two more paintings in the exhibit, similar but not the same at all. I spent some time looking at them, before standing in front of *Bruised and Bloody* again. I left when the clerk said she was about to close up for the evening.

❂

I stood there in Anne's room, overwhelmed. I had prepared a dozen or so questions, but now there were a hundred things I wanted to ask her. I had spent three years living as her neighbour—did she remember the two little girls running around in their bathing suits, selling lemonade or collecting bottles or raking leaves? So what if she did? I had gotten a psych degree to try to figure out why my sister had killed herself, why my parents had divorced—why parents who lose a child almost always divorce—why I had tried to kill myself. Could she tell me why?

And could she tell me why she wanted to paint her husband after she had killed him? Did she feel strange knowing that people looked at, and admired, a painting of her dead husband? Who were the other men? Were they demons? Did she walk around seeing demons? What is that like? Is it the same as worrying, the minute you wake up, what it is you are supposed to be worried about?

Did she look into my face and worry I was demon-possessed? Did she ever just want to lie in bed and pull the covers over her head until the world had forgotten about her? Did she ever feel normal? Did she even believe that anyone is normal? Were there people out there just living their lives, complete happy little humans?

"Most of my family suffers from different mental illnesses—" I said.

"Don't do that," said Anne. "Don't make this about him."

"About—"

"You people always make it about mental illness. Please. Call me crazy."

"I will not call you crazy."

"You want to talk about me being crazy, it's as easy as this. I spent too much time being a human being without thinking about it. I lived my life just trying to make it to tomorrow, not at all believing today meant anything, and you know what? My life was all about him. We got married so young. So so young, he just pursued the hell out of me, he was after me hard and I thought I loved him. I know I did love him. I loved him more than anything there was.

"Yes, I killed him. I killed my husband, and I wish every day that I hadn't. But in a way, this act set me free because now, my life is not about him. And it never needed to be about him, but I don't know if I could have realized this if he were still alive. I lived to be only his wife, and everything I painted, I painted for him, and everyone who knew me knew me only as Mrs. Legion, and if I did anything, it was as if we had both done it, or only he'd done it. And now that he's dead, people still try to make it about him, as if the rest of my life should be all about his death, but I'm a fucking living breathing human being and I suffer every day of my life. I miss him so much. But his death does not define me. I'm the same person I was before I killed him. Maybe I'm crazy, but who isn't crazy and who doesn't wish everything were different. Fuck, I wish they'd let me smoke. Christ, I'm ninety years old."

She paused to look out the window a second. "But why don't we talk about art? I mean you're here because my art did something for you, but even you turn it into some mental health class. I don't want to talk about fucking mental health. I want to talk about art and the way it pulls you out of yourself, tells you things you'd never know if you weren't standing there looking right at it, or if you didn't open yourself up and let yourself actually create something that's bigger and better than yourself. But no one wants to talk about art with a crazy old bat. I used to think when I got really old, people would take me seriously, but they don't even do that. They stare at me, at the way I'm just plain old. But I'm still kicking, so they ask, 'What's your fucking secret?' and they look so greedy, like they so badly wish to be ninety and hunched over with longevity's secrets. But they don't realize I'm still human, and I still hurt the same as they do, only the years have piled up some more. So I tell 'em smoke a pack a day and just make it to tomorrow. There's your secret."

She laughed then, the saddest laugh I'd ever heard, as if it had hurt her to do it. And I told her I was sorry. She told me not to apologize. She spoke in loops, and some of the time I wasn't sure what she was trying to say, but she was speaking to me, fully attuned to me, the person before her. I do not know how long we spoke that first night.

I didn't look for the artist's name until the clerk told me they were closing, and when I read the name I nearly fell over. It was as if my brain refused to believe it was Anne Legion my neighbour, Anne Legion the murderer, Anne Legion who had invited my family into her home for Christmas tea. I stood there searching my brain for another Anne Legion, for any way this could make sense.

"Je suis désolée," the clerk said. "We are closed."

And I felt as if she had rescued me from another world. I asked if I could just buy a postcard before she closed, but she said she was meeting someone and anyway the till was shut down. I went back to the bed and breakfast and googled and googled until it was obvious no one had written about Anne Legion's art. I lay in my bed wondering what this feeling was. I didn't feel happy, that wasn't it, but I felt lifted up, held by a magic I didn't know the world held. And I was desperate for it.

As I lay there thinking, I realized I was no longer thinking about my unhappiness. For as long as I could remember, it was very hard work not being miserable. Even reading a good book, or an afternoon at the symphony, took me only so far, so that as much as I was enjoying it, I was aware that it was only part of a fleeting moment. I was still aware of myself in the midst of it, in a way that made me intensely aware of the life I was heading back to—one of worry and stress and, if I'm frank, hopelessness.

Anne's painting, the hours I spent in front of it, googling it, wishing I had a print of it, lying in bed remembering it, all seemed like a new earth I had floated to where time was not in control, reminding you of all it has done, will do. I felt any number of clichés—free, alive, weightless. I was desperate not to leave that feeling, though even as I lay there it was fading. It changed my world in that everywhere I looked I found myself looking for that *Bruised and Bloody* feeling. It was never where I expected to find it. Art galleries or symphonies or poetry readings. I'd have this anticipation as I entered, this desperateness, but the feeling would never come when I was looking, only when I allowed myself to get lost accidentally, lost in something, some place, someone.

The honeysuckle was overgrown the third or fourth time I went to see her, though I didn't notice until Anne mentioned it. "Did you bring cigarettes?" she asked me, as if we had planned that I would. I said no, though I had some in my purse.

"Shit," she said. "Well. Let's go outside anyway. Then next time they'll be none the wiser." She left the room and went straight for a wheelchair parked at the side of the hallway. "You don't mind pushing an old lady," she said, not really a question as much as new information she was giving me. "So you don't smoke?"

"Trying to quit," I told her.

"Goddamn" she said, and she let her head fall against the back of the chair. I followed the sidewalk. After a few minutes she said, "Sorry about the honeysuckle. I don't know how we let it grow like that."

"Oh I don't mind," I said. "I didn't even notice."

"Damn," she said, and she sat up a little. "I wish you people weren't a bunch of liars. Of course you noticed it. It must have been choking you as you walked up."

"It's fine."

"It's sure as hell not fine. I'll have to tell Paul to trim it before it outright kills someone." She seemed nothing like the old lady she had been the first couple of times we'd met. "Take me inside," she said. "Inside." In her room, she flopped onto her bed as if someone had broken her heart. I sat with her a while, sipping tea, and she kept talking about the flowers.

Finally, I asked if she'd rather I come back another day.

"No, ask me your damn questions," she said. I pulled out my notebook, but then I asked the first question that came to mind. "Where do you find ideas for what you're going to paint?" A poor question, I'll admit, but I was curious. "I mean you have your—I'll call it your dead men collection. So, I guess, how do you choose which men? But you've got other work too, some very abstract and beautiful paintings. So where does your inspiration come from?"

"Come on, Abigail. I thought you were going to be serious about this."

"I am being serious. I'd like to know."

"Well, I could never answer that question."

"Okay. Well. I'm sorry, I guess."

"I am unable to answer that question. You would most definitely need to ask the Anne that paints them. The Anne sitting here is not like the Anne who paints dead men, as you call them. That Anne must leave the world, or comes from a different world, and then does her thing. If you or I tried to do it right here, right now, we'd have nothing of value at all, we'd have colours and wasted paint…"

"So you believe another person paints your paintings."

"Oh don't be stupid. I'm me of course. I'm just a different me when I paint, and sitting here right now, I could never tell you what told me to paint this instead of that, any more than God could tell you why he put such fucked-up humans all over the place."

"God?"

"You know what I mean. I was being poetic. If I just pulled out some paints and painted, life would be easy, but I'd never paint anything other than bits of myself; I'd never put something out into the world big enough to mean anything. I will say this—" she paused and pretended to read a bit from some loose-leaf before finishing. "It better be spontaneous. If you're going to paint, you better be able to say I'd like to paint blank when someone asks. I like to paint dead men—I do. I like to paint and think about the moment of death and the infinite number of things that might be there in your mind when death is there. I like thinking about this because I didn't ever think about it for so long. I didn't ever realize I too would die, being human. And I'm sure if I had, I wouldn't have killed Albert. I would never have gone crazy. I would even say the reason I'm still kicking is because I am exquisitely aware of my own mortality...

"But I also like painting flowers, only I do it abstractly most times. And I'd like to paint people painting, people looking at paintings, really looking. I'd like to paint people being caught up in nature or art or life or death. The ideas come in my sleep, while I'm eating, talking to you, whatever." She crumpled the loose-leaf. "So ask me how I decide what to paint, I tell you I have to decide which of these crazy bits of nonsense in my head I shouldn't paint. If it's not like that, you're not a painter. You are not an artist."

I left telling myself she was crazy, in spite of myself.

Since *Bruised and Bloody*, I've had next to no ideas, other than wanting to write about Anne Legion in a meaningful way. I've always written and have always wanted to be a writer in a way that meant other people were reading and thinking about my writing, but mostly I just wrote about myself, or I wrote suicide letters in depressive fits, which I'd never show to anyone. *Bruised and Bloody* woke me up, gave my writing a purpose. But is it art, writing about someone else's art? Here I thought we were artists bouncing epiphany off epiphany, but now, meeting Anne, I felt like a hack.

I have written this thirteen different times, versions of it. I had them all saved in Moleskins. I'd steal bits from each every time I started again. When I got home that night, I dug them all out and started reading them, but I just felt like a fraud.

I burnt them. I took them outside in the back and burnt them.

My boyfriend at the time came out and sat with me while they burned. It was a strange moment. I don't know where he was in his head, but he didn't ask what I was doing, just put his hand on my shoulder, squeezed gently, then rubbed my back until I leaned into him. I thought for a minute the *Bruised and Bloody* feeling would be there, that ridding myself of this obsession would somehow give me some meaning, but as always, my expecting it kept it firmly at bay. I was thoroughly aware of myself, of my boyfriend, of the Moleskins, the fire. I was firmly in this world, forced to move through it.

Fancying yourself an artist affords a certain luxury. And as much as I felt like a fraud out loud, I had always believed I was an artist. I never felt guilty for escaping into my imagination, for lying still on the couch and thinking about Legion's work, what it was about these paintings that added so much to the world, my world. And all the other moments that brought the same feeling. When you are an artist, these flights outside of reality are acceptable. It is, perhaps, the narcissist in every artist that makes them believe they are creating something of worth in everything they do. Even putting my makeup on in the morning felt like a miniature art project, one which others, if they would only pay attention, would find meaningful.

But Anne's words grew louder in my mind: "You are not an artist," a fist squeezing my brain until all of it was gone. I was left with just me. And when the identity you have clung so hard to for so long is stripped away, it's kind of a terrifying thing. I walked around questioning everything I had ever believed. I still thought about writing, about Legion's art, about Anne, but all of this only furthered the feeling of loss, or of being lost. Each thought was quickly dismissed as the blathering trivia of an idiot. This sounds dramatic, and it is, but I felt unsafe in the world, as if everything solid was sloughing off into an abyss, and I was left standing on a lone precipice trying to reach for anything to put back in its place.

Writing about this is embarrassing. The fury with which I could lose my footing in the world makes me feel fragile and even—can I say this?—crazy. Or at least stupid. I had taken pride in my common-sense view of the world, having been depressed, having seen my sister depressed, having lost someone I loved so young, having survived a suicide attempt. I felt like—I believed—I somehow had a more realistic view of life and what it means to be a person than most. I even think I believed this worldview I had curated gave me a leg up artistically, that I somehow was able to create things worthy of others' time.

❖

Anne Legion died late into the night of October 13, 2017, or maybe the morning of the fourteenth, natural causes being the official cause of death. Nature.

The months leading up to her death had been some of the worst of my life. I was depressed again and none of my usual tricks to get out of a slump were working. I think I felt more hopeless than I had in the months leading up to my attempt to kill myself: even imagining death was no comfort, maybe because I couldn't imagine dying without having figured out who I was, I don't know. But I do know the perceived solace I'd found in death when I tried that first time was not here anymore, and I could barely move.

My boyfriend moved out. He had never officially moved in, had kept paying rent and bills at his own apartment, but he had been staying at my place for a while. He stuck around as long as he could handle it. I feel appreciative of the way he tried so hard to care for me, but I'm glad he got out before I brought him down, too. A depressed person is maybe the best person to care for another depressed person, until they're not, until they lose hope along with you, and then you're just two depressed people.

He left before that happened. Which was fine with me. I felt guilty enough, with him bringing me water to my bed, or food, or whatever, which I never noticed at the time—I'd always be shocked when I finally took in everything he had delivered to my bedside, as if shock is a thing you can feel while depressed. One morning, I decided to brush my teeth, and as I stood in front of the sink staring into the mirror, preparing myself, I noticed his toothbrush was gone, and I was grateful he hadn't tried to talk through anything before making his decision. So he was gone, and I was working hard just to get out of bed and into work every so often.

But something got me out of bed that Friday evening. If I believed in anything, I'd say it was Anne speaking to me from the ether, but it was just one of those moments in the midst of my episodes that bursts through me and seems to convince me I need some fresh air. I chain-smoked around Macleod, getting lost in myself. I probably did think about Anne at least a bit, and that'd definitely make the narrative of this essay meaningful, or something, but the truth is I don't remember what I thought about. I remember ending up on Lone where it meets Grandview Drive and thinking briefly of walking down Grand-view to Lee, but I ended up walking through the intersection and up to Main, where I eventually ended up at Bubba's.

Bubba's is about the best you'll find in Macleod, and that night it was hopping. A band was just finishing up as I walked in, "But I'll be DJing for the rest of the night," the lead said before starting in on their last song. We may have made eye contact as I sat down.

I ordered a beer and a water, "and what the hell, maybe a shot of a tequila." The waitress raised an eyebrow, but jotted it down and scuttled off.

The band was loud enough that I couldn't understand the lyrics, but good enough that most of the bar was paying attention. A crowd of people stood in front of the stage, holding their drinks, bobbing their heads; a few were even dancing. The lead didn't give a damn. He was sweating through his shirt, a grey tee. His hair was long, soaking, so that when he flicked his head, beads of sweat speckled everywhere.

His eyes were closed through the whole song, yet when the second or third verse ended and they broke down in a jam session, he moved around the stage as if it were their practice space in his garage, he had the whole place memorized.

The rest of the band moved in accordance with him. They were tight, but they depended on him, that was obvious. The drummer would point his left stick at him between beats. The bassist moved backwards across the stage to play back to back with him. The lead didn't even open his eyes when they met, just put his head back, resting it on the bassist's shoulder, before flicking his head forward, hair and sweat everywhere. The second guitar watched him the entire time.

The song could have lasted two hours and the bar would have just gone along with it. By the time the jam was winding down and he was getting back to the chorus, I had finished my beer and the waitress had brought a second. I don't even remember the tequila, but the shot glass was empty on the table. I didn't want the song to end, though I wasn't aware that was true until the song ended and the bar was screaming and the lead was bowing along with the rest of them, holding his guitar to the side, flicking his pick to a girl in the front. "Thank you very much," he said, and it seemed like he meant it.

I knew if I sat there long enough, there would be free drinks, but I didn't expect one of them would be from him. "The DJ sent this over," the waitress said, and she put a cherry whiskey paralyzer on the table. I thought I had been watching him—his playlist was bordering on boring, but he was obviously right into it—but I didn't notice him even talking to any of the waitresses. I looked at him while I sipped it, and we made eye contact on the third sip, I'd say. I raised the glass to say thanks. And he called me over with a finger.

A lot of other nights I would have left the drink half-finished on the table and walked home. But I sipped the drink once more, then brought it over to his booth. "What'd you think?" he said.

"It's a paralyzer," I said.

"No, of the song."

"Oh," I said, and I wanted to tell him it had changed my life. "It wasn't bad."

He pulled his headphones over his ears and fiddled with his machines. "We fuckin' rocked it," he said.

"Yeah," I sipped the rest of the drink until it made that slurping sound. "It was pretty great."

"You here all night?"

"Not sure," I said, but I was pretty sure I wasn't going anywhere.

"We'll probably chill at Mikey's after," he said, as if I should have known who Mikey was. "You should come." So I drank until the bar was closed and I rode with him in his car to Mikey's.

There were more people there than I would have thought, but he spoke to me like we were the only ones. He asked what I'd been up to that I'd only made it for the last song. I didn't tell him I had been stuck in my bed for the last three days and didn't know what had pulled me out of it for tonight. I told him I had been out walking. "I love that," he said, and he flipped through his phone and put a cover of "I'm Gonna Be" on the Bluetooth speaker. "What are some of your outlets?" he said.

"Outlets?"

"I'm interested in how humans create things, even if they don't fancy themselves artists."

"Oh," I said, and I pretended like I had to think first. "I'm a writer."

"You're a writer?" he said, and pulled back in his chair, feigning surprise. "I like the confidence."

"What?"

"What do you write?"

"I'm writing about a painting," I said.

"What?"

"There's this artist I really like, and I'm writing about her work."

"Show me," he said in this way that made me think he was excited to be having this conversation. I pulled out my phone and googled *Bruised and Bloody Carcass*. I handed him my phone, and he spent a long time looking it, zooming in with his fingers, swiping around. "It's weird the things that inspire us, huh?" he said, and I felt so embarrassed.

The drummer sat down beside me on the couch just then and said, "Who's this?" The lead held out an open palm to me.

"I'm Abigail," I said.

"No way. Are you fuckin' Delaney Waters' sister?" the drummer said, and I needed to leave. I felt sweaty and couldn't believe how drunk I was. "That chick was the shit in ninth grade," he said, and I have no idea what I would have said, but he continued, "Do you mind?" and pulled out a baggie of cocaine.

"No," I said, and I looked at the lead who shrugged.

The drummer pulled a little mirror out from under the table, took a pinch of the stuff and started crushing it with his Scene+ card, cutting it into three lines, snorting one of them. "Do you need some?" he said to the lead.

"Nah," he said.

And the drummer passed the mirror to me with one hand, holding the rolled fifty out with the other. And I snorted a line of coke.

The night Anne Legion was dying, I was getting drunk and snorting cocaine for the first time in my life in front of a boy I had just met a few hours earlier. I've gone over this night so many times, for what I'm not sure. Well, for connections to Anne, there's no other reason, but that's crazy. There's no way I would have known, could have known, and if I had known, would it have changed anything? I imagine it would have.

"I quit doing blow the night my brother called to say I needed to watch his kids so he could go buy us some," the lead said. "When I got to his place, he was already gone and his kids were just sleeping. The oldest was on the couch."

"Yeah, this shit'll fuck you right up," the drummer said.

"I don't know how long he left them for. I was there within forty minutes or something, but still."

The high was almost immediate. I wasn't drunk anymore, and I could have done anything. I settled into the couch and looked around, and I thought things like, maybe it's not all that bad being a human. I felt like sitting there in Mikey's house was probably the best thing I had ever done. I took my phone back from the DJ and started flipping through Anne's works, pointing out details in each. And I was talking about how she'd captured something in the dead men that no other artist was capable of, if someone wanted to understand what the moment of death was like, they wouldn't come closer than looking at these paintings.

"You'd like to know what death feels like?" the DJ asked me.

"I'm actually friends with the artist," I said, and I told him how she smokes, and she's ninety, and she's not even crazy.

I did more coke throughout the night, so that it was ten a.m. before I knew it was morning and the lead had long fallen asleep. I curled up in the bed where he was sleeping, cuddled into him. He put his arm over my hip.

On Monday, October 16, 2017, Paul called me from the centre. "Ms. Legion has died and it seems she's left you some things," he said.

"What things?" I said, which wasn't at all what I wanted to say, but I needed to sit down and I was doing the dishes.

"Well, the paintings, for one," he said. "And her notes—"

"Her notes?"

"All those papers," he said, and I went a little crazy thinking about what those would say. "And it looks like a letter."

She had so many paintings. She had been painting the whole time she was at the centre, and they kept all of them in storage. I didn't know this until she left them to me. They are interesting. More dead men, for sure, but most of the ones from the centre were honeysuckles and other flowers and still lifes, which somehow still feel gory. There are quite a few wild abstract things I haven't spent enough time with. I hung *Bruised and Bloody* in my living room for a day, but decided to donate it—on loan—to the little art gallery in Macleod. Having it there in my home with me was too much. Her notes, I'm still going through. I will keep them forever. The letter was short:

> Abigail,
>
> If you ever finish your essay or whatever it is your writing, tell them this: It's important to be careful about what you think you know for sure.
>   Don't make me into any sort of heroine.

But it sent me fluttering through the world for months. I could no longer sit still. I dreamed all the time and I walked, and I couldn't wait to finish work so I could go out and think. I wrote more than I had ever in my whole life, and I'm still writing.

In the last few versions of this essay, I tried to make a list of things I knew for sure. The lists were long at first, but they always felt sentimental and melodramatic. I've whittled it down to this: I don't know anything for sure other than that it is very hard work being a human being.

IN A WAY THAT DOESN'T
MAKE ME CRINGE

A novel comes to mind about which the author said she wanted to add at least one example of a lasting marriage to the tradition. She said she wrote the entire thing because she worried about a gang of extraterrestrials reading a sample of humanity's literature and calculating a rate of next to 100 percent of marriages ending in divorce. She could think of very few books, and even fewer movies, in which whole families were happily glued together, thought the literature proposed marriage to be a certain way of being miserable. If you weren't desperate for divorce, or at least cheating with your wife's best friend, one of you would die and the other would heroically mourn the first's death until he/she fell magically in love again. At which point they'd start in on a doomed marriage.

Back when I read it, I thought how nice it is that my wife and I, if someone were to write about us, would add to the happily married side of the pile, and maybe the extraterrestrials wouldn't think we human beings were all that crazy. I straighten my tie and wipe my palms, trying to remember who the writer was, what she would think of us now, nervous and sweaty all over again.

I married the love of my life, I'll admit that. We married young, claimed each other as soulmates, but we were also filled with all the naïveté of newlyweds that made us believe—each time we fought or felt the other was treating us unfairly—that we had made a huge mistake. She would say things like, "Sometimes I wonder if I really should have jumped in like this," and as stoic and determined as I claimed to be, this killed me. I would pout off to the car and drive halfway to Mount Pleasant, dreaming up these scenarios of pulling into a hotel and meeting some beauty and starting some wondrous little fling, or just driving until I ran out of gas and being picked up by another beauty and starting off for our blissful life. These were ridiculous, I knew, and I'd always turn back and head home to apologize. But always, between that U-turn and home, I would try to figure out if one could really find the love of one's life so young. Could I fall in love at nineteen, marry at twenty-two and love that person forever? Could she love me?

She'd come sobbing to the door and we'd make out over the threshold of our tiny house, make our way to the bed, where she'd make me believe it was possible to be in love forever. We'd spoon all night and I'd feel unstoppable. But it didn't ever last and I started to believe—like most of humanity's art apparently—that there was no way one person could spend their entire life loving only one other person.

Yet here we are. Though I'd never have guessed it. Standing here, waiting for everything to start, I try not to think of all that.

"You okay?" Abigail has snuck into the room I've been told to hide away in, my Abigail.

She was, as they say, an accident, which I'm sure E.T. would assume is the case for all children, but I could see the relief in Madison's face when she told me. And somehow I felt like we should have planned her, as if she were the inevitable piece that had been missing. We could easily love each other forever with a heap of crying cuteness between us.

Madison had terrible pregnancies, morning sickness long after the literature said it would subside, outrageous weight gain all over, even her feet, acne, and a relentless misery. But still, I couldn't stop watching her. It was as if the universe had heard my petty questions and so opened up and pushed me to her. I would not stop looking at her, thinking about her, touching her in ways I had never before, as if the ways her baby was changing her were showing me the depths to which I had not explored. Even the little pimples I could feel under my fingers were exciting.

She was a wreck, took a sick leave a month before she was due, but I could feel her settling into my new devotion, hesitant at first, not believing I could love her like this. I too found her watching me as I read on the couch or did the dishes, as if she couldn't believe my happiness, was trying to catch me out. I'd feel her staring. I'd let her, smile into the sink, then blow her a quick kiss, watch her blush.

"Of course I'm okay," I tell Abigail. "I'm fine. You look stunning." I can watch her trying to deny it in her mind, a habit she's long had, but I believe is getting over.

"Thanks Dad," she says. "But no one'll be noticing me."

"Abigail," I say.

"Why would they?" she says. "I'm not looking for attention anyway."

She is beautiful. All the mess and tangles of hurt, the missed opportunities of child rearing, did a number on us. For a very long time, I couldn't look at her without anger and blame, my own pain flooding up. So to look at her now, today, ready to embrace her parents once more, all of that garbage floating off into the distant past, I'm taken by her, by her courageous beauty.

When she was born, she looked nothing like either of us. She was a great mystery to me, though I loved her so, and loved her more for tying me to her mother. But the unfamiliarity of this tiny baby made it impossible for me to imagine anything about her future, the way I had imagined a miniature version of Madison running about before her birth. Every stage of her life had this mystery, I think, for probably everyone she knew.

Except maybe Delaney.

"They won't be looking at me when they see you walking next to me," I tell her.

"Dad, you'll be fine. I mean you've done this all before, right?"

"I know. I know. I'm just so glad you're here."

"I know," she whispers, maybe about to cry. "Me too."

She very nearly wasn't here, but that's not anything I want to think about right now, though when have I ever been able to stop rolling it around my head once I've started down the road thinking about it?

Delaney wouldn't... Goddammit, Delaney. She wouldn't have been here anyway. Couldn't have been. And she won't ever be anywhere now. This will always be true, I've come to realize. No matter how much time has healed us, how many have moved on, she will never be present.

Truthfully, I think I always worried that Abigail might try to kill herself. I think she always believed we didn't love her, or at least that we loved Delaney more than her. She lived a pensive childhood, always deep inside herself, trying to sort out what people actually meant by what they were saying, or doing, as if her childhood innocence was left balled up in the womb.

There was a time when she was so young she couldn't yet say her Ls. "I love you, Abby," I'd say to her. And she'd say, "How come?" She'd look up at me and ask me, "How come you yuv me?" Just saying it wasn't enough. She needed proof. In fact one of my biggest regrets, easily the one I think of most often, was not having an immediate answer. It is natural for a father to love his daughters, so natural that when asked for a reason, all I could muster was a bumbling, "Because you're so beautiful."

Delaney might have accepted that; I think she always believed she was beautiful. Abby just turned her eyes away from mine, picked some fluff off her shoulder. She was dismissing the idea even at three years old, Delaney barely even born.

How do you explain why you love somebody? You make me so happy. I can't imagine life without you. These years without you have been so miserable—I'm talking about Madison now, obviously. How different these loves are, yet still as complete. You make me want to be a better man. You keep me up at night imagining summer walks and spring picnics. I can't sip a latte without remembering our first date, all those years ago. I can't shop for groceries without wondering if you still eat those rice cakes, can't drive in the country without playing our old tunes, can't do anything, or go anywhere with another woman, without comparing it to how I felt with you.

Is even love so selfish that the only way to explain it is to say I feel happier when I'm with you than without? And what if the other feels less happy? And how can we know? And what if it changes? Again? Do I fight for her because she makes me happy? Or should I fight for her happiness, which may or may not always include me? Which I'm almost sure I would not, if it did not in fact include me. Is that love? Needing someone else to—

"It's gonna be perfect, Dad," Abigail says. She keeps her eyes on mine, still sorting out what I'm up to. "You guys are made for each other, everyone knows that."

"I know. Yes we are. Of course."

"Dad, you can't get cold feet now. After all this."

"I know. I'm not. Just nervous. I can't imagine a life without your mom."

"Tell me about it," she says, and she touches her forehead.

I must have figured, what were the odds of both my girls doing it? So once Delaney—it's harder for me to say it with Delaney—once she hanged herself in the closet, I stopped worrying about Abigail. Fully stopped. As if I had never worried before.

Delaney was such a shock. Such a huge shock. Engaged. Happy. Though obviously not happy. Over the days and years that have followed, I've run through her whole life a thousand times, and I should have known she wasn't happy. She was so obviously unhappy. But so was I—was?—so was her mom. And Abigail, I guess. Delaney's unhappiness just hid out in full sight. Her weird obsession with death, after the wreck out on our street. She talked about that for years, and seemed to enjoy funerals. She'd joke about her mom and I being old, getting old, what her and Abby would be like when we were gone. And she was so mean. To everyone. Herself. Everyone. But in this stupid witty way that made it all funny.

When her fiancé ended it, she just hung herself. She must have thought about it before that, she must have. But I can also imagine her, Delaney, thinking it, and setting out to do it, in the same breath.

Abby found her. Poor Abby. I always forget this. She told me she had been writing her own suicide notes for years before Delaney, and so felt as if Delaney had stolen even that from her. What miserable parents we were.

"I'm just kidding," Abby says. "I'm just happy you guys. I dunno. Found each other. Again," she says. "And yeah. I'm here to see it." Exactly the thing to say to make me cry.

It took me so long to figure out what her note was saying. I still have nightmares where I'm standing, reading the note, while Abby's suffocating in her Volvo. Damn it.

I wanted a book, I think. Something from Abby. And I went over there at some time I knew Madison would be gone, and there was the note on the floor by the stove.

Tell Dad I loved him. The past tense doing the trick. I should have known from the first sentence, but I must have been able to deny it. This has already happened, I was thinking. There must be rules against it happening twice. Damn it. Loved. She loved me.

I must have flown through the city. I don't remember any of the drive. I was in the kitchen, then I was out at Blue Sand Trails, pulling her out of the Volvo, doing CPR until the ambulance got there. Don't remember calling them either.

Madi and I were forced to tolerate each other if we wanted to be a part of Abby's recovery.

I asked Madison later—much later, probably around when we decided to be official again, as Abby called it—what she thought when she saw me in the hospital waiting area.

Overwhelming relief, she said, though she asked me what the hell had happened as if it were all my fault, I reminded her.

"I had to blame someone," she said, and she slapped my shoulder lightly, a bitty little smile on her face. But I left the comment hanging there too long and she started to cry. She went from the joke to crying so fast all I could do was offer her my pocket square.

"Why couldn't I cry like this with Delaney," she's said. She's said this quite a few times. She wanted so badly to cry back then, but refused to cry in front of me, with Delaney.

"What the hell happened?" she asked, standing in the middle of the waiting room.

"I don't know," I told her.

"You don't know?" she said, looking around at the worried strangers. "Who the hell brought her here then? You called me didn't you? 'You should get down to the general.' That's all you said. What the hell, Jeremy? What happened to Abigail?"

"Here." I passed her the note.

She read the first lines. "Oh my God?" she said.

I stood, but even now I don't know what I was going to do. And she took off down the hall, not running, but I knew I was to sit back down.

"You did cry," I would tell her.

"But not with you. I couldn't with you."

This was one of the times I was convinced we were doing the right thing by getting back together. She blew her nose into my pocket square, then wiped her cheeks, eyes, with the clean side, and handed it back. I slid it into my pants' pocket, squeezed her hand in mine. The past opened up before me in a tidal wave that came crashing down on us. It swept me up in all these memories I thought were gone forever, so that in that moment, in the Starbucks on Main, I knew we were right to be together again.

The thing you'll notice, though—whoever you are, the aliens reading this—is that we humans are easily capable of believing a thing to be certain one day, and believing the opposite to be true the next.

That is to say: we had a lifetime of pain and regret and divorce behind us that seemed to prove we shouldn't be together, and a snotty pocket square was hardly stand-up evidence against it.

We recycled plenty of old arguments, about the girls mostly, and invented new ones about whatever we could think of, but Abigail was getting better, asking us to give her space even, and Madi and I still wanted to see each other.

"Well, I'll be here around six anyway," I said. We were leaving Starbucks after Abigail had explained that we wouldn't need to babysit her anymore. I no doubt had convinced myself that I still wanted to meet with Abby, just to be certain, or what have you. But when Madison said, "Oh good. I'll meet you," I thought to myself, Yes, I knew you would. And I said, "Swell then," like I used to when the girls were young.

Our new arguments never made me angry but awoke something in me that would acknowledge she was right. Not in a sitcom way, but in a way that made me feel as if I were somehow growing. I felt desperate to apologize to Madison after a night of thinking, and determined to make it through the next date. How strange to use these words—*dating, official, my place, yours, love*—

"You can't cry yet, Dad."

"Found each other again," I say. "I like that. And I'm glad I—"

The usher—my grown nephew—sticks his head through the door. "It's about that time," he says.

"Deep breath," says Abigail, and she takes one herself.

I have never felt more connected to Madison than I do now. Even after Delaney—after Delaney, when Madi relied on me for nearly everything, from bathing her to reminding her to eat. There was a disconnect there. And I suppose a resentment growing in each of us.

But today I love Madison in a way that doesn't make me cringe when I say it, that makes me nervous and sweaty, but also plain old giddy to walk down that aisle, to wait for her at the altar. Again.

A QUARTER SHORT

The day Tommy Sprinkler had to split his lottery winnings with a total stranger, there were too many people in line at 7-Eleven, too few people working. He stood there counting and recounting his change, trying to sort out whether he'd have enough for the candies he'd chosen, the salt 'n vinegar chips and a Coca-Cola. Each time he'd have it nearly counted, the blinking lights behind the counter would distract him—he'd stare up at them and forget how many nickels he'd just counted. He counted them so many times he started shaking the change in his clenched fist, imagining it floating in the air between his fingers as he moved his hand up and down. Finally, he opened his hand and the change fell to the floor, rolling this way and that.

"Friggen!" he screamed, and all those people turned to stare at him picking up nickels off the floor. "What would all you people be doing if I was all of a sudden Tommy Sprinkler, Millionaire," he muttered. The people checked their phones. One lady picked her kid up from the floor and kissed them on the nose.

Tommy Sprinkler had bought and paid for a lotto once before. The jackpot was up to seventy-nine million, seven being Tommy's favourite number, and nine being his second. He slipped his beef jerky back in the little box on the shelf and bought the lotto.

He bought it on Wednesday and spent all of Thursday waiting for Friday, going over what he'd do if he won. He had to keep his cool, he knew that. When he'd spot the seven, the nine, the thirty-five, the fifty-three, sixteen, nineteen, forty-nine, he'd slip the lotto back into his pocket and he wouldn't tell nobody. He'd cash his ticket in loonies and get a truck to deliver them to his apartment and he'd swim in the happiness of golden coins on his skin. He wondered if that would be enough, just knowing he could buy whatever he wanted if he wanted.

But his mother would eventually come over and see the mess. She'd scream and yell and tell him to clean it up, put it somewhere safe. But wouldn't she be proud of her son when he was a multimillionaire. She'd say they oughta celebrate and they'd head off to Bubba's for a couple of steak sandwiches.

They almost never got steak sandwiches 'cause they almost never had any money, but they had them once because a lady tipped his mom a hundred bucks, around Christmas time last year, before he finally got his own place, for putting a lot of sweat into the lady's manicure. When the lady left, his mom said they oughta celebrate and they went to Bubba's for steak sandwiches, and Tommy decided it was his favourite food, as long as he could scrape the peppercorns off before eating.

Tommy called his mother sometime after she would have eaten lunch, before supper.

"Can we go get steak sandwiches?" he said.

"What the hell, Tommy. What do you think?"

"Come on, Ma. We never go for steak sandwiches."

"Who's gonna pay for them? I can't pay for them."

"I'll pay you back."

"Oh, Tommy."

"I promise."

"Oh, what the hell."

"Fuck yeah."

"Watch your mouth, goddammit. I'll meet you there."

"Long as it's not raining."

Tommy felt an unwavering confidence in his fortune. He had already turned his lotto into one steak sandwich, and imagine how happy he'd be when it became as many steak sandwiches as he could ever eat.

"Why'd you want a steak sandwich so bad?" his mom asked, after they'd ordered their diet Pepsis, after she'd told him he should've changed his shirt if he was going out.

"We're celebrating," he said.

"You get a job?"

"Better," he said. "I bought a lotto."

"What the hell, Tommy," she said, and she said this is just the kind of joke that made her kick him out in the first place, even though God knows she's killing herself worried over him in that damn place anyway. She said she can't spend her life trying to figure out how he's gonna feed himself or keep that damn apartment or do anything at all. She said she sometimes thinks he'd get her to wipe his ass for him if he thought she'd do it. She said she's sorry she's being hurtful, but she knows he's a smart and normal boy—man, even—somewhere in that head of his.

"Come on, Ma," Tommy said, though he could tell she thought he wasn't listening to her.

"Come on, what?"

"Can't I just eat a steak sandwich without you screaming at me?" He could see the waitress hauling the steaks out to them. He thought he was saved, for a minute. "I got a good feeling about this lotto," he said. "I feel it in my belly."

"You're probably just starving hungry," she said in that angry whisper that was almost worse than the yelling.

"Oh my God. Thanks," he said to the waitress. "I'm starved."

"Thank you," his mom said.

Tommy Sprinkler scraped the peppercorns off his steak and took a bite. It was almost exactly as he'd hoped it'd be, as he'd remembered. He smiled as he chewed, and he wondered if a steak sandwich a day is all it would take.

"What should I do with my millions, Ma?" he asked.

"Oh, Tommy," she said.

"What would you do?"

"I have no idea—"

"I'd probably go get—"

"I'd figure out how to fix your damn brain issues."

"Yeah," Tommy said. He closed his eyes for the next bite.

"I didn't mean—"

"No. Yeah. We could find all those people working on time travel. How they go so fast they end up going backwards—"

"Tommy."

"And we could get 'em to take us back to the first time, that first day, the only day I can ever remember and you could run out and say get outta here Tommy. Before the goddamn lightning smites me down and blasts me back to second grade and chars up my goddamn watch right off my wrist."

"Oh Tommy. Seriously."

"And we could stop at the second time on the way fuckin' back. And I'll tell you to shut the hell up. To back the hell off. Don't face your fears, Tommy, I'll tell myself; don't go outside in the goddam fuckin' storm to enjoy the goddamn rain on your face. Hide Tommy. Go shiver in the bathtub shaking like a fuckin' shitzu. Save yourself. Save your second charred-up watch. Save your—"

"Tommy."

"We could find Sarah and flash her my millions and see if she still wants to break up—"

"Who? Tommy, settle down."

"Or what's her name. Who's fat as ever now. Make her say sorry she stopped talking to a millionaire retard—"

"Tommy." Ma stood up, her chair scraping across the floor.

He put a big hunk of steak in his mouth, chewed so his mom couldn't help looking at it as he tore it apart. "What kinda brain issues you talking, Ma?"

"Tommy, you shut that big mouth of yours."

"Fuck."

"Thomas."

"This steak is gross anyway," he said, and he spat out the last bit of it back onto his plate and left his mom sitting in Bubba's on her own.

Dark clouds were rolling in as he stepped out of Bubba's, but he couldn't go back in, not after his dramatic departure. He walked as fast as he could, and at the first rumble he sprinted the rest of the way to his apartment. He called Ronald once he'd finally caught his breath. "Ronald. Ronald," he said. "This is crazy. But can you come to my place?"

"I dunno, man. I'm pretty tired."

"Okay. Okay. That's fine. I'm fine. I'm just sorta freaking out a bit."

"Might not even storm—"

"I feel it. You can feel it. Like it's some kinda panther trying to claw up your chest and biting your neck and your whole body feels like it's being torn apart—"

"Okay. Okay, man. I'll be right over."

Tommy Sprinkler went into his bathroom to stare at himself in the mirror, his own eyes staring back into themselves being the easiest way to prove this was all real. But at the first crash of thunder a few minutes later, he slipped into the tub and closed the curtain and shivered away.

One of his quarters rolled under the magazine rack so he couldn't reach it, but he managed to save the rest. He put his candies to the side, set the chips and pop on the counter. "This enough for all this and a lotto?" he said.

The clerk was nice enough to count it out. "Short. Uh. Eighteen cents. You're short eighteen cents."

Tommy stood there for a second, trying hard to recount all the change in his head.

"Here," the woman with the kid said. "I've got a quarter," and she slid it across the counter.

BEFORE A LOST SOUL

The moment Miss Dwyer looked at the photograph of her son, the moment it was handed to her as a gift in her front entrance and she looked at it, she couldn't at all believe what she was feeling. Tears and snot and gasping and knees that wouldn't hold.

"My gosh," the pastor said, grabbing her arm to hold her up, but she flopped to the floor anyway, leaving the pastor holding her hand above her head. He held it. He stood holding her fingers in his hand while she cried.

"I don't know why I shot it," he said. "I had heard the sirens, though they were in the air for a long time before they actually registered, being so taken by the—by your son. I was still sitting on the road when the officer asked me to move. They would need to cover the body. I guess I tried to tell you all that in the letter," he said. He pointed to the letter he had taped behind the photograph. "I'm sorry," he said.

"I can't believe it," said Miss Dwyer, or at least she was thinking it over and over.

"When I saw the story in the *Sun*, I felt led to find you," he said. "To let you have it."

"I just can't believe it," she kept saying to herself. She pulled her hand out of the pastor's, held it over her mouth, tried to look at the thing through her tears. "I don't want it," she said, and flicked it away. It flipped up and landed in front of her on the floor, the swelling heap of her son's body under the yellow tarp right there. She flicked it again and the pastor tried to catch it.

"Give me that," she said, and she grabbed the photograph and threw it behind her.

"If there's anything I can—"

"Can you please just go?" she said. "Please."

He watched her for a moment, but made himself leave.

She hid it away, but the photo had burrowed its way so far into her brain that she could think of little else, the way it all mixed together, pushing her backwards. She had heard Lisa—the only girl he'd ever brought home—say once that she thought Earl would be a good cop. Miss Dwyer could hear them in the living room from the kitchen, and it sent her careening down a winding road into the future: her son in uniform, Lisa by his side, maybe some little grandbabies running around. Of course he'd have to quit that weed nonsense, and whatever else he was up to whenever he hid away for days on end. Sometimes she'd sit in his room, the mounds of clothes on the floor reminding her he was just a stupid kid, the smell of it all the closest she'd get to knowing him in any real way.

She had first thought the boy in the driver's seat was her son, staring down at his lap, the way his little nose turned up just so. But then her son was thirty-six now, and the boy was, oh, who could tell? Just a few years older than the age her memory places Earl before he left. Before he packed his backpack and left, a ridiculous note on his desk: *I'll be gone for awhile.* No *I'm sorry, Ma.* No *Love you, Ma.* No explanation. Just five words. Six words he had turned into five, in such a hurry to get lost he couldn't even think.

The whole damn photograph played tricks. The headlights burning red, as if they were as angry as she and couldn't help themselves, the house in the background so obviously white, though it was covered in that stupid purple from the flashing police lights, the boy so unaffected by the body six feet away. The way nothing was how it was supposed to be—she could almost fool herself into thinking it wasn't a body, it wasn't her son under the tarp. But then how could it be anything different? How could the photo change anything, this last photo of her son, the first she's had since he left?

She nearly brought it to the small memorial they held at Macleod Funeral Services Centre, but what kind of person would even think to do something like that? She ended up using a blown-up version of his twelfth-grade yearbook photo, hardly recognizable to anyone who would have known him now. Though she had no idea who would have known him now. She tried his dad's old number, but it was disconnected, probably decades ago. She tried hard but couldn't think of anyone else. She placed an obituary in the *Sun* inviting friends to the service, but regretted it immediately, hoping for an intimate and quiet send-off.

Four men attended, and a woman came running in late carrying her high heels on one finger. She joined a man with a week-old black eye. None of the attendees seemed to know each other besides the couple. Miss Dwyer didn't recognize any of them, but for the pastor, of course. She sat in the second row and stared at her son's photograph, his dark blue urn, until the facilitator came in to start the service.

He came bouncing into the service hall, then seemed to slow when he noticed the turnout. "Are we ready to start?" he whispered to Miss Dwyer.

She nodded.

"Many people ask me how I can handle working here," he started, "but I think I have one of the most important jobs in the world, ushering souls from this world to the next. Miss Dwyer has asked for a non-religious ceremony, and I'd like to respect that, but I simply cannot help thinking of the afterlife whenever I stand before the friends and family of a lost soul."

He kept on, and Miss Dwyer sat patiently through it, waiting for the tears to come. She thought maybe she'd spent them all in the days leading up to this. Her body ached to be free of this room, these strangers, but she couldn't cry... until she felt an arm slip around her shoulder and looked to see the pastor sliding into the pew next to her. With a shoulder to rest against, she cried so hard she thought she might faint. The pastor rubbed her back gently until the facilitator invited Miss Dwyer up to the microphone. She turned in the pew and gathered herself before whispering over the pastor's shoulder, "Would anyone like to say any..."

The group looked down at the floor while Miss Dwyer looked between them.

"Hank and I saw the story in the paper," the woman said, standing mid-sentence. "It really affected us. Hank especially." She opened her mouth as if she might keep going, but sat down after looking at Hank, still staring at the ground. She rubbed his back as if he were the one grieving.

One of the men stood up. "I was Earl's boss," he said, and Miss Dwyer thought he might run out the door next. "We didn't know each other that well. But... I guess he was a hard worker. The office'll miss him. And I guess I felt like I needed to come say that."

There was a long silence. The pastor started to say something, though Miss Dwyer didn't know what. Just as he started to speak, the last man interrupted. "I'm sorry," he said, still sitting in his pew. He ran both of his hands up his face and back through his hair. "Fuckin' eh, I'm sorry," he said, and he did get up, practically running out the exit.

The pastor watched him through the window on the door, then turned to Miss Dwyer. "I didn't know Earl," he said, "but I was at the accident." He kept his hand on her back. "I just wanted to say his death—I'm sorry Miss Dwyer—his death changed my life. And I think..."

Miss Dwyer could feel herself pulling away from him. Who was he? And couldn't he tell her anything about her boy? Couldn't any of these people tell her anything? Who was this man, this boy, her son, that no one could even say anything about him? At all.

"Excuse me," she said, and she slipped down to the far end of the pew, hurried to the back of the chapel and out through the door. She walked straight out of the funeral home, leaned against the outside wall, put her head against it and looked up at the clouds, wished she had a cigarette. She had a full pack in her purse—goddammit her purse.

As she leaned against the wall, she noticed a woman in a car in the lot staring at her. She squinted at her. The woman kept staring for a second, as if she couldn't see that far anyway and didn't know she was staring, then quickly looked down at the steering wheel. Then she looked back up at her, back down at the wheel.

Miss Dwyer went inside to get her purse, her cigarettes, but when she got to the chapel doors, she could see the pastor and the funeral director through the little window. They were laughing about something, the pastor relentlessly scratching the tip of his nostril, the director leaning on the ugly podium. There was no way she was going in there, so she went to the reception area. The couple was there, whispering to each other. She avoided eye contact, walked to the refreshment table and grabbed two butter tarts. She took one bite and almost gagged, then took her tarts and headed out to her car.

The woman was still there. She looked up at Miss Dwyer when the funeral centre's door opened, but quickly looked away again. Miss Dwyer had no time for this. She scurried through the lot to her car, got in, and tried to eat the rest of her tart. She had taken only one more bite when the woman knocked on her window. Miss Dwyer cranked the window down.

"Are you... Were you here for Earl's funeral?" the woman said.

"Who are you?"

"I'm... I guess... I was his girlfriend."

Girlfriend. It never occurred to her that he might have gone and gotten a girlfriend, though of course it should have. Why shouldn't he have had a girlfriend? Of course he'd have a goddamn girlfriend.

"I'm Tina Slinn," she said.

"Do you have a smoke?"

"Fuck. I wish."

They looked at each other.

"Are you... How did you know him?" the girlfriend asked.

And Miss Dwyer just stared at her, studied her little nose, her eyes, those lips.

"I'm sorry," his girlfriend said. "Fuck. I don't even know what I'm doing," she said, and she started to walk away.

"I'm—I was his mother."

"Okay," she said, stopping to look at her now. "I thought—I mean you look—I thought so," she said.

"Go get my purse."

"What?"

"I left my purse in there. I have cigarettes."

"You want me to go get your purse?"

"It's in the chapel. Front pew."

"Fuck."

They laughed for a second, sort of.

And the girlfriend turned and went into the funeral home.

Miss Dwyer got out of the car and leaned against the driver-side door. The clouds were too happy. The sun was too bright. The birds were too loud. The girlfriend came out with the purse much quicker than she thought she would.

"They didn't like that I took it," she said.

Miss Dwyer took the purse and dug around till she found the cigarettes, dug for way too long before she said, "Do you have a lighter?"

"No— Oh, wait. Yes, I do," she said, and she took off to her car. Miss Dwyer opened the cigarette package, threw the plastic on the ground. Earl's girlfriend found the lighter with no problem and came back and handed Miss Dwyer a black Bic.

"Thanks."

"Yeah. It was Earl's."

"What do you mean?"

"Well, he—"

"He still smoked?"

"No. Not really. He bought it 'cause I always lose mine. Kept it in my glovebox."

This. This is exactly what she had wanted those strangers to tell her. Anything about her boy, her son. Earl. He transformed into a whole different person in her mind as she flicked the lighter a few times until it caught and she lit the thing. He grew up into the kind of person who maybe thought about somebody else sometimes as she took the first drag, not just the boy—

"You can have it."

Miss Dwyer studied the lighter for a second, then turned to the girlfriend. She was looking at it, too, then she looked straight at Miss Dwyer, her greenish eyes studying her right back. "You keep it. It's yours. I've had these stupid things forever," Miss Dwyer said.

"You sure?"

"Since I quit. Cold turkey."

"Shit."

Miss Dwyer held the pack out to her. Tina grabbed the lighter and lit one, put the lighter in her back pocket.

They leaned against the car and smoked, blowing the smoke up above their heads.

"He called me less than a month ago," Miss Dwyer said. She took a drag and held it in, "I didn't answer. I never answered. He was just—"

"He—"

"He was just… I don't know. I didn't know. Was he good to you?"

"He was… honestly, he was one of the best humans I've ever known."

And Miss Dwyer started crying. Not like in the chapel, but just well enough that she thought maybe having a smoke with his girlfriend was going to change everything. Maybe she really could forgive herself, one day.

"He looked like you. He was so kind. Like too kind. He—"

"Did you love him?" Miss Dwyer asked out of nowhere.

"He was the best man I had ever been with," Tina said. "By far."

And when Miss Dwyer looked at her, she was crying too. She hugged her. She was tense, at first, but as they hugged, Miss Dwyer could feel Tina relax, rest her face against the top of Miss Dwyer's head.

"Yes," his girlfriend whispered after a long while. "I really fuckin' did."

ACKNOWLEDGEMENTS

I would be remiss if I didn't begin by thanking the many staff members and strangers in the Starbucks in Chapters/Indigo at the south end of Regina. In fact: I tried to start elsewhere, and I couldn't get anything down on paper. Afterall, I wrote at least 90 percent of the work in these pages while I was sitting next to the fireplace there. I cannot tell you how many baristas I have met and befriended over the years, how many of them would ask how the book is coming, or school, or the kids, life. I cannot tell you how many strangers—other customers—I have used as inspiration for characters, or scenes, or—well, I don't know what else. The point is: I don't believe I would have finished the book if not for this particular Starbucks. The white noise of strangers mulling about in there: it is the perfect background for this book. If you are reading this because you recognize me from the coffee shop, thank you. For real.

It took me over ten years to gather the stories in this book, and I had some very generous help in doing so: Michael T began the first lecture in my very first creative writing class saying something like, "Maybe some of you want to sell a million fantasy novels; maybe some of you want to be included in a textbook like this," and he held up the *Norton Anthology of Short Fiction* (or something). I immediately decided the latter was what I wanted as he continued to tell us neither was very likely. I don't know if my work will ever grace the pages of any university textbook, but I do know Professor T—who insisted we call him Mike—read all of these stories before they ever should have been shown to anyone. He was always graceful in his critique yet was able to zero in on the garbage bits with absolutely no remorse. If there are any good bits in these stories, they are likely there to impress him.

Medrie P made me believe my writing was worthwhile. She, too, could pick out bits that needed work, but she always pushed them forward kindly. I feel inspired every time I leave a conversation with her.

Thanks, Randy L, for supporting my work as an artist, for writing such beautiful things, and for supporting me as a person when I didn't know who else to ask.

Thank you, Susan J, for bragging about my work when you didn't need to.

Thank you, Tea and Jamie and Harley and anyone else who joined those little writers' meetups. Those workshops pushed this book to the finish line.

A great big thanks to Lisa Bird-Wilson. I feel like I owe you everything.

And thanks to the Saskatchewan Writers' Guild, SK Arts and Coteau Books (RIP).

Thank you, Chelsee, for giving me the time to write this.

Thanks to Silas and Emma and Karine at Nightwood Editions.

Thanks to [SPACES], Dave at Swift, Flowing and Grain Magazine for publishing my work over the years.

Thank you, Chantelle, for believing in this book, and in me. I love you very much.

And thank you, Derby, Dot & Bella. You are the very best.

ABOUT THE AUTHOR

Tim Blackett is a Canadian writer whose work has appeared in *Briarpatch*, *[spaces]*, *Grain Magazine* and a small Saskatchewan journal called *Swift, Flowing*. He holds a Bachelor of Theology and a BA in English from the University of Regina, as well as a certificate in creative writing from Humber College. *Grandview Drive*, placed second in the John V. Hicks Long Manuscript Award (2019), and the titular story was longlisted for the Carter v. Cooper Short Fiction Award (2012). Blackett lives in Regina, SK.